Praise for the National Bestselling Bookmobile Cat Mysteries

"With humor and panache, Cass delivers an intriguing mystery and interesting characters."
—*Bristol Herald Courier (VA)*

"Almost impossible to put down . . . the story is filled with humor and warmth." —MyShelf.com

"[With] Eddie's adorableness, penchant to try to get more snacks, and Minnie's determination to solve the crime, this duo will win over even those that don't like cats." —Cozy Mystery Book Reviews

"A pleasant read. . . . [Minnie is] a spunky investigator."
—Gumshoe

"A fast-paced page-turner that had me guessing until the last dramatic scenes."
—Melissa's Mochas, Mysteries & Meows

"Reading Laura Cass's cozies feels like sharing a bottle of wine with an adventurous friend as she regales you with the story of her latest escapade."
—The Cuddlywumps Cat Chronicles

Also by Laurie Cass

Lending a Paw
Tailing a Tabby
Borrowed Crime
Pouncing on Murder
Cat with a Clue

Wrong Side of the Paw

Laurie Cass

BERKLEY PRIME CRIME
New York

BERKLEY PRIME CRIME
Published by Berkley
An imprint of Penguin Random House LLC
375 Hudson Street, New York, New York 10014

ISBN: 9780451476562

First Edition: August 2017

Printed in the United States of America
1 3 5 7 9 10 8 6 4 2

Chapter 1

There are many tasks that I find difficult. Braiding my annoyingly curly hair, for starters. Differentiating equations and putting down a good book before one in the morning are also beyond my capabilities. Another thing I've found hard in each of my thirty-four years? Choosing a favorite season.

Summer is easy to enjoy with its warm freedoms, but winter offers skiing and ice skating and the sheer beauty of a world transformed by a fleecy blanket of white. And though spring is exciting with its daily growth spurts, right in front of me was a glorious hillside in its early autumn colors of green with sprinklings of red and orange and yellow, a scene so stunningly beautiful it was hard to look away.

"Fall it is," I murmured to myself.

I was standing at the bookmobile's back door, which was wide open to let the unseasonably warm air of late September waft around the thousands of books, the hundreds of CDs and DVDs, the jigsaw puzzles, my part-time clerk, myself, and Eddie, the bookmobile cat.

"Mrr," Eddie said. On his current favorite perch,

the driver's seat headrest, he stretched and yawned, showing us the roof of his mouth, which was the second least attractive part of him. Then he settled down again, rearranging himself into what looked like the exact same position.

Julia, who was sitting on the carpeted step under the bookshelves that served as both seating and a way to reach the top shelves, looked up from the book she was reading. "What does he want now?"

One of the many reasons I'd hired the sixtyish Julia Beaton was because of her tacit agreement to pretend that Eddie was actually trying to communicate with us. Julia had many other wonderful qualities, among them the gift of empathy, which was a huge plus for a bookmobile clerk, and an uncanny ability to understand people's motivations.

Those two traits had undoubtedly contributed to her success as a Tony Award–winning actress, but when the leading roles started to dry up, she'd retired from the stage and she and her husband moved to her hometown of Chilson, a small tourist town in northwest lower Michigan, which was where I now lived and worked—and there wasn't anywhere on earth I'd rather be.

Though I hadn't grown up in Chilson, I'd had the good fortune to spend many youthful summers there with my long-widowed aunt Frances, who ran a boardinghouse in the summer and taught woodworking during the school year. It hadn't taken me long to fall in love with the region, a land of forested hills and lakes of all sizes, and I soon loved the town, too.

Which was why, not long after I'd earned a master's degree in library and information sciences, when I found a posting for the assistant director position at the Chilson District Library, I spent half the night and all the next day working on a résumé and cover letter. I'd sent the packet off, crossing my fingers, and after a grueling interview and a couple of nail-biting weeks, I'd been ecstatic to be hired.

Since then, not all had been what anyone might call rosy, but the bookmobile program I'd proposed had become a reality a little over a year ago, and in spite of sporadic funding problems, library director issues, and the occasional need to appear in front of the library board to answer pointed questions, I was a very happy camper.

Eddie, on the other hand, did not look like a contented cat. Instead of the relaxed body language he'd been exhibiting moments earlier, he was now sitting up, twitching his tail, and staring at me with a look with which I was intimately familiar.

"What he wants," I said, "is a treat."

"He had treats at the last stop," Julia pointed out.

"Which is why he thinks he deserves a treat at this one, too."

"If he has treats at every stop," she said, "he's going to get as big as a house."

I'd first met Eddie a year and a half earlier. In a cemetery. Which sounds weird, and probably was, but Chilson's cemetery had an amazing two-lake view. Janay Lake to the south, and to the west, the long blue line that was the massive Lake Michigan.

The day I'd met Eddie had been another unseasonably warm day, and I'd skipped out on the spring cleaning chores I should have been doing and gone for a long walk up to the cemetery. I'd taken advantage of a bench placed next to the gravestone of an Alonzo Tillotson (born 1847, died 1926) and had been startled by the appearance of an insistent black-and-gray tabby cat.

In spite of my commands for him to go home, he'd followed me back to my place. By the time I'd cleaned him up, whereupon I found that he was a black-and-white cat, I'd fallen in love. Even still, I'd dutifully run a notice in the local newspaper's lost and found column and had been relieved when no one called.

Eddie was my first pet ever; my dad had suffered horrible allergies and until last year I'd never felt the connection a human and a pet can have. I'd also never realized how opinionated and stubborn a cat could be.

"He's already pretty big," I said to Julia, "but the vet says he's a healthy weight."

"Mrr," said the cat in question, starting to ooze off the headrest and toward the driver's seat.

"Thanks so much," I muttered. "I love it when you sleep there and shed all over the upholstery so I get your hair on the seat of my pants."

Eddie thumped himself onto the seat. "Mrr!"

"I think," Julia said, laughing, "that he took offense to that big comment."

"Who you calling big?" a woman asked.

Julia and I turned. Up until that point, the bookmobile's stop had been empty of patrons. I smiled, pleased that we weren't going to turn up completely dry. Of all the facts and figures that my library board scrutinized, the numbers from the bookmobile got the most attention. So far, the trends were upward ones, but I didn't for a moment assume that all would be well forever.

"Hey, Leese," I said to the woman, who was almost a foot taller than my efficient five feet. Her height was the same as that of my best friend, who owned a restaurant in Chilson, but instead of Kristen's slender blond Scandinavian inheritance, Leese Lacombe's ancestors had endowed her with a broad build, an olive skin tone, and brown hair almost as curly as my unruly black mop.

Leese, a few years older than me, possessed a razor-sharp brain, a quick wit, and a prestigious law degree. She'd spent more than a decade playing by the rules in the downstate corporate trenches, and moved back north a few months ago to start up her own law office, one that specialized in elder law. To keep costs down, she was using her home as an office and had taken to borrowing books from the bookmobile instead of making the half-hour drive into Chilson. A July article in the local paper about her practice had generated a number of clients, and it looked as if she was on her way to success.

"What's new with you?" Julia asked, standing to get the stack of books Leese had requested online. I was still tweaking the bookmobile schedule, but at that point we were visiting each stop every three weeks. Though that wasn't a very long time for most people, it could be an eternity for bibliophiles, and we were getting used to bringing along huge piles of requested books and lugging back the correspondingly huge piles of returns. I doubted any bookmobile librarian ever had needed to buy a gym membership to get an upper-body workout.

"New?" Leese set her returning books on the rear checkout desk. "I'm glad it's almost October, for one thing. My summer neighbors have slammed their trunks for the last time."

Julia and I nodded, understanding the feeling. We lived in a part of Michigan that was the summer playground for a large number of folks from the Detroit, Grand Rapids, and Chicago areas. Some people visited for a weekend or a week; others had seasonal residences.

The population of Chilson and the entire Tonedagana County more than tripled in the warmer months and summer came with a complicated set of issues. Most of us were glad to renew the friendships that had been put on hold the previous fall—not to mention the fact that many businesses depended on the summer tourist dollars—but October came with an undeniable sigh of relief. No more parking problems, no more waiting in line for a restaurant table, no more waiting anywhere, really.

"It is nice to have our town back," Julia said. "We'll be tired of looking at each other by April, though."

Leese laughed, and it was a surprisingly gentle sound from such a large person. "Undoubtedly. But without the busy months, would we appreciate this quiet time?"

The question was an interesting one. I gave up trying to shift Eddie from the driver's seat and walked down the aisle to join the conversation. "So it's part of that old question, how can we value the highs of life if we don't know what the lows are like?"

"Exactly!" Leese gave me a high-wattage smile and I knew exactly what was going to happen next. She would sit on the carpeted step, Julia would pull around the desk chair, I would perch on the edge of the desk, and the three of us would dive into a long, leisurely discussion when we all had better things to do. But it was nearly October, the summer folks were mostly gone, and it was warm enough to prop the door open.

What could it hurt to let the bookmobile chores wait a few minutes longer?

Julia pulled the chair around and Leese sat on the step. "It's the swings in life that make things interesting," she said.

"Oh, I don't know," I said, hitching myself up onto the edge of the desk. "Isn't that some Chinese curse? 'May you live in interesting times'?"

"Would you rather live when it's boring?" Leese challenged.

Julia laughed. "Minnie Hamilton couldn't live a boring life if she wanted to. She's attracted to trouble."

"Am not," I said automatically. "I'm just—"

"Do you know what this tiny woman did earlier this spring?" Julia demanded of Leese. "In the middle of a massive power outage, she managed to hold a bang-up successful book fair."

Leese looked at me with interest. "I heard about that. Wasn't Trock Farrand the headliner? I didn't know you were involved."

"Minnie's show, from top to bottom," Julia said. "When the original big-name author canceled, Trock heard about it and flew out from New York."

"He's a friend, that's all," I said, knocking my shoes together. "He wanted to plug his new cookbook." Trock, host of a nationally televised cooking show, owned a summer place just outside of Chilson, and in spite of the differences in our ages, background, and interests, we'd struck up a solid friendship.

Another solid thing was the relationship between Trock's son, Scruffy, and my friend Kristen. I had the inside scoop that a proposal was in the near future, and I was doing my best to play innocent.

"Whatever." Julia waved off my comment. "And just a couple of months ago, Minnie figured out that—"

"Hey!"

Julia frowned. "I'm ranting, Minnie. Please don't interrupt when I'm in full flow."

But it wasn't Julia that I was scolding. "Where are you going?" I asked my cat.

When we were en route, my furry friend traveled in a cat carrier strapped to the floor on the passenger's side, but once I set the parking brake, Julia unlatched the wire door, setting him free to roam about the interior. Though he'd run outside a couple of times the first year of the bookmobile's service, since then he'd shown little interest in leaving the bus before we did.

Eddie, being a cat, paid no attention to my question, but continued to sniff at the open doorway.

"Is he going to make a run for it?" Leese asked, amused.

"Not a chance," I said. "He wouldn't want to get too far from his cat treats."

Eddie's ears flattened and Julia laughed. "I think you hurt his feelings. You should apologize before he does something drastic."

"I shouldn't have to apologize for telling the truth." But she did have a point. A miffed Eddie was not a good situation. He had claws and knew how to use them, especially on paper products. Facial tissues, paper towels, toilet paper, newspapers, and even books weren't safe when Eddie was in the mood for destruction.

"I am sorry," I told my cat, "that you take offense to a fact-based statement."

"Huh," said Leese. "Not much of an apology, if you ask me. Not sure he thinks much of it, either."

Eddie was standing at the top of the stairs, staring out, twitching his ears and nose.

"Hey, pal," I said, sliding off the desk. "Inside only. You promised, remember?"

"That was before you insulted him," Julia said. "All previous deals have now been canceled."

"Come here, Eddie." But just as I leaned down to grab my fuzzy friend, he hopped out of reach, jumping to the bottom step.

"That'll teach you to make fun of a cat," Leese said, laughing.

"Especially an Eddie cat," Julia added.

We were parked in a large church parking lot, at least a hundred feet from the closest road, and hadn't seen a car in the last ten minutes. I wasn't overly worried about Eddie getting dangerously close to traffic, but there was a long line of shrubs at the far side of the lot and I could just see Eddie crawling into that prickly mess and not wanting to come out.

"How about a treat?" I crouched at the top of the stairs. "Come back right now and I'll give you a whole pile." Not a big pile, but still. "Here, kitty, kitty."

Eddie, catlike, was focused on his new mission, whatever that might be, and launched off the bottom step and into the bright October sunshine.

I groaned and went after him. Over my shoulder I called, "Can someone bring me the treats? He might come if I shake the can."

Once outside, however, I realized Eddie wasn't headed for the shrubbery. Or the roadway. Instead he was trotting straight for the only vehicle in the parking lot, a battered pickup truck. Dents and scrapes of all shapes and sizes were scattered along the doors and sides, some serious enough to have scoured the paint down to the metal.

I leapt to the stunningly obvious conclusion that the vehicle was Leese's and wondered what a former corporate attorney was doing with an open bed truck. At previous bookmobile visits I was pretty sure she'd been driving a midsized SUV.

Mentally shrugging—I paid about as much attention to cars as I did to daily temperatures in Hawaii—I trotted across the parking lot, ten yards behind my cat in a very short parade of two. "Eddie, come back here, will you? I thought I only had to run on workout mornings with Ash. I'm not sure I'm ready for more. Think of me, will you? I'm sure you've done that once or twice."

Most days, my inane conversation caught Eddie's attention, slowing him enough for me to catch up. This time, if anything, he sped up and he sniffed the air and trotted ever closer to the truck.

"Here kitty, kitty," Leese called as she climbed down the bookmobile's steps. "Come get a cat snack." She rattled the cardboard can of annoyingly expensive moist morsels, but Eddie trotted onward.

"That your truck?" I asked.

"For now." She made a face. "It's a long story."

Eddie, still ignoring the siren call of cat treats, jumped onto the truck's rear bumper, then up onto the edge of the tailgate. I slowed from my half run and started planning how best to snag my cat. Cornering Eddie was a lot easier than capturing him. "I think he wants to go for a ride."

"I'll give it to him with my blessing as soon as my SUV is fixed."

Eddie's ears swiveled. Laughing, I edged a few feet

closer to the truck. “I think he’s rejecting your generous offer.”

“He’s a cat of good taste.” Leese gave the treat can another shake. “That thing’s a piece of junk.”

“Mrrr,” Eddie said, then jumped off the tailgate and into the truck’s bed.

Reaching the side of the truck, I stood on my tiptoes and peered in. All there was to see was a large tarp and a black-and-white cat walking over the top of it in an ungainly fashion.

“Fred Astaire, you are not,” I told him. “Please don’t make me come in there after you.”

“Mrrr,” he said, but his tone was different from the usual communicative chirp he gave. It was low and long and almost a growl. He started pawing at the edge of the heavy canvas and tried to poke his nose under it. Of course, he was standing on the edge, which made things difficult, but Eddie didn’t like to do things the easy way.

I turned to look at Leese, who was now standing next to me. “What’s under your tarp?”

“No idea,” she said shortly. “It’s not mine. Tarp or truck.”

Two minutes earlier, she’d been ready to give away a truck she didn’t own? “I don’t—”

“Mrrroooo!”

I winced as Eddie’s howls penetrated my skull and sank deep into my brain.

Enough was enough. I walked around to the truck’s back end and put one foot on the trailer hitch. Grabbing on to the tailgate, I climbed onto the back bumper, swung one foot over into the pickup’s bed and then the other.

Eddie was howling for all he was worth and had

managed to burrow his front half under the tarp. I crouched down and took a gentle hold of his back half. "Come on, pal. Let's go, okay?"

But when I stood, cat in hand, his claws were still extended and they'd snagged the tarp's edge, yanking the canvas to one side and revealing what Eddie had been after.

"Oh!" I stumbled backward. "Oh . . ."

Because Eddie had uncovered a body. A dead body. Of a man. A man about sixty years old. With staring eyes of blue.

I scrambled over the tailgate, holding a squirming Eddie close to my chest, and dropped to the ground, panting, not wanting to see any more.

Leese was standing quiet and tall, her hands gripping the edge of the truck, her mouth working as if she was trying to say something. For a long moment, nothing came out, but when it did, her voice was a raw whisper.

"It's my dad."

Chapter 2

Julia, who'd been standing in the bookmobile's doorway watching the scene unfold, was the first to recover enough to call 911. After she'd told the dispatcher the circumstances, given our location, and received instructions that all of us should stay away from the truck, she hung up and took a long look at Leese.

"You need to sit down," she commanded, using her strongest stage voice. "Minnie, go inside and bring out the chair. We'll sit Leese over there."

She was indicating a spot near the bookmobile's front bumper, in the sun and out of the light breeze. It was also out of view of the truck, which was certainly intentional. *Nicely done*, I thought, and hurried to do her bidding. First, though, I put Eddie, who I'd been clutching so hard he was starting to squiggle something fierce, into his carrier.

When I came out with the chair and put it on the sunny grass, Leese was speaking in short, awkward, and repeating sentences. "He can't be dead, I just saw him last week. Why is he in the truck? I just saw him last week. Why is he in the truck? I don't understand. He can't be dead."

But she was biddable enough that it wasn't any problem for us to maneuver her into the chair. Her ruddy face was a peculiar shade of pale and her hands, typically strong and sure, were shaking and searching for something to do. Once she was sitting, her hands gripped each other and didn't let go.

"Water," I murmured.

"I'll get mine," Julia said quickly. "You stay out here."

She vanished around the corner of the bookmobile, and I was glad she'd volunteered, because if I'd fetched the water, I would have had to see the truck, and then I'd remember those staring blue eyes, and—

"Hard to believe it'll be October the day after tomorrow," I said. Talking about the weather was banal, but it was always there to talk about, and getting Leese to talk about anything had to be better than letting her thoughts circle around inside her head.

Leese blinked. "What?"

"The weather." I sat cross-legged on the grass in front of her. "It's so warm, it feels like early September."

She barked out a short noise that might have been a laugh. Probably not, but maybe. "You're right. It is warm enough for early September."

"Do you think this means we'll have a mild winter?"

Weather discussions were easy and, if you encouraged them even the slightest bit, could fill hours of time. We didn't require hours, but I did see a need to distract Leese from what lay across the parking lot for a little while.

One of the downsides about living in a rural area was the time it could take for emergency vehicles to respond. Thanks to my boyfriend, Ash Wolverson, a deputy with the Tonedagana County Sheriff's Office, I knew where the sheriff's satellite offices and the local fire and EMS stations were located, which was why I knew it would take at least fifteen minutes for anyone to get to us. We were in the far northeast part of the county, the least populated part with the least amount of emergency services, and even law enforcement can drive only so fast.

So Leese and I chatted about the weather and talked about the advantages of snow tires. I'd just started to edge into asking tentative questions about her father when an ambulance rolled up.

We stood as two EMTs got out of the vehicle. The driver, a blond woman in her forties, glanced from Leese to me to the bookmobile and back to Leese. "We got a report of a—"

"Over there," I interrupted, not wanting to hear the words she was about to say. "In the bed of the truck."

They nodded and moved away, and as they were pulling back the tarp, a police car pulled into the parking lot and a deputy I didn't know climbed out.

After that, things moved quickly and, in retrospect, inevitably. Why I hadn't put two and two together, I did not know, but it wasn't until Leese was put in the back of the police car that I realized two things. One, that her father had been murdered, and two, that Leese was a prime suspect.

"I don't understand," I said to Julia, as we watched the police car drive away. Leese had been quiet throughout the entire episode. Now crunched up into the backseat, she was staring straight ahead.

I looked at the EMTs, who were sitting on their vehicle's bumper. The sheriff's deputy, a man I didn't know, had asked them to wait to take the body away until a forensics detective arrived and cleared the scene. Judging from their slumped shoulders and crossed ankles, they were clearly bored. I thought about asking if they wanted to borrow some books, but figured they probably shouldn't be reading on the job.

"There's a lot about this I don't understand," Julia said. "But there is one thing I know for certain."

"What's that?"

"That you'll figure it out."

I shook my head. "This is beyond me."

Julia rolled her eyes dramatically enough so that, if we'd been in a theater, the people in the back rows could have seen it. "Leese is a friend. You know she didn't kill her dad. And you won't let her be arrested for something she didn't do. Ergo, if the police don't resolve this fast, you'll jump in where no law enforcement officer would dare to tread and risk life and limb to save your friend."

I did my own eye roll, a very slow version. If I couldn't match the quality, at least I could outdo her in quantity.

"Tell me I'm wrong," Julia said.

But since she was essentially right, I couldn't.

I'd anticipated a night of fitful sleep, tossing and turning and starting awake in the middle of the night from haunted dreams of staring eyes and flashing police lights, but instead I slept like a rock from the moment my head hit the pillow to the moment my alarm went off.

Though I wasn't sure that sleeping so soundly after the shocking events of the previous afternoon said anything positive about my character, I was pleased to wake up well rested and practically perky.

"What are you going to do today?" I asked Eddie, who was snuggled between my elbow and hip. "Hey, here's an idea. How about if you help pack? This warm weather isn't going to last much longer and we don't have any real heat in here, remember?"

"Mrr," my cat said, and, without moving a muscle, wormed his way deeper into the covers.

"Fine." I slipped out from underneath the sheets. "Just don't blame me if your favorite cat toys get left behind."

In my jammies and socks, I padded across the small bedroom and into the tiny bathroom. Everything was miniaturized because our current abode was a houseboat, the cutest little houseboat imaginable, and it was our home through the warm months.

When the weather turned cold, I dragged my stack of cardboard boxes out of the storage locker that came with my boat slip rental at Uncle Chip's Marina, packed, and hauled everything that I didn't want to get covered with a winter's worth of dust up to my aunt Frances's boardinghouse.

I wasn't sure if I truly remembered my uncle Everett, the long-dead husband of Aunt Frances, or if I just thought I remembered him from looking at old family photos. My aunt had met him in college and it was soon after he died that she'd turned the Pixley family's summer place into what it was now.

More than once I'd been told there was an exact total of one traditional boardinghouse left in the world, the one being the place my aunt ran. I had no idea if that was accurate or not, but I did know that I loved its wide front porch, its pine-paneled living room with its fieldstone fireplace and shelves of jigsaw puzzles and board games, the massive kitchen, and the back screen porch that looked out onto a tree-filled backyard.

When I told people about my unusual living arrangements, I typically saw furrowed brows and heard murmured concerns about building equity and establishing credit. I would say something about paying off college loans, which seemed to satisfy the questioners, but the truth was I loved the winters I spent with my aunt. We were more than relatives; we were friends.

Then again, sometimes it was hard to believe that Aunt Frances and I were close blood relations. I was short; she was on the tall side. I had pale skin; she tanned easily. She was also amazingly skilled with her hands and was equally capable of building a six-panel door and of cooking a perfect lemon meringue pie. I much preferred ordering takeout over doing dishes, and still wasn't exactly sure what a router did.

But none of that seemed to matter, because we laughed at the same things and agreed on a basic fact of life—that worrying didn't do much good. Aunt Frances was a lot better at not worrying than I was, but I was working on being more like her.

Of course, not worrying was getting a little harder, since Aunt Frances had agreed to marry her across-the-street neighbor, the distinguished Otto Bingham. Not until next spring, she kept assuring me, but I saw no reason for them to wait and had started saying so. The stalling was starting to make me a bit nervous.

"There's no hurry," Otto would say.

"No?" I'd ask, arching my eyebrows. "Don't tell me you're getting cold feet." After all, I was the one who'd originally shoved Otto in my aunt's direction and I felt a degree of responsibility for the pending nuptials.

"We have a few details to work out," my aunt would say vaguely.

"Like what?" I'd demand. "Why waste time? Just go down to the magistrate and get it done. Why are you waiting?"

My aunt would look at Otto, Otto would look at her, and they'd exchange one of those happy-couple smiles. Then they would determinedly change the subject and I'd be given the choice of being an incredible pest or letting the subject drop.

"I should start being a pest," I told Eddie. Now showered and dressed, I was rubbing my freakishly curly hair dry with a towel. Aiming a hair dryer at my head would create a frizzy mess that could only be solved by a ponytail and a hat. "I bet I could be a really good one. After all, I've been getting lessons from you for a year and a half now."

Eddie, who was on the bed in the exact same position he'd been in fifteen minutes earlier, opened one eye, then shut it.

"What was that?" I asked, doing my best to make the bed with him still flopped on top of it. "Did you say something?"

He pulled himself into a tight ball, rolled over, and said absolutely nothing.

I laughed and kissed the top of his head. "Have a good day, my friend. I'll see you tonight, okay?"

"Mrr."

After a quick breakfast of cold cereal and orange juice—which hit my self-imposed limit of morning dishes to wash at three, because spoons counted as dishes to me—I shouldered my backpack and let myself out into the morning.

The town of Chilson rose from the shoreline of Janay Lake on a shallow slope at first, then up steeper and steeper. The houses perched on the top of the hill had amazing views and property tax bills to match.

Uncle Chip's, the marina where I moored my boat at a cut rate in exchange for updating their budget projections, was on the east side of town, the side where normal people with normal jobs could still find affordable homes to buy.

The west side was massive houses and mansionlike lakefront cottages, a mix of new money and old money left over from the years that steamers running up from Chicago stopped at the natural harbor created by the entrance of Janay Lake into Lake Michigan.

On bookmobile days, I always drove the mile from the marina to the library, since lugging Eddie and our lunches that far would have been too hard on both me and my friendly feline. The bookmobile's maiden voyage had included a stowaway Eddie, who'd quickly become an integral part of the operations. If I didn't bring him along on every trip, there would be innumerable unhappy patrons, something that was best to avoid. On library days, however, unless the weather was horrific, I walked. This hadn't been a running morning for the Ash and Minnie team, so the walk to work and back would likely be my only exercise.

The bizarre warmness of the last few days was still holding and I barely needed the nylon shell jacket I'd tossed on over my library clothes of slacks, dressy T-shirt, and loose blazer. This time of year the sun came up just before eight o'clock, and if I timed things right, I'd see the sun rise above the horizon as I entered the library.

As I walked briskly off the dock and headed up the

sidewalk and toward downtown, I glanced at the house closest to the marina. When I'd moved to Chilson, it had been a ramshackle mess, a hundred-year-old family cottage long since chopped up into apartments. For decades it had been given about as much tender loving care as you'd expect from an absentee owner who seemed to care primarily about getting the rents on time.

Rafe Niswander, a friend of mine, had bought the place about four years ago. The whys of that purchase still had the coffee-drinking geezers at the local diner scratching their heads every morning, but there was no denying that Rafe was doing a fantastic job of renovation.

From top to bottom and stem to stern he'd redesigned, rewired, and replumbed. He'd fabricated crown molding to match the original, haunted building salvage stores, and researched period colors. And then he'd stare at whatever he'd done, declare it unworthy, and rip half of it out.

He'd managed to wangle an occupancy permit out of the county's building official, but no sane person would want to live in a house that had milk crates for kitchen cabinets and a persistent drywall dust issue. None of this, however, seemed to bother Rafe. If a casual observer asked how he could live in a permanent construction zone, he would shrug, start whistling the Seven Dwarfs' "Heigh-Ho" song, and get back to work.

When the project was done, it would be a showpiece, but the diner geezers were laying long odds on any completion date within the next five years.

Yesterday I'd heard the buzz of a floor sander when I'd come home and had stopped by to tell Rafe what had happened on the bookmobile and to remind him to wear his dust mask, a reminder I was sure he'd ignored. This morning he must have left early for his job as principal of the middle school, because the house was dark. I shied away from imagining the dust he'd created the night before and headed up the hill.

Ahead of me lay a downtown that edged into quaintness but thankfully stayed on the side of reality. The home-grown blend of old and new, brick and wood, stylish and traditional, was part of the charm of Chilson and I thought, as I almost always did while walking to work, that I was the luckiest person alive.

I unlocked the library's side door just as the sun shot over the horizon, and let myself in.

"Minnie? Is that you?"

Of course, no life was perfect.

Strong-mindedly, I resisted the urge to turn and flee and, instead, pasted a smile on my face. "Good morning, Jennifer," I said, advancing into the lobby. "How are you on this gorgeous morning?"

The new library director, standing tall behind the main counter, didn't return my smile. "Well enough, I suppose."

My former boss, Stephen Rangel, had given me a lot of latitude to do my job, for which I was still grateful. He'd also been humorless and mired in the necessity to follow rules, however arbitrary they might be. Plus, he hadn't been a fan of the bookmobile and had provided only a grudging support throughout the early stages. ("Minerva, are you certain you're up to this?" "Minerva, the library board only approved this project because you'd found a generous donor. How, exactly, do you plan to fund the operations?" And so on.)

We'd all expected Stephen to stay in Chilson until

his retirement and he'd even confided he'd been grooming me to be his replacement. That shock had barely faded when he'd stunned everyone by announcing that he'd accepted a library director position in another state.

My coworkers had pleaded with me to apply. I'd seriously considered it, but in the end decided to pass on the opportunity. If I moved up to director, there was no way I'd have time to drive the bookmobile and I wasn't ready to give that up.

On the other hand, if I was now the library director, I wouldn't be facing the sleek and citified Jennifer Walker, who was sending waves of disapproval at me for no reason that I was aware of. Back before she'd started, I'd patted myself on the back for having been responsible for the library becoming the temporary home of a very rare and valuable book, thinking that the new director would be impressed at my connections and abilities. If she had, the feeling hadn't lasted.

"What can I do for you?" I slipped my backpack off my shoulder. Into the returns bin went the books I'd finished reading, *Station Eleven* by Emily St. John Mandel, *Let's Pretend This Never Happened* by Jenny Lawson, and *I Capture the Castle* by Dodie Smith, a comfort book published in 1948 that I'd reread for the umpteenth time.

"I asked you to reduce the bookmobile's budget," Jennifer said. "I expected a draft this week, yet here it is Friday and I haven't seen anything from you."

After Stephen's departure, the staff had breathed a collective sigh of relief. No more didactic pronouncements, no more unfunded mandates, no more unrealistic expectations. Though I'd respected Stephen, I'd never managed to like him, and I'd looked forward to a deeper relationship with the new director.

This hadn't happened yet.

The last of my books *thunked* into the return slot. Jennifer had, in fact, asked me to reduce the bookmobile's budget. She'd also asked for it to be done by the middle of October, and this morning my phone said it was September. Just barely, but still.

Why she wanted the bookmobile's budget reduced was a question she hadn't yet answered. Thanks to a generous donation last winter, we had over two years of operations money in addition to a healthy budget for vehicle maintenance. There was also a small, but growing, fund for the future purchase of a replacement bookmobile.

To my way of thinking, clearly the sensible way, there was absolutely no reason to touch the bookmobile's budget. But Jennifer had been hired by a beaming library board and it was my job to do as she asked.

"I've been working on some ideas," I said, turning to face her, "and I'll have a budget completed by your deadline, which was the middle of October."

"When I said the middle of October," she said to the air above my head, "that was the latest I want to see it. I fully expect to get a completed budget ahead of that time."

"Oh." I stared at her. How on earth I was supposed to have known that, I wasn't sure. "I didn't realize."

"No? Everyone says how on the ball you are, Minnie. I assumed that would include early delivery dates of things I request."

If I'd been a mind reader, sure.

I looked up at the bottom of her chin. "I'll have it to you next week," I said. "If I'd known you wanted it earlier, I would have sent it to you earlier."

"It's not a matter of wanting." She smoothed the front of her jacket. "It's a matter of your performance. As soon as you finish, please e-mail it to me." With that, she and her high heels clicked down the tiled hallway.

I watched her open the door to the stairwell and, as she clicked up the stairs to her second-floor office, shook my head and headed to the staff break room. Normally, at this time I was the only one in the building; the only time I'd ever seen Stephen in his office before nine o'clock was the Monday after a time change when he'd been out of town and neglected to turn back the clocks in his house.

But at least Jennifer was headed upstairs. If the last few weeks were any indication, she wouldn't be back down until after the library opened to the public at ten.

After a quick stop in the break room to start a pot of coffee, I went to my office, dropped off my backpack, grabbed my favorite coffee mug, the one emblazoned with the logo of the American Bookmobile and Outreach Services, and returned to fill up with the fuel by which the Chilson District Library operated: caffeine.

A few sips of the steaming hot nectar of the gods later, I began my morning the way I'd been doing ever since Jennifer had moved into Stephen's office, by walking through the library and seeing what was what. Our new director had a habit of zeroing in on the slightest negative, and if I could head off those comments, maybe she'd eventually realize that the library wasn't a total disaster or a complete mess in need of a huge overall.

"Not a mess at all," I murmured, looking around and

marveling, once again, at the gorgeous setting. We'd been in this building, which everyone still called the new library, for almost exactly four years. And even then it hadn't been new. The residents of Chilson, when faced with the question of whether or not to fund the expensive renovations of a vacant and century-old school for the purpose of giving their jammed-packed library more space, had overwhelmingly voted to fund the project and the result was a place of pride for everyone.

The designers had opted to expand on the Craftsman style of the original building, giving us oak-paneled walls, oak ends on the shelving units, metallic tiles around the drinking fountains, and a working gas fireplace in the reading room. We had a computer lab, a Young Adult lounge area, and meeting rooms with projectors and a catering kitchen.

It was flat-out gorgeous, but Jennifer continued to find faults, so I cruised the entire place, adjusting picture frames with the precision of an art gallery manager, making note of which shelves needed books to be soldiered to the front, and making sure Gareth, the maintenance guy, hadn't missed a single speck of dirt when vacuuming.

Satisfied that I'd done everything I could to avert Jennifer's wrath, I returned to my office and fired up the computer. Though I hadn't exactly lied to Jennifer about the bookmobile budget—I did have some ideas—they remained just that and I needed to move the ideas into the practical realm if I was going to make my new boss happy.

I stifled a thought that popped into my head (*Nothing I do is going to make her happy*), tossed down some more caffeine, and started working.

A couple of hours later, the sound of voices and

footsteps penetrated my consciousness. I leaned back, stretching, and got up, mug in hand.

"Oh, no," I said, entering the break room, dismay clear in my voice.

"Hah!" Kelsey Lyons, one of our part-time clerks, grinned at me and pushed the coffeemaker's start button. "I was here first. Timing is everything and you don't have it this morning."

Though our library ran on coffee, the strength of the stuff varied widely. Donna, our seventy-one-year-old marathoner and snowshoer, preferred it weak enough that you could see through it. Holly, one of my best library friends and about my age, liked it in the middle. Josh, the IT guy, also a good friend and within a year or two of Holly and myself, preferred it the way I did, strong, but not so strong that it could pass for espresso.

Kelsey, on the other hand, would probably eat the grounds raw, but it was an unwritten rule that whoever emptied the pot could make the next one whatever strength they wished.

"Rats," I muttered.

"You snooze, you lose," she said, her face all sunshine and roses. Clearly, this was not going to be her first cup of the morning.

"Oh, man." Josh, mug in hand, came to a halt in the doorway. "Please tell me you made this pot, Minnie."

"Sorry. I was two minutes late."

He sighed heavily. "Knew I should have waited to install that program."

"Cut it with water," Kelsey said.

"That's what you always say," Josh said, shoving his free hand into a pocket of his cargo pants. "And it always tastes like crap."

Up until a few months ago, the stocky Josh had been a diet soda guy, shoving dollar bills into the soda machine like there was no tomorrow. Since he'd purchased his first house, however, that habit was a thing of the past.

He frowned at the coffeepot, then turned and frowned at me. "Hey, did I hear right about what happened on the bookmobile yesterday?"

Kelsey, who was in the act of deftly pulling out the coffeepot and letting the brew drip straight into her mug, asked, "Something happened? Is the bookmobile okay?"

It warmed my heart every time I realized that people were concerned about the bookmobile's health. The library staff cared about the bookmobile. The library board cared. The downtown merchants cared. Complete strangers cared. Even people who didn't have a library card cared, a concept that baffled me, but I'd stopped trying to understand that one.

"The bookmobile is fine," I said. "It's just . . ." My eyes were suddenly filled with moisture. I looked down, took a quick breath, and smoothed out my face. "Remember I told you about Leese Lacombe, that attorney who moved back north last summer? Specializing in elder law?"

Though I got two blank looks, I kept on going. "Anyway, yesterday was so warm we left the bookmobile door open. Eddie got out and, well, he found Leese's father in the bed of the pickup truck she was driving."

"What do you mean, Eddie found him?" Kelsey pulled away her mug and plopped the pot back down. "If her dad was with her, he couldn't have been lost."

"You're not getting it," Josh said. "He was dead."

"He was . . ." Kelsey blinked.

I nodded. “The ambulance came, the police came, and eventually the medical examiner came.”

Kelsey gave her head a little shake, rearranging her short blond hair. “I don’t understand. What was he doing there? Had he died and she was taking him to the hospital or . . . something?”

“I don’t know.” I flashed on an image of Leese in the back of the police car, determinedly looking forward.

“The guys downtown are saying she killed him.” Josh shrugged. “Not saying she did, but that’s the talk.”

“Why is it that men talk,” Kelsey asked me, “but women gossip?”

“Don’t tell me you’re still hoping that life is going to start being fair,” I said, smiling a little. “Do your kids know you’re so unrealistic?”

She laughed. “It’s because of them that I keep on hoping.”

“Speaking of hope,” Josh said, “I heard that Jennifer is trying to find money for more computers in the lab.”

“Oh? She’s been asking me to cut the bookmobile’s budget.”

Josh smirked. “Then I guess we know where that money is going. And who better to get it than the computer lab?”

Though I’d been in the act of reaching out to fill his coffee mug, I abruptly yanked it away. “No way am I pouring you coffee after a remark like that.”

He grinned. Josh, better than anyone other than my friends Rafe and Kristen and my brother Matt, knew exactly how to push my buttons. And he probably enjoyed it more than any of them. Well, except for Matt.

"If you'd wanted to be Jennifer's favorite," Josh said, "you shouldn't have let your cat puke all over her shoes."

I tried to keep a straight face, but ended up laughing. The day Jennifer had interviewed with the library board, we'd had to abort a bookmobile run and Eddie ended up in the library for the day. In spite of my efforts to keep him contained in my office, my fuzzy friend had wandered out, made a beeline for the candidate's Italian shoes, and rid himself of some troublesome hair balls.

"Eddie has excellent taste," Kelsey said, giggling.

I sensed the turn the conversation was about to take, and though I wouldn't have minded joining a Jennifer-bashing session, I couldn't. Assistant directors didn't do that kind of thing. Or at least they shouldn't. "She's working a lot of hours."

"Check it out," Josh said to Kelsey. "She's sucking up to the boss when the boss isn't even here." He made a vacuum cleaner noise.

"Nice," I said. "That pretty new manager of the wine store is getting to be a regular patron. If she asks about you again, I know what I'll tell her."

"Yeah?" he asked cautiously. "What's that?"

"Now Josh," I said as patronizingly as I could, "you know I always tell the truth." I bestowed a wide smile upon him. "And now I have to get back to the business of the library. Cheers." I toasted my friends with the sludge in my mug and headed to my office.

But though I'd intended to sit down and get straight to work, I stood at the window for some time, trying not to worry about Leese.

Chapter 3

For the first time in I couldn't think when, Rafe and Kristen and I had planned to get together for dinner.

Back when I'd first moved to Chilson, the three of us visited every restaurant in Tonedagana County, most of the eateries in Antrim, Charlevoix, Cheboygan, and Emmet Counties, and a few down in Grand Traverse County.

It had started as a casual resolve not to eat in the same place twice, quickly morphed into a Thursday night event, and had solidified Kristen's resolve to open a restaurant of her own. Since then, however, the three of us, who'd become friends on a beach before we were teenagers, had become so busy with our own lives that coordinating our schedules took a monumental effort.

When Kristen's restaurant opened, the two of us established a Sunday evening habit of me arriving after the dinner rush for dessert in her office. Often we ate crème brûlé, but sometimes it was a new recipe she wanted to try out.

Rafe and I, because his house so was close to Uncle

Chip's Marina, saw each other frequently. I'd stopped last week to check out his progress on the downstairs bathroom and caught him crouching on the floor and frowning at the beadboard he'd put in the previous week. The tallish and lanky Rafe stood, brushed sawdust out of his straight black hair, and asked what I, as an impartial observer, thought of the knots showing through the paint primer, and had appeared annoyed when I'd said I couldn't see any knots, even when he was pointing directly at them.

To distract him from an unnecessary scrutiny of his work, I'd suggested the three of us go out to dinner, just like in the old days.

"What's the matter?" he'd said. "Did my man Ash finally figure out that you were never going to learn the infield fly rule and he couldn't take it any longer?" He'd grinned. "Or have you finally realized that you're deeply in love with me and are only waiting for the right time to break it off with him and fall into my arms." He spread his arms wide and made loud kissy noises.

I rolled my eyes. "Eww. No, they're down a couple of deputies and he pulled night shift this month." My boyfriend was also taking classes at the local community college; it was a minor miracle our paths ever crossed. Still, I saw him more than I'd seen my previous boyfriend, an emergency room doctor. If Ash's shift hadn't been too exhausting, we got together to run or bike a few mornings a week, but mornings were growing darker and darker and I wasn't sure how much longer that would last.

I tried to remember the last time Ash and I had done even a semiromantic thing together. Dinner? Movie? Snuggling in front of his fireplace? It had been weeks, but I couldn't pin it down. Why wasn't I making sure those things happened?

Suddenly, I realized that Rafe was staring at me with an odd expression. I felt my face turn warm and quickly said, "Kristen's flying solo now that Scruffy is back in New York, but we could add a fourth. Who are you seeing these days? Invite her along."

Rafe's love life was a complicated thing. As far as Kristen and I could figure, three months was the maximum he'd dated anyone. We figured that's how long it took a woman to realize that she was never going to change him. Of course, his versions of the multitude of breakups varied from "Too clingy" to "Couldn't stand how she laughed" to "Didn't like beer," but Kristen and I knew too many of the women to believe any of his explanations.

"Right now I'm footloose and fancy free." He'd dropped to his hands and knees to peer at the woodwork, but looked up at me, flashing his smile, a bright white against the permanently tanned skin he'd inherited from his distant Native American ancestors. "Want to hear what happened with Stacey?"

"No." I had no idea who Stacey was, but I was already on her side. "Do you want to do dinner or not?"

In the end, it turned out he did. For the next two days we had a three-person round of texting about dinner details and it was seven o'clock when Rafe parked his battered Jeep Cherokee at the Weathervane in Charlevoix. Originally a grist mill, its riverside location next to a drawbridge was a big attraction in summer, when the number of boats passing through from Lake Charlevoix to Lake Michigan seemed to rival the number of cars driving over the bridge itself.

Since the weather was still mild, we sat on the deck.

Kristen and I ordered wine, and our designated driver sighed and ordered a beer. "Don't give me any more," he told our waitress. "No matter how much I beg." He gave her a huge grin.

When she smiled back, Kristen and I exchanged glances. Rafe's long-standing habit was to flirt outrageously with female waitstaff, and more often than not, at the end of the meal he'd have a new number in his cell phone and a smirk on his face.

"Plan number one," I said to Kristen.

"On it." She gave a thumbs-up.

Rafe looked from one of us to the other. "There isn't a snowball's chance that either one of you is going to tell me what's going on, so I won't waste my precious time in asking."

"Should have figured that out years ago," Kristen said.

I nodded. "Think of the things you could have accomplished with the energy you've expended so uselessly."

"Moved mountains." Kristen made a shoving motion.

"Learned two new languages," I said.

"Invented a cure for the common cold."

"Perfected cold fusion."

Rafe opened his mouth to make a smart remark, but instead turned to smile at our approaching waitress. "Thanks," he said as she handed around the drinks. "I don't suppose you have a table where I can sit and eat without being insulted."

"Pay no attention to my husband." Kristen hopped her chair close and slung her long arm around his shoulders. "We're still working out the best medications for him to take."

"It's that weird-shaped pill that's giving him the

trouble," I told the waitress in a confidential tone, leaning over to tuck my hand under Rafe's elbow. "You know, the *blue* one?" I winked at her.

"Oh," she said, suddenly catching on that we were talking about an erectile dysfunction medication. "Oh. Well, I hope it works out for . . . um, for all of you. I'll be back in a few minutes for your order."

When she was back inside, Kristen and I spluttered with laughter.

"Aren't you the funny ones," Rafe said sourly, but he said it with a smile.

"We are, aren't we?" Kristen held up her glass. "To the reinvigoration of the Thursday Night Rcstaurant Review Crew."

As we tinked glasses, Rafe pointed out the obvious. "It's not Thursday."

"Which makes us even funnier," Kristen said. "Drink up, my dear boy. It's the only one you're getting until we're home, no matter how many times you bat those long lashes at our waitress."

He looked across the table and fluttered his eyes violently.

"Not a chance," I said, tucking my wineglass close to my body.

"Don't even." Kristen took a sip of her burgundy. "This stuff is too good for you." She glanced at me. "For you, too, but I have high hopes."

It was a fond hope of Kristen's that I'd turn into a wine connoisseur so we could have long esoteric conversations about vintage and growing conditions and the best way to harvest grapes. I doubted she would ever succeed since my wine preferences were based on two things, price and the cuteness of the label, but who was I to tell her to give up a dream?

"Speaking of you," Kristen said, "I've heard ten different stories about what happened yesterday with you and the bookmobile and Leese Lacombe and how her dad died. What's the real deal? Unless you don't want to talk about it."

"Not really," I said. "Not right now anyway."

As a relative newcomer to Chilson, I often had to rely on natives to give me the historical details that were so often necessary to understanding relationships and motivations. The town wasn't tiny, not by Up North standards, but it wasn't uncommon to realize, halfway through a conversation, that you were talking to someone about their cousin. Years ago, I'd learned to get a background check on everyone I met from Kristen, or Rafe, or my aunt Frances, or Donna at the library, or sometimes all four.

"Did Leese go to Chilson?" I asked. Rafe had graduated from high school two years ahead of Kristen and me.

"She was in the elementary school," Rafe said, "but then her mom got a job in Petoskey and they moved."

"I remember," Kristen said, snapping her fingers. "Number eight on Petoskey's softball team. She was a power hitter. Whenever she came to the plate, our outfield moved way back."

All very interesting, but I wanted to get back to what Rafe had said. "You said her mom got a job in Petoskey. What about her dad?"

As I asked the question, I focused hard on the sailboat coming up the channel, trying to guess exactly when the bells on the drawbridge would start dinging, when the traffic lights would turn red, stopping traffic back all through downtown Charlevoix, trying hard to watch what was going on in front of me so I didn't have to remember what I'd seen.

"Leese's parents split up a long time ago," Kristen said.

"Dale and Bev got divorced when Leese was little," Rafe said. "I remember Leese being the first kid I knew whose dad didn't live with them."

The bells went off and the traffic lights switched to red. As the bridge's deck started to rise, bells ringing, I said, "Them? Does Leese have siblings?"

"Only child," Kristen said. "At least directly. When her dad showed up to games, sometimes he had two little kids in tow. Stepbrother and stepsister from his second wife."

"Brad and Mia." Rafe tapped his glass. "Brad's a brew master at that new craft brewery on the north side of Petoskey. Not sure what Mia does."

"Figures he'd know the guy who makes beer," Kristen said to me. "But I'm surprised he doesn't know about Mia. She was a cute little bug of a kid, and she grew up pretty. I lost track of her after she got out of high school."

Rafe pulled out his cell. "Of course, now that you mention it, I think she's a Facebook friend. Hang on." He tapped at his phone's screen a few times, tapped again, then said, "Sure, here she is." He handed his phone over to Kristen.

"No kidding," she said. "Mia's in charge of Information Technology for what's-their-face, that company in Charlevoix. You know, that one that makes something for cars."

A girl computer geek? I'd have to tell Josh. I squinted at the screen, which was hard to see in the glare of the setting sun. "Does it say anything about her liking the White Sox?" Because if she did, there was no point in introducing her to Josh, who was a die-hard Detroit Tigers fan.

"No, but she did grow up to be gorgeous." Kristen gave me the phone and I studied Mia's picture.

"Wow, she is hot." I passed the cell back to its owner. "And you haven't dated her?"

Rafe shrugged. "Not my type."

Laughter erupted on the female side of the table. "I didn't know you had a type," Kristen said, "other than that she has to be breathing and younger than your mom."

Rafe looked at Mia's Facebook photo. "Pretty enough," he said, "but she doesn't talk much. She's a friend of a friend. We run into each other at parties, is about it."

"Her mom's sooo not like that," Kristen said. "Carmen. I remember at softball games, Carmen would be there with Dale. He'd be yelling at the umpire like the jerk he was—not to speak ill of the dead, but the truth is the truth—and she'd be right there with him, both of them in the guy's face."

"You remember that stuff?" I looked at Rafe. "Do you remember the parents of your opponents?"

He tapped the side of his head. "Like a steel trap."

"It's a small-town thing," Kristen said. "If a kid is athletic, they'll play every sport they can. I did soccer, basketball, and softball." She shrugged. "A lot of girls did those same sports, so you see the same kids over and over. You get to know them and the people who show up to watch them."

In Dearborn, where I'd grown up, the student body

was roughly a zillion times bigger than the size of Chilson's high school. If I'd wanted to play a varsity sport, which I never had, the odds of me actually making a team were about the same as Eddie never shedding any of his variegated black and white hairs. Up here, if you wanted to play, about all you had to do was keep a decent grade point average.

"What did Leese's dad do for a living?" I asked.

"Builder," Rafe said. "I worked for him one summer. Sort of. Not my favorite job and he was a horrible boss." Rafe twisted in his chair and glanced around. "You two ready to order? Our waitress is right over there." He flashed her another smile and made a come-along gesture.

"The magic is gone," I said, watching. "Look, she barely smiled back."

"Poor Rafe." Kristen sighed. "This could be the start of a long dry spell for him."

"In spite of the lies you already told her, five bucks says I'll get her number before we leave." Rafe reached for his wallet.

"That's five each." I drew the appropriate bill out of my pocket and Kristen did the same. If we spent any time with Rafe, a five-dollar bet was almost a guarantee, so we'd come prepared.

"Not fair," he grumbled, but slapped down two fives onto the center of the table to match the ones we'd laid out. "But you can't interfere."

The waitress approached. "So what can I get for you three?" she asked.

"Ladies first," Rafe said, nodding in Kristen's direction.

I smiled to myself and settled in for an entertaining

evening. My concern for Leese and the events of the previous day faded to the back of my mind.

Almost.

The next day was a bookmobile day, and our formerly perky trio of two people and a cat was decidedly unperked. Our shared dour mood could have been due to the weather, which though still warm, now included a layer of clouds so thick it was hard to believe the sun had come up and so low that if it dropped a few more feet it would be fog.

It was an indication of things to come. Thanks to the long periods of constant cloud cover in this part of the state, fall and winter were times when seasonal affective disorder roared through Tonedagana County at an epidemic level. Snow, with its reflective brightness, helped abate the worst of the symptoms, but I knew more and more people who were purchasing light therapy lamps. The results, I was told, could be impressive and I was thinking of getting one for my office.

But today, I was pretty sure it wasn't the weather that was dampening our collective spirits. No, I would have bet the five dollars I'd won from Rafe that it was the memory of what had happened the last time we'd been out—finding Dale Lacombe's dead body.

As we drove, time and again I tried to think of a conversation to start, and every time I came up with something that seemed too stupid to bother with. We didn't need to talk about the weather; it was right there in front of us. Same thing with the changing colors on the trees. You can only point and say "Pretty!" so many times without feeling like a toddler overusing the one word in your vocabulary.

I could feel Julia glancing over at me every so often, and I knew she was also wrestling with what to say. Neither one of us wanted to talk about it, and neither one of us wanted to remember it, but the discovery of Dale Lacombe's body was all we could think about.

Then, just a few miles before our first stop, I knew what I had to do. It was going to be ugly and I risked ridicule, but Julia and I had long ago made a pact that what happened on the bookmobile stayed on the bookmobile. I took a deep breath and started singing.

Julia's head snapped to the left so fast I was worried about whiplash. "Seriously?" she asked.

I nodded and launched into the second line of the theme song to *Gilligan's Island*. It was one of the few songs I knew from start to finish. My brother and I had been huge fans of the sitcom. Somewhere along the line, I'd also developed hand gestures to go with the words, but I couldn't do those while driving.

Shaking her head and smiling, Julia started singing along and we pulled into the parking lot of the Village of Dooley's fire station just as we finished the closing line. Timing is everything.

"Mrr."

"Was that a criticism?" Julia asked, unbuckling her seat belt and leaning forward to unlatch the door of Eddie's carrier. "Or were you asking for an encore? When you don't enunciate your consonants, it's hard to tell the difference."

"Mrr!"

"Saying the same thing only louder doesn't help me translate," she said, watching as he leaped from floor to console to dashboard. "And don't I wish I could move like that."

"He's young," I reminded her. "When you were

three and a half, you could probably—" I stopped and studied her. Though tall, lanky, and graceful, Julia had never struck me as the athletic type. "Sure is a nice day, isn't it?"

She hooted with laughter. "You are one of a kind, Minnie Hamilton."

"Mrr," said our new dashboard ornament.

"You, too, of course." Julia stood and patted him on the head, making his face bounce a little. After two pats, he ducked away, jumped down, and trotted to the rear of the bookmobile, where he sat down and stared at the back door.

"Does he think we're going to keep it open again today?" Julia sounded amused.

"Please don't ask me what a cat thinks," I said. "Especially that one. His head may be big, but I'm not sure he's always using the brains he has up there."

Just then the bookmobile's door opened.

Julia laughed. "Here you are, assuming he's scamming for a chance to get outside when all the time he was serving as a watchcat, warning us of approaching patrons. And here's our first of the . . . oh." Her voice gave an unusual squeak. "Good morning, Leese. It's . . . nice to see you."

"And you." Leese's face, which two days earlier had been a cheerful and rosy-cheeked tan, now looked worn and pale. She heaved herself up the last two steps, leaned down to give Eddie a pat, then stood tall, squared her shoulders, and looked at me.

"I know this isn't where I usually meet the bookmobile, but I found the route schedule on your website and drove out here. I'd like to talk to you for a few minutes, if you have time." She nodded at Julia. "Both of you."

The door opened again and small feet clambered up the stairs. "Is the bookmobile kitty here?" a high-pitched voice asked.

"I want to pet Eddie!" called a different child's voice.

"Say good morning to the bookmobile ladies first," said a man.

"Good morning, bookmobile ladies," kid number one said.

"Morning," said kid number two. "Can I pet Eddie now?"

Julia glanced at Leese and me. "Talk away. I'll take care of them," she said, and moved off to do so.

"Shall we adjourn to my office?" I asked, and we walked to the front. I unlocked the driver's seat and rotated it to face the back.

Leese sat on the carpeted step and looked up at me. "I owe you some explanations," she said.

But I was already shaking my head. "You don't owe me a thing, so please don't say anything you're not comfortable telling."

She half smiled. "And that's why I owe you; because you don't feel I owe you anything."

"That almost makes sense," I said, "but not quite. Either way, feel free to not explain."

She looked at the floor, then up at me. "How about if I want to?"

"Different story altogether. If you need a friend, if you need to talk, then talk away."

"Thank you," she said quietly. "My local friends are old ones, but they've built lives that don't have room for me right now. And though I'm making new friends, that takes time."

"I know." And I did. I'd had the luck to fall back

into instant friendship with Kristen and Rafe when I'd made the permanent move to Chilson, but it had taken months and years to develop new relationships. Small towns meant small tight circles of friends, and if you didn't have children in school or a workplace to meet people, finding friends could take a lot of work.

She waited a beat, then nodded. "First I have to thank you for calling and checking up on me. I should have called you back right away, but . . ." She sighed. "I wasn't up to it and I'm sorry."

I remembered the message I'd left for her to call. I'd worried a little about the silence, but had decided to wait another day or two before trying again. "No need to apologize," I said.

"Okay, then. First off, no matter what you hear, they didn't arrest me. I was held for twenty-four hours in the county jail for cause, and was released after the medical examiner's preliminary findings came out. My father had been dead longer than they'd thought. With so much time having passed between the murder and finding him in the truck, the window of opportunity expanded exponentially."

I'd followed her words, but got lost in the syllables toward the end. "So what you're saying is anyone could have done it?"

"At this point they're not even saying if it was murder."

"Um . . ."

She rolled her eyes. "I know; why else would his body end up in the truck if it hadn't been murder? The sheriff is just being cautious, I suppose."

"Cautious" wasn't a word I would have used to describe the almost frighteningly capable Sheriff Kit Richardson, whose toughness was legendary. Some of the stories about the fifty-something sheriff had to be apocryphal, but with my own eyes I'd seen her take down a man a hundred pounds heavier and a foot taller with little more than a fierce glance. And she was an Eddie fan, so all in all I found her to be a role model of the highest order.

"They'd like to arrest me, though," Leese said conversationally.

My eyebrows went up. "You sound pretty calm about it."

"Only on the outside. My guilt would be an easy resolution for them. Father and daughter get into an argument, daughter kills him—either accidentally or not—and she hides the body in his truck until she can find a way to get rid of it." She made a tossing gesture. "The Mitchell River Valley is only a couple of miles from that church where you stopped the other day."

I didn't need a map to see what she meant. Planning the bookmobile route had carved Tonedagana County's features deep into my brain cells. "They think the state forest is a good place for . . ."

"For disposing a body?" She shrugged. "It's a big place. Winter's coming on. With a little work you could bury a body and have it hidden until spring, if not longer."

I shied away from thinking about the logistics and zeroed in on something else. "That truck was your dad's?"

She made a noise that wasn't quite a snort but wasn't exactly a laugh, either. "For the first time in years, I asked my dad for a favor, and that's the piece of crap I got. It needed more work than my SUV did."

My eyebrows wanted to go up, but I kept them firmly in place. "You and your dad didn't get along?"

"Let me think how to answer that." She stretched her legs out straight, her heels thumping the floor. "And the answer is no, not since I was three years old. That's when he took off for greener pastures. If I was lucky, I saw him every other weekend. If I was unlucky"—she grimaced—"I saw him more often."

"Rafe Niswander and Kristen Jurek are friends of mine," I said. "Kristen said you're a great softball player."

"That, from the blond bomber?" This time Leese's smile looked real. "I'd love to see her again. And Rafe, too. Is he still as cute as ever?"

I blinked. Somehow I'd never thought much about Rafe's looks. Of course, now that I was thinking about it, he did have a lot going for him. White teeth, high cheekbones, easy smile, thick black hair, and a flat stomach that didn't reveal how much beer he seemed to consume. "He's mostly annoying."

"Same old Rafe, then." She laughed softly.

"They said your dad came to a lot of your softball games."

"Only until it became obvious I wasn't good enough to get a college scholarship. After that, my stepmother was the one who brought my step-sibs to the home games."

That hadn't been how I remembered Kristen telling it, but no doubt Leese had a better memory for those events. "What was with your SUV?"

She made a face. "The transmission went out a week ago. My car guy said if I didn't mind waiting, he could get me a rebuilt one cheap, but I'd have to wait until the summer people were gone."

Wincing, I said, "Even a rebuilt is expensive, isn't it?"

"Which is why I sucked it up and asked my dad for

a loaner. My law practice is going to take a while to be profitable and I don't want to spend more of my savings than I have to."

"He had an extra truck?"

She nodded. "He's one of those guys who always looks like he's having a party, there's so many vehicles in the driveway. But when I asked to borrow one for a couple of months, he tried giving me this long sob story about how he needed all the trucks for his crew. I got tired of it halfway through, opened my wallet, pulled out some bills, and held them out. The look on his face was priceless. I was so proud of myself for shutting him up that I almost laughed."

Her gaze drifted away. "I got a friend to drop me off at his house later that day, and when I drove off in his truck, he didn't even come out, just stood in the doorway watching me with his arms crossed. It was the last time I saw him until . . . until two days ago."

I came around and sat down next to her, putting my arms around her as she started to sob. Because even if her father hadn't been much of a dad, he was the only one she would ever have.

And now he was gone.

Chapter 4

Early the next morning, Ash and I arrived at the Round Table at the same time, me walking up to the downtown diner from the marina, him getting out of his SUV, which he'd driven from the sheriff's office, all of two blocks away. I might have made fun of him for this, but he looked exhausted. The only problem working the night shift, he'd said, was that he couldn't sleep during the day. I was proud of him for stepping up to volunteer, but was starting to be concerned about the toll it was taking on his mental state, not to mention his body.

His shoulders were rounded with fatigue, and his handsome, square-jawed face, typically ruddy with health and good cheer, was an odd shade of gray. But when he caught sight of me, he straightened up, smiled, and held the glass door open for me. "Ms. Minnie," he said, bowing and waving me in.

"That reminds me of something I've always wanted to ask," I said. We walked past the PLEASE SEAT YOURSELF sign and slid into our regular booth.

The round table after which the restaurant had

been named decades ago was in the back. It was also empty, as it usually was on Sunday mornings until the churchgoers started filing in. Monday through Saturday, however, it was the unofficial official table for a geezerly group of men, a group certain they had the answers to the world's problems.

I avoided that table as much as possible. They thought I was a youngster who needed much instruction, particularly from them, and this made me so cranky that, whenever they snared me in a conversation, I could almost feel the smoke coming out of my ears.

Ash knew all this, and for my protection and theirs, he'd suggested meeting for a Sunday breakfast instead of Saturday.

The menus were sitting upright on the table behind the basket of jams and jellies. Ash pointed in their direction. "Going to walk on the wild side and have something new?"

"Maybe next week. But let's get back to the question I've always wanted to ask."

"You're not going to make me think, are you? Because I'm pretty sure my brain went to sleep when I clocked out."

"I can drive you home, you know."

"No, I'll be fine." He smiled. "Back to your question. Animal, vegetable, or mineral?"

"You two are up bright and early." Sabrina, the restaurant's forever waitress, put down two water glasses. "Coffee coming up for Minnie. How about you, Ash?"

"Decaf," he said sadly.

"Working night shift again?" She took an order pad from her apron and pulled a pen from her graying bun of hair. "Then you'll want the oatmeal with dried cherries and walnuts. Single biscuit on the side with gravy?" He nodded and she wrote. "The usual for you, Minnie?"

I almost said yes. "No. Let's try something different. Your pick."

"Oatmeal pancakes with cherry pecan sausages for Miss Minnie." She slid the pad back into her pocket. "Back in a jiffy with the coffees."

"That's it," I said, tipping my head after the retreating Sabrina. "My question. When does a woman stop getting called 'miss' and turn into a 'ma'am'? Is it when she starts getting gray hair? Is it when she starts paying more attention to comfort than fashion? Is it when she has children? Grandchildren? Where's the line?"

He laughed, showing the dimples in his cheeks. "You're making this more complicated than it is."

It wouldn't be the first time I'd done so and undoubtedly wouldn't be the last. "Explain, please."

"What really matters," he said, "is the age of the people involved. If the woman is older than you, she's a ma'am. If she's younger than you, she's a miss."

"That's it?"

He nodded.

"That's pretty simple." I thought of a possible complication. "Are you sure that's a universal truth? I mean, maybe that's just the Wolverson Theory."

"Nope," he said. "Guys talk about this stuff all the time. It's a national consensus."

I laughed. "Nice try." Although the image I got of a bunch of cops huddled together in the back corner of a break room, raising their hands and vowing to accept the etiquette of addressing women was a good one, I was old enough to know that men talking about such a thing was more far-fetched than Eddie learning how to say thank you.

Sabrina approached with two steaming mugs. "Here you go," she said, setting down the mugs. "Your breakfasts are next in line so it won't be long."

"How's Bill these days?" I asked.

For once, the back corner booth was empty of her husband, Bill D'Arcy. He was a newcomer to Chilson, having moved north less than two years ago, and was what you'd kindly call taciturn. Bill spent most of his day hunched over his laptop moving stocks and bonds around the world and making more money than I would have dreamed possible.

He'd established himself as a regular at the Round Table soon after he moved north, and in addition to becoming the love of Sabrina's life, after his car hit the outside wall of the restaurant, he confessed that he had early-onset macular degeneration.

Sabrina glanced at Bill's normal seat. "The treatments are doing okay. He's still losing his sight, but it's slowed down. Or so the doctors say."

The muscles in her face shifted and I could tell she was struggling not to cry. Just as I was starting to reach out to touch her hand, to give what comfort I could, she said, "Of course, there's a bonus to it." She grinned. "He won't see me getting old and fat." Smirking, she slapped her hips with the palms of her hands and headed back to the kitchen.

I wondered whether, if and when the time came, I'd be able to joke about health issues with my future spouse. This led, in a natural way, to picturing Ash and me thirty years from now. But I couldn't get the image in my head. Not at all.

"Who would have guessed," Ash said.

"Guessed what?" I wrapped my hands around the ceramic mug, soaking in the warmth, and abandoned my previous line of thought.

"That they seem to be making progress on macular degeneration," he said. "Twenty years ago, when my grandmother got it, they said there was nothing to be done, that she was going to go blind in a year and that she should make adjustments accordingly."

I took a long sip of coffee. I'd once heard an interview with a woman who had, for various bizarre reasons, suffered a long bout of temporary but complete deafness, and when she'd recovered from that, had endured a time of temporary but complete blindness. Of the two, she'd said, deafness had been far harder to manage. She'd sounded sincere, a down-to-her bones sincere, but I'd found it hard to believe. After all, if you were deaf, you could still read. There was Braille, sure, and audio books and surely friends and family would read to me if I went blind, but if the ability to wander through the library and pick up a random book ceased, I was afraid I'd be cranky the rest of my life.

"Either one would be hard," I murmured.

Ash frowned. "Either one what? Either eye? Grannie had it in both."

Explaining the pathways my thoughts had taken in those two seconds would have been a pointless conversation that might have ended in him learning a bit too much about how my brain worked, so I said, "It's great they're making progress with the disease." Saying that vague, but true, statement reminded me of another topic. "Speaking of progress, is there anything new with the death of Dale Lacombe?"

Ash glanced at his watch. "Twelve minutes."

"For what?"

He grinned. "For you to ask me about Lacombe. Hal was wrong; he said it would be less than five."

"Oh, funny hah hah." I said it sarcastically, but eked out a smile. Detective Hal Inwood and I had met numerous times for a variety of reasons. At first he'd done his best to pat me on the head and tell me to let the grown-ups do their jobs, but eventually he'd come around to realize that I had a brain that could, on occasion, be useful to him and to the sheriff's office.

"And you know perfectly well I can't talk about an active investigation." Ash unrolled the paper napkin wrapped around his silverware. "Not sure why you're wasting your time asking."

"But this is different," I said, doing the same unrolling thing. "You must be able to tell me something. I was there, remember?"

"Nice try." He spread the napkin across his lap. "Let's talk about the biking route we're going to take next time I get a day off."

"Leese is a mess." The napkin in my hand crunched up into a ball. "She's worried that you're going to arrest her and there's no way she could have killed her father."

"Oh?" Ash's expression went still. "Why do you say that? Were you with her the day before?"

"Well, no. She couldn't have done it, that's all."

Ash looked at me.

"I know, I know," I said, sighing. "Given the right circumstances, practically everyone can kill. All I'm saying is that Leese wasn't in those kind of circumstances. That these weren't them." A sentence that almost made sense.

"Breakfast for two, hot and hardy." Sabrina put our plates on top of the paper place mats. "Can I get you two anything else?"

Ash and I both pushed our mugs toward her.

"Birds of a feather." Sabrina laughed. "Be right back."

She went to fetch the coffeepots and we looked at each other. I half shrugged an apology, because I really shouldn't have asked him to divulge anything about the investigation, and we started eating.

But the pancakes tasted a little flat, and the sausage sat in my stomach like an uncomfortable rock. The cause, I was sure, wasn't the kitchen.

After I waved good-bye to Ash in the diner's parking lot, I considered the rest of the day.

It was early enough to go home and crawl back into bed with Eddie for a nap and still wake up before the hour hand on the clock came around to double digits, but now that I was up and nicely caffeinated, I was wide awake.

I could do essentially the same thing, but stay awake and read the next book on my To Be Read pile, but that was my plan for the afternoon. Not that I had a problem reading all morning and all afternoon—I'd done it before and would do it again, happily and with no guilt whatsoever—but I was feeling the need for some human companionship.

Kristen would still be in bed, and I was going to see her in a few hours anyway. I could stop by Rafe's house, but now that it was October, it was bow season and he'd be sitting up in a tree until noon. I toyed with the idea of using the key he hid on a nail underneath the back porch. I could let myself in and . . . and do what? Move his minimalist furniture around? Find his current set of plans and red mark it with suggested changes?

It was tempting, and if Eric Apney, my nearest boat neighbor and a new friend of Rafe's, was still around, I might have gone ahead, but practical jokes weren't much fun by yourself, and Eric had pulled his boat out of the water a couple of weeks ago.

I thought about walking over to Holly's house. Or to Josh's. Or to any number of other friends. Or up to the Lakeview Medical Care Facility, where I knew a number of elderly folks through the new outreach program I'd been developing at the library, but it wasn't even nine o'clock—a little early on a Sunday morning for a drop-in visit.

I grinned into the morning air and started walking. Because there was one place where I'd always be welcome any time of the day or night and that was suddenly the place I wanted to be.

"Minnie!" Aunt Frances wrapped me up in a big hug. "I didn't expect to see you this morning. If I'd known, I would have laid another plate."

"Top of the morning." Otto, who'd stood when I'd walked into the boardinghouse's big kitchen, smiled at me. "Have you been out walking? You have a nice rosy tint to your cheeks."

"Had breakfast with Ash at the Round Table," I said. "But I will take some coffee . . . No, you sit. I'll get it." I waved them both back into their chairs and opened the mug cupboard. "What's new with you two?"

The silence that followed felt heavy. I turned and looked back at them just in time to see a long, communicative glance be exchanged.

"What's the matter?" A sudden fear jumped into my skin. Aunt Frances and Otto were both in their mid-sixties, which didn't seem nearly as old as it used to be, but it was also an age where things could start to go seriously wrong.

"Nothing's the matter," Otto said. "We were just making some decisions, that's all."

Silent relief sang in my ears. "Oh? About what?" I poured my coffee and sat at the round table that filled one corner of the kitchen.

"The wedding."

"About time," I said, nodding. "I can't believe you haven't tied the knot yet."

"No need to rush into these things," Aunt Frances said.

"If you're going to do it at all, you might as well do it right," Otto murmured.

I squinted. "There's a right way?"

"In any given circumstance, yes," my aunt said. "And we've concluded that what's right for us is for me to move into Otto's house after we get married."

"The wedding is set for April," her fiancé said.

"In Bermuda," Aunt Frances said.

I'd been turning my head from one to the other, like a spectator at a tennis match, but I stopped and stared at my aunt. "Bermuda?"

"I've always wanted to go," she said.

"You have?"

"For years and years." She looked at Otto with so much love that I could almost see it in the air.

"A destination wedding." The more I thought about it, the more it sounded like an excellent idea. I wasn't so sure I liked the idea of her moving out of the boardinghouse, but I'd think about that later. "I like it. I like it a lot."

"Good. And now it's time to get to church," Aunt Frances said, pushing back her chair. "Would you like to come along?"

I blinked. Church? For years, the only times my aunt and I had attended church was Christmas Eve and Easter, if we were in town. I glanced at Otto, who must have been the reason behind this change.

He smiled at me, and I felt a rush of affection for this man who was making my aunt so happy. After all, sometimes change could be good. Sometimes even very good. I pushed away my concerns about the future of the boardinghouse and smiled back.

"Sure," I said. "That sounds nice."

That evening, Leese whooped with delight. "It's the blond bomber!" She threw her arms around a grinning Kristen. "As skinny as ever and I bet just as sassy."

Kristen hugged her back. "Sassier every day, just ask my staff. And I hear you could have been partner at that multi-name law firm downstate. Nicely done."

The two former competitors slapped each other on the back one more time, then the three of us pulled around stools to sit at one of the stainless steel counters in the Three Seasons kitchen. Out in the dining room, we heard the distant grumble of the vacuum cleaner being run by Kristen's maintenance guy.

It was a standard part of Sunday evenings for me to stop by Kristen's restaurant for dessert, and though we'd never expanded beyond the two of us, that didn't mean we couldn't. I'd called Kristen in the afternoon, asking if she objected to me bringing along a visitor.

"Male or female?" she'd asked.

"Female."

"Is she fun?"

"Do you seriously think I'd bring someone who wasn't?"

She'd acknowledged my point and readily agreed. Now, I watched the two of them catch up on fifteen years of life events.

"Could have made partner," Leese said, nodding acceptance at the glass of red wine Kristen held out, "but that would have meant having to, you know, work downstate. I was tired of all the traffic and the lights and the noise."

It was a familiar story for people who'd been raised in the north country. Young people often headed downstate to Grand Rapids or the Detroit area to find jobs and to get away from a place where everyone knew—and expected to know—everyone else's business. After a few years of expressway rush hours and half-hour waits in line at the grocery store, many yearned to return, but only a fortunate few were able to do so.

I looked at two of those lucky ones, reached for my wine, and kept listening.

"You couldn't talk them into opening a branch up here?" Kristen poured her own glass and pushed the cork back into the bottle.

Leese sipped her wine, made appreciative noises, then shrugged. "If I'd tried hard enough, maybe. But I was tired of the office politics and the quest for billable hours. I went to law school so I could help folks, not to make a huge pile of money."

"Hear, hear!" Kristen toasted Leese. "I wish you good luck and a small pile of money. And if anyone asks me for a lawyer recommendation, I'll send them your way."

"She specializes in elder law," I said.

"And cottage law," Leese added. "It's like estate planning with a twist."

Kristen grinned. "You're in the right place, my friend. Half the talk I overhear in this restaurant is about how the kids and grandkids will be able to afford the property taxes on the family cottage. Get me some business cards and in the spring I'll start handing them out like dinner mints."

I read Leese's slightly puzzled look and explained. "The name of Kristen's restaurant is also a descriptor of when she's open. Three seasons."

"You're closed in the winter?"

"Hate snow," Kristen said. "Always have. In a few weeks, maybe less, I'll skedaddle down to Key West. During the week I spend a lot of time in a hammock inspecting the insides of my eyelids, and on the weekends I tend bar for a friend."

"Sounds like a good plan." Leese smiled. "How long have you had this place?"

"Going on four years."

"Have you been in the restaurant business since high school?"

I kept my gaze firmly on the shiny countertop, wondering what version of the story Kristen would tell this time.

"Nope." My best friend hesitated, then said, "After I got a bachelor's degree in biochemistry, I got my doctorate. Then I spent a miserable couple of years working for a big pharmaceutical company. I came home one Christmas and spent the whole time whining about my job. Someone got tired of hearing me complain and said if I didn't want to be unhappy the rest of my life I should think about doing something else."

At the end of the sentence, Kristen kicked me.

I kicked right back. My recollection of that conversation wasn't the same as hers, but whatever.

"Less than a year later, I'd opened this place," she said, spreading her arms wide. "I work my tail off spring through fall, then bask in the sun most of the winter."

For once, she'd mostly told the truth. The only thing she'd left out was the intensive and exhaustive training she'd embarked on before opening her own place and the brilliant way she'd convinced the bank's loan manager to sign off on the commercial loan—by bringing him lunch.

The two chatted for a few minutes about former softball teammates: about who moved away, who was still around, who had kids, and who didn't. Then Kristen asked, "What about your family? Is your dad still—"

This time I kicked her a lot harder.

She slapped a hand over her mouth. "I am so sorry," she said through her fingers, her blue eyes wide with regret. "I forgot, I just totally forgot."

Leese half smiled. "I'd forgotten, too, for a few minutes, so don't feel guilty, Kristen. It's not a good look on you."

"But I am sorry for being so stupid."

"This wasn't nearly as stupid as you were in that tournament when your team played Traverse City St. Francis."

Kristen sighed. "I still dream about that game. How could I have been that dumb?"

"Don't worry," I said. "I'm sure there will come a time when you're even more stupid. Just have patience."

"What would I do without you to prop me up?" She shook her head in fake wonderment.

Leese smiled, looking at us. "You two act more like sisters than just friends. It reminds me of my . . ." Her words trailed off.

"Of your stepsister?" I asked gently. "Your stepbrother?"

"The police are questioning Brad and Mia." Leese pushed her empty wineglass away and shook her head at Kristen's gesture toward the bottle. "They're talking to my stepmother, Carmen."

"But they must know you didn't have anything to do with your father's death," I said.

Leese's sturdy shoulders had slumped. "It's not their answers so much as the questions."

"What do you mean?" Kristen asked.

"It's not Brad or Carmen I'm worried about," Leese said. "It's Mia. She's been doing fine for years, but something like this . . ." She shook her head. "Bad enough that our father is dead, that would be hard enough for her to deal with. But having him dead like this? And for the police to put me in jail for a day, and then to grill her as if she had something to do with his death?"

I exchanged a questioning glance with Kristen, then phrased my next question as tactfully as I could. "Mia has had issues?"

"It was when she was in high school," Leese said. "My baby sister was diagnosed with anorexia." She looked at us, tears glistening in her eyes. "She was hospitalized and she . . . almost died."

Not knowing what to say, I reached out and took her hand between mine.

"Something like this," Leese whispered. "It could send her backward. It could kill her."

Kristen stood, came around the back of Leese's stool, and hugged her from behind. And we stayed like that, saying volumes without saying a word, for a long time.

Finally, I broke the silence. "We'll figure this out," I whispered to Leese. "I promise."

Chapter 5

I sat at my computer the next morning, determinedly searching for ways to cut the bookmobile's budget in a way that didn't sacrifice services. Halfway through the morning I came to the conclusion that my self-appointed task was impossible unless fuel prices dropped to twenty-five cents per gallon or unless I cut my own salary by a significant amount.

Stephen, my old boss, hadn't been big on pay increases, and inflation was far outpacing the raises we'd reluctantly been given over the last few years, so I wasn't keen on a wage cut. I was on pace to pay off my last student loan within a year and I wanted to bulk up my savings before I even considered buying a house.

When noontime rolled around, I'd found a way to revise the bookmobile's route that would save fifty miles and the accompanying driving costs. It wasn't much, and it would take some rearrangement of the outreach efforts to the homebound folks I'd picked up, but it was the only real thing I'd found to cut. It wasn't enough to make Jennifer happy.

I pushed my chair back, stretched until my neck and shoulders gave satisfying pops, and grabbed my coat.

Out front, I stopped at the main desk. "I'm headed to Shomin's. Does anyone want anything?"

Donna looked up from the books she was sorting. "Reva's salad with extra dried cherries, please. And that apple vinaigrette dressing."

"So healthy," I said. "Why can't I be more like you?"

She smiled. "Someday you probably will. Until menopause I ate like a college student."

"Is that when you started running marathons and doing all that snowshoeing?" When she nodded, I said, "Then I have fifteen or so years left to enjoy myself. Hot diggety!"

Donna laughed. "If you do exercise the right way, it's enjoyable."

"Then I must be doing something wrong," I said, grimacing.

"Oh, I don't know, when I see you and that adorably handsome Ash Wolverson out running or bicycling together, you don't look as if you'd been dragged out there by force."

"It's an act," I told her, heading toward the front door, and wondered how many levels of truth there were to my words.

One of the big wood and glass doors opened and Mitchell Koyne slouched in. Mitchell, one of the tallest men I'd ever met, was a library regular. He was Rafe's age, or thereabouts, and while the two of them weren't bosom buddies, they had enough in common that I grew concerned about the universe if they spent more than one consecutive hour together.

"Hey, Minnie."

I glanced at the wall clock over the door, not that I truly needed to. "Afternoon, Mitchell." One of Mitchell's curious habits was that he never set foot in the library before noon. For years, Holly and I had tossed around theories on how Mitchell managed to eke out a living. Summers he worked as a laborer on construction jobs; winters he worked at a local ski resort. In spring and fall he helped put in and take out docks. None of that could have provided much income. Of course, since he lived in an apartment carved out of his sister's attic, he probably didn't need much.

No one expected much from Mitchell other than weird questions and the occasional bit of trivia. Not that Mitchell was dumb—far from it. He read far more widely than I did, wasn't afraid to ask questions, and retained the essence of everything he had read or taught. He was blessed with a combination of innate intelligence and, until recently, a complete lack of ambition.

Mitchell's über-laid-back attitude toward life had changed when he'd started dating Bianca Sims, a real estate agent out of Petoskey. Bianca seemed normal enough, so we were all curious if the romance was going to last.

I looked up, way up, at Mitchell, weirdly pleased that no matter how hard he was working at his jobs in hopes of impressing the fair Bianca, his library schedule was still the same. Today he was dressed in his typical worn jeans, ratty sneakers, ancient T-shirt under an untucked plaid flannel shirt, and a cap with a logo for the Traverse City Beach Bums, a minor league baseball team.

"Guess what?" Mitchell asked.

"You've painted your pickup truck all one color." His truck was easy to identify from a distance because the hood, body, doors, and bed had all come from different junkyards at different times and were a variety of colors.

He frowned. "Why would I do that? There's hardly any rust anywhere. Guess again."

"Do I get a hint?"

"Nah, I'll just tell you. I've been promoted!" He bounced up and down on his toes, grinning widely. "At the toy store downtown. They're making me manager."

For a stunned second, I couldn't think of a thing to say. Finally, I managed to get out, "That's great, Mitchell."

"Yeah, I'm going to get health insurance and everything. Pretty cool, huh?"

"Very." And it was cool. "Congratulations."

"And now that I'll be full time with benefits, want to know what I'm going to do with my first paycheck?"

Not in the least. "What's that?"

His grin went even wider. "I'm going to pay off my library fines. All of them."

"You're . . . what?"

"Hah. Thought that would surprise you. But I mean it. I'll come in on payday with the cash."

Mitchell's fines were the stuff of legends. Over the years his monetary transgressions from overdue and lost books had come close to the four-figure mark. It had mainly been because of Mitchell that Stephen had created a hard-and-fast rule of not allowing any borrowing from any adult account with overdue fines more than a dollar.

This had resulted in Mitchell spending lots of time in the reading room, poring over his choice of books, magazines, and newspapers, which wasn't exactly what Stephen had intended, but as I'd told my former boss over and over, ours was a public library and Mitchell was part of the public.

Not having Mitchell's name at the top of the fine list, though, was going to take some adjustment.

"That's outstanding," I said. "Let me know when you come in, okay? I want to take pictures so I can send one to Stephen."

Mitchell held up his hand for a fist bump. "Good plan."

He continued inside and I headed out into the half-hearted October sunshine, a little wistful. It was good that he was becoming a more stable citizen, of course it was good, but a part of me was already regretting the disappearance of the old Mitchell.

I was in the break room, putting my lunch onto a plate, when Jennifer walked in. "Have you been to Shomin's Deli?" I asked. "Their sandwiches are outstanding."

Jennifer glanced at the container while smoothing the line of her black and white checked jacket. She wore this over a white silk shell, on top of a black pencil skirt and high-heeled boots. It was a sleek look, and if I'd tried to wear that same outfit, I would have felt like a little kid dressing up in Mommy's clothes.

"Chalkboard menu?" she asked. "Wooden booths with hooks at the end for hanging coats?"

She made it sound provincial and sadly out of date. "That's the one," I said cheerfully. "Have you tried their Reuben? People say it's the best in the state."

"I don't care for corned beef." She flicked another

glance at my lunch. "When you're done, I'd like you to come up to my office for a few minutes."

"How about now?" I stood, shoved my sandwich into the fridge, then did my best to make idle chitchat as we walked down the hallway and up the stairs, but when you're the only one asking questions ("How was your weekend?") and the responses you're getting are single syllables ("Fine"), the conversation tends to lose momentum quickly.

My last effort, that of asking Jennifer if she'd ever vacationed in this part of Michigan, died a quick death as she opened the door of her office and pushed it wide.

"Oh," I said. "Oh. This is . . . new."

It certainly was. The formerly wood-paneled walls had been painted a sleek gray; the carpet was a speckled black and gray. The deeply stained desk and chairs were now a shiny black. The draperies had been replaced with starkly white Venetian blinds, and the light fixture was a flat fluorescent panel that clung to the ceiling for dear life. The murky abstract paintings she'd added did little to bring any brightness to the space.

"Isn't it wonderful?" A smiling Jennifer admired the space. "This is the office I've always wanted. I went a little over what the library board gave me for a budget, but I have no problem making it up out of my own pocket."

At least it was her wallet and not the bookmobile's budget. I struggled to find something kind to say. I didn't want to blurt out to my new boss that her dream office belonged in Chicago and not northern Michigan. That in spite of the accessory heating Stephen had purchased, the room was going to feel cold until May.

"I'm glad," I finally said, "that you're happy with how it turned out."

"Thank you." She sat at her desk and held out a hand, indicating that I do the same. "Please, have a seat."

"Um, thanks." I looked askance at the object she was pointing toward. Until then I hadn't been exactly sure it was a chair; it could easily have been a piece of modern art, something sculpted to look sort of like a chair to make a point about post-modernism in the twenty-first century.

Gingerly, I lowered myself and perched on the edge of what had to be the seat. "I've made some cuts to the bookmobile's budget," I said, trying to preempt her. "I should have preliminary numbers to you by the end of the week."

"That's exactly what I want." Jennifer leaned forward, putting her elbows on the glossy black desk and lacing her fingers together.

I flashed back to the many times Stephen had summoned me upstairs and then used the exact same body language, which had always meant he was about to tell me something I didn't want to hear.

Déjà vu all over again, I thought, and waited for the bad news. It didn't take long.

"She wants you to do what?" Holly, in the act of spearing leftover macaroni and cheese onto her fork, stopped mid-stab and stared at me.

I toed the refrigerator door shut and dropped my lunch onto the table. "I'm supposed to go upstairs to give her daily updates."

Through a mouthful of peanut butter and jelly, Josh asked, "Why can't she come down and see what's going on herself? I mean, if we were a big city library, maybe, but here? Sounds like a waste of time."

Though I agreed with him, I didn't want to create any more discord and I was already regretting what I'd told them.

Holly forked in a bite and swallowed. "What else did she want? She's the master of efficiency. She wouldn't have dragged you up there for just one thing."

"I think part of it was the new interior design theme."

"Old news." Josh waved his half-eaten sandwich at me. "I saw it the other day when I had to go up there to hook her computer up again. I kind of like it."

"He showed me pictures," Holly said, squinching up her face. "Nice for Manhattan maybe, but it doesn't fit here."

"Who cares if it fits or not?" Josh frowned. "It's her office. Can't she set it up the way she wants without getting crap?"

He had a point, but Holly wasn't going to let him win the round. "If it's in a public space, no," she said. "There are expectations that public decor is suitable to its surroundings."

"Expectations by who?" Josh asked.

From the sneer in the back of his voice, I could tell those two were about to launch into one of their habitual arguments. If I hadn't met both sets of their parents, I would have assumed they were siblings. Ones that had never gotten along. To distract them, I said, "Jennifer also wants a written monthly report to take to the board."

"What's the point of a monthly report," Holly asked, "if you're already doing an annual one? Sure, the annual came from Stephen, but everyone knows you wrote most of it."

The board didn't, but I let her keep her illusions. "There's value in keeping her up to date. Plus the annual report will be easy with the monthly ones in hand. If I have twelve monthly reports, practically all I have to do it staple them together and make a new cover."

"Sure," Josh said. "Like you're going to do that."

He was right, of course. No matter what, I'd spend hours and hours working on the annual report, laboring over what should be included and what should be left out.

"Doesn't she know how hard you work?" Holly said, a little too loudly. "Doesn't she know that the last thing you need is more things to do, especially stupid things?"

The conversation was headed straight into Jennifer-bashing territory, so I hunted for a new topic. "Do either of you know Leese Lacombe?"

"Is that Brad's sister?" Josh asked. "Isn't she the one they arrested for killing their dad?"

"Dale Lacombe was murdered?" Holly's eyes went wide. "Where have I been that I hadn't heard?"

If I'd been smarter, I would have changed the subject to something less fraught. Whether schools should teach cursive writing, say, or whether our current taxation system was fair and equitable. "Leese didn't kill anyone," I said. "Anyway, no one has said it was murder."

And since I really didn't want to talk about Dale Lacombe—*those pale blue eyes*—I cheated. "Did I tell you two that Jennifer has asked me to cut the bookmobile's budget?" Cheating, definitely, but it worked like a charm.

Eventually, I did get to eat my lunch. Which was a good thing, because going foodless for long stretches without getting cranky was not one of my gifts.

After I ate, it was time for a stint at the reference desk. Late afternoon was my favorite time to be the reference librarian because that was the time the schoolkids came in to research their projects.

The kids typically fell into two camps: the kind who had never talked to a librarian before and didn't quite realize I was human, and the kind who thought my job was completely unnecessary, reference librarians having been replaced by the Internet years ago.

I had a couple of each type that afternoon, all four of them boys in the twelve-year-old range, and all four had a list of things in the library they had to use.

"This is a stupid assignment," one of the boys said, looking at the grimy, crumpled list in his hand. "No one needs libraries anymore. Everything is on the computer."

I pointedly glanced around the room since almost every table was occupied by one or more people. The kid didn't clue in. I considered giving him the Neil Gaiman quote of "Google can bring you back 100,000 answers. A librarian can bring you back the right one," but let it go. From the set of his chin, I could tell the kid wasn't willing to listen to Neil Gaiman or to the possibility of joyful serendipity that only browsing through book stacks could bring.

"Not everything," another of the boys said. This one wore a Green Bay Packers hat, which illustrated his willingness to stand out. "There are lots of books in the library that aren't on the Internet. I mean, they're there, but you can't read them without getting someone to buy them for you."

"Who wants to read a bunch of dumb books?" his classmate said. "How many of those stupid Harry Potter books do you need?"

"Either way," I said, cutting in before the argument went the way of Holly and Josh's discussions, "your assignment still needs to be done. Let me show you some tricks to remembering the Dewey decimal system."

All four of the kids got such pained looks on their faces that I laughed. "Don't think of it as having to remember more numbers," I said. "Think of it as a shortcut to finding what you want."

"Never thought of it that way," said one of the boys.

"Me, either," said a taller female voice.

I turned and saw Leese leaning against the reference counter. She smiled. Sort of. "When you're done, can I talk to you for a minute?" she asked.

At my nod she pulled out the nearest chair, dropped into it, and started flipping through a book that had been left there ten minutes ago, one I'd yet to return to its home in the 590s. Though I was pretty sure that my friend had no interest in the history of taxidermy, you never knew.

I pulled my attention back to the already restless kids. In spite of wanting to hurry them through their assignment so I could talk to Leese, I did my best to make sure they understood why there were numbers in front of and behind Mr. Dewey's decimal. At the end, it was possible that half of them might retain ten percent of what I'd said, so I considered the tutorial a success.

"What's up?" I sat in the chair next to Leese.

She turned a page of the book, which showed a

picture of a stuffed weasel, then shut it, saying, "Oh, I was in town to get some paperwork recorded at the county building, so I thought I'd stop by."

I squinted at her, not quite believing the story. "You said you wanted to talk to me."

"What's that? Oh, sure. Well, I meant, you know . . . just chatting."

Right. "Leese, if you want to talk about anything, you know I'll listen. I'm a good listener, just ask Eddie."

She smiled at that, but still didn't say anything.

I slid forward on my chair so no one else would hear me. "If it's about your dad," I said softly, "I'll listen. If it's about the police investigation, I'll listen. If it's about not being able to find pants that fit, I'll listen." And I would. Not only because I felt a vague sense of guilt that Eddie had been the one to discover Dale's body and hence drag Leese into trouble, but mostly because she was a good person and a friend.

For a long moment, she didn't say anything. Then, at last, she half turned toward me and said, "The final autopsy report on my dad is done. My attorney got a copy of it."

"Oh," I said. "That must be . . ." But I had no idea how that must have been. Painful? Difficult? Weird?

Leese gave a twisted smile. "Yeah. Exactly. It's bizarre, is what it is. Autopsies are done down in Grand Rapids, at Spectrum, after they're brought downstate by the county's medical examiner investigator."

More bizarreness. I suppressed a shiver and waited for her to go on.

"One of the main conclusions was that the time of death was approximately twelve hours before the

EMT squad arrived that afternoon, with a three hour possibility of error either way." She paused and went on. "The cause of death was a broken neck."

"A . . . what?"

Leese looked off into the distance. "A neck broken so badly that the spinal cord was severed, which caused a nearly instant death. Apparently a broken neck doesn't always mean death, but in this case it did."

"But . . ." I didn't know where to go with my question so I just let it hang there.

"I know," Leese said. "How did someone with a broken neck get into the back of the truck? Especially considering how his neck was broken."

"What do you mean?"

Leese shuddered. "His neck wasn't the only thing broken. One scapula, a collarbone. The pelvis. Metatarsals and metacarpals. And his skull was fractured."

I closed my eyes briefly. "What could have caused all that?"

"A fall," Leese said quietly. "That was the report's conclusion anyway. And from quite a height, at least thirty feet. Other factors are involved, too. The surface he fell onto, for one. They'll be analyzing his clothes and skin."

Of course they would. Maybe they'd find that Lacombe had fallen onto landscaping dirt specially ordered from a South American greenhouse that grew only exotic orchids, orchids that only one person in all of Michigan cultivated. Or maybe they'd find he'd fallen onto asphalt of the kind that paved every road and driveway in this part of the state because there was only one asphalt plant.

Questions bubbled up inside me. Were they trying to build a case against Leese? Would they wait for the forensics evidence to come in? From Ash, I knew that would take days to weeks, not the hours or minutes as shown on television. Would they start talking to her neighbors? Talking to her friends? To her clients?

Leese shifted. "So did he fall, or was he pushed? And how did he end up in the back of that truck?" She shook her head. "I'm a start-up business. Brand new. I can advertise all I want but what's going to grow my practice is personal recommendations. Word of mouth."

She toyed with the corner of the book. "In the last two days, I've lost two clients. They didn't say why, but I believe it's the suspicion that I killed my dad. The police came with a search warrant and went through my house, and—" She eyed me. "You hadn't heard that, had you?"

"No." And I didn't like it one bit. That could only mean they were still considering Leese as a serious suspect.

"As far as I know, they didn't find anything incriminating." She gave a half laugh. "But the word is getting around. If I lose more clients, if I can't get any more, I'm done. I can work without income for another few months, but I have to get more clients by the end of the year. I . . ."

Her voice cracked. She stopped talking and looked at me, her panic tamped down, but still visible in the taut lines around her eyes. "What am I going to do?" she whispered.

"Wrong question," I said.

She blinked. "What?"

"The question," I told her, "is what are *we* going to do. Because I'm going to help you."

"You . . . are?"

"Absolutely. And I know exactly how to do it."

Chapter 6

A little more than two hours later, I was done with work—leaving at five o'clock on the dot for the first time since I'd been hired—and was pulling into Leese's driveway, the last one on the road before the asphalt turned into a dirt track.

Made of fieldstone, Leese's house was snugged underneath a set of maple trees whose leaves were just starting to blossom into crimson. It had diamond-paned windows, a wide front porch, and a set of adorable eyebrow windows on the second floor.

She'd put a tasteful sign out front announcing the presence of LACOMBE LAW, SPECIALIZING IN ELDER AND COTTAGE LAW, and put an identical but smaller sign on the front door, clearly indicating where clients should enter.

As she'd instructed, I didn't go in that way, but instead went around to the back door, which was right at ground level. I knocked a few times, opened the door, again as instructed, and went inside and up the few stairs to the kitchen.

One glance around the cream-colored room was

enough to tell me that Leese was far more interested in cooking than I could ever imagine being. In addition to the shelves full of cookbooks, the knife block was fully occupied with actual knives, and there were countertop appliances whose functions I wasn't completely sure about. There was also a plugged-in Crock-Pot issuing tantalizing smells.

Leese noticed my sniff. "Clam chowder," she said. "For when you're done. You didn't eat already, did you?"

I shook my head, since no rational adult would consider a can of soda and a granola bar anything close to a meal. "It smells great."

"Good. Gives you something to look forward to." She paused, then said, "Good luck, I guess."

The warm weather was holding, so there was no need to zip my coat as I walked down the driveway. I went out to the road and walked along the shoulder—the closest sidewalk was back in Chilson, about twenty miles away—and a few minutes later arrived at the driveway of Leese's closest neighbor.

It was a ranch house with vinyl siding, clipped foundation hedges, and a recently sealed asphalt drive. The landscaping was so tidily maintained that not a single leaf lay on the broad expanse of lawn. Not a shred of personality showed and it made me a little twitchy.

Earlier, I'd asked Leese if she knew them, and she'd said their names were Alice and Bill Wattling. "We wave at each other when I drive past," she'd said. "They seem nice enough."

My idea to help Leese had been to talk to her neighbors, to see if any of them had noticed any vehicles stopping by her house at the time her father's body must have been placed in the truck. This was a little difficult because we didn't know the exact time we were talking about, but Leese had narrowed it down.

"There was nothing under the tarp on Wednesday night," she'd said at the library, "because I'd gone grocery shopping and put some of the heavy stuff in the back. I would have noticed if . . . you know. And Thursday was the bookmobile day."

All of which meant that Dale's body had been moved between the time Leese had arrived home from the grocery store and when she'd left for the bookmobile on Thursday afternoon. She'd finished her grocery shopping just before the store closed at 10 p.m. and had left for the bookmobile after a post-lunch phone call with a prospective client.

That all worked out to about sixteen hours the truck was out in the driveway, unattended. Since it was unlikely anyone would have done the deed in broad daylight, what we were after was any information about Wednesday night.

Or early Thursday morning, I amended in my head, because if I'd been trying to sneak around, I'd do it at 3 a.m., a time far too late for most people to be up and too early for people working the night shift to be home.

Other people lived on the street, but the Wattlings were by far the closest. I trod up the prefabricated concrete steps and I pushed the rectangular doorbell button, lit from inside by a slightly creepy orange glow.

Inside, a low electronic chime gonged hollowly. Footsteps approached and the door swung open. "Alice said she saw someone coming up," said the man I assumed was Bill Wattling. "Whatever you're selling, we're not buying."

This was the neighbor who seemed nice? He was fifty-ish, with cropped graying hair and a mustache that badly needed a trim. The dress pants and plaid buttoned shirt he wore indicated some sort of professional job.

"Hi," I said, being friendly, but not friendly enough to hold out my hand. "I'm Minnie Hamilton, assistant director of the Chilson Library," I told him, figuring it never hurt to establish myself as a person worthy of trust, and if you couldn't trust a librarian, the world might as well end. "I'm a friend of your neighbor, Leese, and I'm guessing you've already heard about her father."

Wattling's face was closed and uninformative and he didn't say a thing. Nonetheless, I plunged ahead.

"What we're hoping to find out," I went on, "is if you saw a car or any headlights, or heard anything unusual last Wednesday night or early Thursday morning. Because that must have been when her"—*those pale blue eyes*—"when her father's body was left in the truck."

"That's your story?" Wattling asked, snorting. "That someone did a body dump? Nice try, but I doubt the police are going to go for it."

"Leese didn't kill her father," I said, strongly and firmly, almost the Librarian's Voice, but not quite. I reserved that for truly difficult situations. This was just uncomfortable. "Someone made it look like she was involved, that's all. And I'm sure the police will be asking these same questions, so you might as well tell us, too."

"If the cops come," he said, "I'll tell them the truth. That no one came past either night." He took a quick step back and shut the door in my face. From inside,

Wattling turned the deadbolt and I flinched at the noise.

From his point of view, Leese had already been tried and convicted. The only thing left was the sentencing.

I trod back down the steps, down the driveway, and planned what I'd say to Leese about the Wattlings. "Those folks might have been nice at a distance, but up close they're clearly not folks you'd want to spend a lot of time with. I mean, have you seen the flooring in their entryway?" I practiced a scrunched-up face. I hadn't actually noticed the flooring, but I was willing to bet Leese had never seen it, either.

Girding up my strength and resolve, I moved on to the other even more distant neighbors, and though not all of them were as disapproving as Bill Wattling, none of them had seen or heard anything that would help.

Leese's father had been killed at a time they all said had been quiet and peaceful. Which didn't make sense, because someone must have delivered his body, and that should have resulted in headlights and, if not voices, at least some noise.

I trudged back to Leese's house in low spirits. I wanted to help her, but I was running out of ideas. What we needed were some brilliant plans, a lucky break, or both, and what I was getting was a north wind in my face.

Shivering against the chill, I put my head down and headed back to Leese's house.

The next day was a bookmobile day, but I'd arranged the fall schedule differently. Every third Tuesday, the bookmobile didn't leave its garage until noon and trundled back home a little after eight. I wasn't keen on driving around in the dark, but having an afternoon/evening run was giving us a chance to reach folks who worked during the day.

Jennifer hadn't approved of the idea, saying that people who wanted to come to the library would find a way. I hadn't cited the reasons why driving to Chilson after a full day of work might be difficult—an unreliable vehicle, the need to take care of children or elderly parents, sheer exhaustion, lack of gas money, and more. Instead, I'd just said I wanted to try this new route and eventually she'd allowed me to go ahead.

Two months in, I was considering the rearranged route a success, but it was a long day, one that left me more tired than I'd expected. When I'd mentioned this to Holly through yawns one Wednesday morning, she'd rolled her eyes and said, "That's because you're still coming into the library at eight in the morning. Do us all a favor and take that morning off, okay?"

I'd said I'd consider her advice, and when my aunt Frances told me much the same thing, in much the same tone, only a little harsher ("You're going to fall asleep and drive into a tree, silly girl. Take that morning off or I'll tattle on you to the library board"), I sighed and admitted they were probably right. That, and my aunt would definitely have tattled on me. She knew every member of my board and wouldn't hesitate to use her influence if she thought I was being truly stupid.

So that morning, instead of waking to the beep of an alarm clock, I woke up to a cat's paw patting the side of my nose.

"Good morning, Eddie," I said. "What can I do for you?"

He said nothing and continued to pat.

I reached out from under the covers to bat his paw away. "What are you doing?"

"Mrr," he said, and started using his other front paw on my nose. There is no stubborn like a cat being stubborn.

"What's wrong with my nose?" I was lying on my side, facing the outside wall of the houseboat. Eddie was snuggled between my shoulder and the wall. "You've never complained about it before."

He kept on patting. The first fifty-two pats I hadn't minded, but the fifty-third one annoyed me. I rolled onto my back to get away from The Paw. Eddie instantly laid his front half across my neck and started purring.

"Seriously?" I asked. "This is why you were shoving at my nose?"

His mouth opened and closed silently and his purr motor revved into high gear.

There was no doubt: I lived with the weirdest cat in the universe. "This is cozy and all," I told him, "but I have this feeling you're going to creep closer and closer to my face and some morning I'm going to wake up suffocated by Eddie fur and then won't you be sorry."

"Mrr," he said quietly, which I took to mean he would be careful not to suffocate me because he couldn't do without me. It was a nice thought, but he was more likely telling me to be quiet so he could get back to sleep.

"Okay," I murmured, and I drifted off into that happy place that wasn't quite sleep and wasn't quite wakefulness. Then, just as I was spiraling down into certain slumber, my phone rang with Ash's ring tone.

Trying not to disturb the snoring Eddie, I reached out with my unencumbered hand and felt around on the nightstand. Just before he went to voice mail, I found the phone and hit the answer button. "Good morning."

"And to you," he said, sounding amused. "Are you still in bed?"

"Me?" I slid out from underneath Eddie, kicked my feet free of the covers, and stood up. "No. Why would you say that?" I looked outside and saw that the sun was just up. "Do you want to go out for breakfast? I don't have to be at the library until noonish."

"I was hoping for a favor. Remember that Shakespeare book you were talking about? I mentioned it to a buddy on the day shift. He's leaving for vacation after work, and he said he'd like to read it. I don't remember the title, but it was written by some guy named Bill."

"Bill Bryson," I said. "Title is *Shakespeare: The World as Stage.*" It was a relatively short biography of the playwright, and funny to boot. "I can drop it off."

"Thanks, that would be great. Just leave it up front and tell them it's for Luke."

"I can be there in twenty minutes." Because I wasn't about to present myself publicly without a shower and some food in my stomach.

Ash laughed. "You were still in bed, weren't you?"

"Just trying to keep Eddie happy," I said, and hung up.

If I'd known what was about to happen at the sheriff's office, I might have crawled back inside the covers and let Eddie do whatever he wanted to my nose. But since I had no clue, I took a quick shower, dressed even quicker, and grabbed a granola bar on my way out the door.

After a fast walk through downtown, during which I'd waved at Cookie Tom, out sweeping his sidewalk, and told him I'd be back later to buy some bookmobile cookies, I was in the front lobby of the sheriff's office, standing at the glassed-in front desk and trying not to stand on my tiptoes to look taller.

Yes, I was vertically challenged, but that was nothing to be embarrassed about and there was no reason why a six-foot-tall male shouldn't consider a woman a foot shorter as a strong, intelligent, and capable human being. I'd come to this realization years ago and since then had made a solid effort to stop trying to appear taller than I was. Why pretend to be something I was never going to be? Besides, high heels made me walk wobbly.

The deputy at the counter slid the glass open. "Can I help you?"

"Hi, I'm Minnie Hamilton and—"

"Oh, hey." The stocky, brown-haired man nodded. "You're that librarian who's dating Wolverson. He said you were bringing in a book for Luke?"

I glanced at his name tag. RODGERS. The name didn't ring any bells. I'd met a number of Ash's fellow deputies, but there were dozens. "That's right," I said, putting the volume on the counter and sliding it over. The book was mine, one I'd picked up at the used bookstore in town, so I wasn't going to worry about when I got it back. "Hope he enjoys it." And since I was in the building, there was no reason not to see if I could get some good information. "Is Detective Inwood around? If he has a minute, I'd like to talk to him."

"Let me check." Deputy Rodgers picked up a phone receiver and stabbed at a few buttons. "Morning, Hal. You have a visitor, Minnie Hamilton. Do you want—" His eyebrows went up and his gaze swiveled back to me. "Sure, I can do that." He hung up the phone and looked at me quizzically. "Hal said to send you to your room."

My room? Funny. "The detective and I have a history." I headed to a door that led back to a maze of offices.

The deputy buzzed the door unlocked and I pulled it open. A few steps down the hall, I turned to the right and went into the interview room I'd been in so many times before.

Just as I sat at the chipped laminate table, the gray-haired Detective Hal Inwood came in. He'd spent decades as a police officer downstate, retired, moved up north, and had started tapping his toes with boredom within three months. When he would retire for good was a common topic of discussion in the sheriff's office, and though I hadn't asked, someone was probably taking bets on the date.

"Good morning, Ms. Hamilton." The detective pulled out the chair across from me and sat. "Let me guess. You're here to discuss your donation to the Police Officers Association of Michigan."

"I'm sure it's a worthy cause, but I was hoping for some information about Dale Lacombe's murder."

"Why am I not surprised. And you should not be surprised when I tell you that I cannot talk about an active investigation."

"But—"

"Ms. Hamilton, please. We know how to do our job. We have been working diligently to find Mr. Lacombe's killer, and—"

"You're looking in the wrong place," I said. "Leese didn't kill her dad. Why are you wasting your time trying to pin it on her?"

Inwood sighed. "We are not, as you say, trying to 'pin it' on Ms. Lacombe. We are following proper police procedure, which will ensure that all appropriate action is taken."

"Appropriate?" I asked, my voice a little loud. "Who decides what's appropriate? Because if you think it's appropriate to search Leese's house, you're nuts."

Inwood gave me a long look. "All avenues of investigation—"

"Will be explored," I cut in to finish. "Yes, I know, but please tell me you're looking at boulevards and highways, too."

I wasn't exactly sure what I meant, and I don't think Inwood did, either, because he had a blank look when the door to the room burst open and Deputy Rodgers rushed in.

"Hal, you have to come out front. Right now."

Inwood stood. "Ms. Hamilton, please stay here." Before I so much as twitched, he left the room.

"Well." I sat back, wondering what was going on. Ten seconds later, before I'd had any real chance to dream up possibilities, a door down the hallway crashed open.

"This way, please," I heard Inwood say. "We'll get you settled down and we'll talk." Inwood and Deputy Rodgers walked past, a young woman between them.

"It was me," the woman said, stuttering the words out through heaving sobs. "I did it, it was me."

"Yes, miss," Inwood said. "In here, please." Moments later, a door shut. Firmly.

I stood then, hearing footsteps, sat down fast. Deputy Rodgers poked his head inside the room. "Um, Hal's going to be busy for a while, so you might as well go."

"Who was that?" I asked, tipping my head toward the now-muffled sobs.

He glanced in the same direction. "Mia Lacombe. Dale's daughter."

This didn't sound good. With a suddenly dry mouth, I asked, "What was she saying she did?" Horrible sentence construction, but I couldn't take it back. The deputy didn't reply, so I stood up and asked again. "What did she do?"

Rodgers shifted his gaze to look over the top of my head. "She confessed."

No, I told myself. It can't be true. "To what?"

"Killing her father."

Chapter 7

"It can't be true." Leese's voice sounded far away. "Mia would never have done that. Never."

Out on the sidewalk, I shifted my grip on my cell phone and tried to think of a better way I could have told my friend that her stepsister had walked into the sheriff's office and hysterically confessed to patricide. In person would have been better, but I hadn't wanted Leese to hear the news from someone else.

"That's what the deputy said," I confirmed, then thought of a bizarre possibility. "What does she look like?"

"Not like me at all. Straight and short dark hair unless she's back to dying it some weird color. She's skinny and short. Taller than you, though."

That wasn't saying much, but her description matched the young woman I'd seen. So much for the possibility of mistaken identity. "When I saw her, she was crying and saying 'It was me, I did it.'" There was no answer at Leese's end, so I kept on going. "As far as I know, she's still talking to Detective Inwood. He's a decent guy, but he's not concerned about winning the Nicest Police Officer Award."

"Right," Leese said. "Can you do me a favor and tell them I'm coming? Tell them I'll be acting as Mia's attorney and that I'm fifteen minutes out."

"Of course," I said, and tried not to remember that Leese lived twenty miles from Chilson. "Is there anyone you want me to call?"

"No," she practically shouted. "Do not call Carmen. Do not call Brad. Let me figure out what's going on. I'll call them myself when I learn something. Carmen will go all weepy and Brad will stomp around looking for something to do. Neither one would be any help."

"Got it," I said, though I wasn't sure I agreed with her. Still, it was her family and she should know what was best. "Is there anything else you'd like me to do?"

"Sure." Over the phone I heard a car door slam and an engine roar to life. "Figure out who really killed my dad."

"On it," I told her. "Drive carefully, okay?"

"Every day," she said, and the phone went silent.

After blowing out a long breath, I looked up at a thick bank of low clouds, and went inside to give Leese's message. Once that was done, I came back out and tried to think what to do next. I could stay and offer moral support to Leese, but I wasn't sure I'd be allowed to stay in the room with them.

More than once in the last year or two, I'd had people tell me to let the police do their jobs. They were right; I should have confidence in our local law enforcement and in our justice system. And I did, truly I did. I just didn't think they moved quickly enough. Detective Inwood and even Sheriff Richardson could only be in one place at a time and there were only so many hours in a day.

I looked up the street to the big clock the chamber of commerce had installed last summer. Looked again, because I couldn't fathom that it wasn't even nine o'clock. Was the freakishly expensive thing broken already? I pulled out my cell phone, but it told me the same thing, that it was ten to nine.

"Three hours," I murmured. There were three hours before I had to start the bookmobile's route. What could I do in that amount of time that would be useful? What could I learn? What could . . .

"Duh," I said out loud, startling the elderly man who was walking past. "Not you," I said, flashing him a smile. "Me. Have a nice day."

Because I'd figured out what to do. I was a librarian. What I needed to do was research.

"Dale Lacombe?" Bianca Sims, girlfriend of Mitchell Koyne and one of the most successful real estate agents in the area, studied me. She was blond, intelligent, and energetic, and I was still trying to figure out what she saw in Mitchell. "What kind of information?" she asked. "I heard his guys are going ahead with working on the houses he'd contracted to build, if that's what you're after."

Sort of, but not really. "I came to you," I said, "because Mitchell says you know all the builders in the area."

A soft smile drifted across her face. "He's so sweet. I can't believe how lucky I was to find him."

If my former boss had known Bianca was looking for a guy like Mitchell, I was sure he would have made the wedding arrangements himself in hopes of getting Mitchell to spend less time in the library.

"If I had to guess, I'd say Mitchell feels the same

way about you," I said, and her smile went even soppier. As I thought about what I'd say next, it occurred to me that I'd never smiled that way about Ash. Not once. "I'm interested in Dale's business. Leese Lacombe, his daughter, is a friend of mine and I'm helping with the obituary."

Or I would offer to help the next time I talked to Leese.

"Happy to help," Bianca said. "His death was a shock to everyone."

Especially Leese. I scribbled on the notepad I'd brought along, testing the pen and trying to push those staring blue eyes out of my memory. "Do you know how long Dale had been a builder?"

"Let's see." She leaned back and tented her fingers. "From what I remember people saying, he started working for a landscaper after high school. Then he got his builder's license and worked for a contractor for a few years before going out on his own. So I'd say Lacombe Construction had been in business for at least thirty-five years."

Longer than I'd been alive. "If he was in business for that long, he must have had a good reputation."

At first, Bianca didn't say anything, then she abruptly pushed herself back from her desk. "I need coffee. Want some?"

In short order, we were standing next to her Keurig coffeemaker, watching first one, then two, mugs fill with the piping hot staff of life. "How much do you really want to know about Dale?" Bianca asked.

A loaded question if I'd ever heard one, and I considered my answer carefully. "The truth," I said.

Bianca offered me sugar, which I declined, and

creamer, which I accepted. "Dale Lacombe," she said, "built cheap houses and charged a lot for them."

"Ah." A number of things suddenly started making sense. Rafe's reluctance to discuss Lacombe. The relationship that Leese, my by-the-rules friend, had had with her father.

"How he found so many suckers," Bianca went on, "I don't know, but he made a good living taking money from people who knew nothing about having a house built. He was always low bid, and you know what? You get what you pay for."

Her cheeks were starting to turn pink and I looked at her with a new interest. The two of us had met a small handful of times, but they'd mostly been chance encounters, and I now realized I'd never talked to her one-on-one. "You didn't care for him, did you?"

"Certainly not for his business practices," she said. "But there's a lot of overlap between how you conduct your business and how you conduct yourself. I mean, if a guy owns a company that regularly builds houses with leaky roofs because he can't be bothered to lay down the subroofing properly, it's easy to believe he's not going to visit his mother after she's admitted to a nursing home."

"He really didn't visit his mom?"

She grinned. "No idea. But I wouldn't have put it past him. I got so tired of problems with his houses that these days I stay away from listing or selling them."

"He was married before," I said. "To Leese's mother."

"Sure." Bianca nodded. "I know Bev. She still says she divorced Dale because the windows in the house he built for her parents leaked whenever there was a strong west wind."

I frowned. "The winds around here are almost always westerly."

"Exactly."

As Bianca continued with story after horrific story about the houses that Dale built, I started getting the feeling that the suspect pool for Dale's murder was a lot larger than I had imagined.

Just before sunrise the next morning, I looked at the bicycle Ash had pulled out of the back of his SUV. "So this is why they call them fat tires," I said.

"Hard to call them anything else." He held the bike upright and nodded at it. "I already put the seat to your height. Go ahead, get on."

I looked at the thing askance. "Why am I suddenly reminded of the first bike I had that wasn't a tricycle?"

Ash grinned. "Because you're a kid at heart. Get on."

He'd just come off his night shift and I was still amazed that he had the energy to go biking. "We can do this some other day," I said. "You must be tired. And I have to be at the library in a couple of hours, so we don't have much time."

"Keep talking like that and I'll think you're chicken." He made rooster noises.

"Peer pressure?" I asked, taking the odd-looking bike out of his hands. "That's what you think is going to get me on this thing?"

"Whatever works." He pulled a second fat tire bike from his vehicle. "I borrowed these bikes from . . . well, let's just say I borrowed them."

I gave him a sidelong look because I had a good idea where the bikes had come from. For various reasons, every year the garage of the sheriff's office ended up with a tremendous number of items, things ranging from power saws to filing cabinets to sporting goods. "Ash . . ."

"Don't be such a worry wart," he said. "I talked to the sheriff, told her that I wanted to try out these bikes. We might want to keep a couple of them for off-season access to some of the trails around here."

I'd never heard of fat tire biking until late last spring, when I'd started noticing them on the bike racks of visiting vehicles. I'd been standing on the sidewalk, giving one a quizzical look, when the owner noticed my expression. He'd immediately launched into an enthusiastic explanation, telling me that the four-inch-wide tires were ideal for spring, fall, and even winter bike riding, that the ultra-wide tires gave great traction in mud and snow, and that riding one was more fun than humans should be allowed to have.

I might have believed him if he hadn't been wearing white socks with his sandals, which to me indicated a complete lack of judgment. After all, if he felt free to wear that in public, could I really trust his opinion on bicycling? On anything?

"We can go up the hill to the cemetery," Ash now said. "Then take the trail that heads to the state forest. We'll be back in forty-five minutes if you get moving."

"That hill is so steep I can barely walk up it."

"I've told you a million times to stop exaggerating. Honest, it'll be easy on these things."

"Trust," I mused, climbing onto the bike. "So hard to win, so easy to lose."

"Have I ever steered you wrong?"

"Not yet," I said darkly. "But there's always a first time."

"Not today." He climbed astride his bike and put

a foot on one of the pedals. "So are you coming or—hey!"

I whirled past him. "Last one to the corner pays for the next breakfast," I called over my shoulder.

"Cheater!" he yelled, but I didn't consider it cheating; I thought of it more as evening the odds. After all, he was bigger, stronger, and fitter than I was. Any physical race that we started at the same time would be won by Ash unless the contest was evened up a little.

We reached the corner, me winning by the slightest hair, and we headed up the hill.

"This isn't so bad," I panted when we were halfway up.

"Told you," he said, not out of breath at all.

"I hate it—when you—do that," I managed to get out.

"Do what?"

I shook my head, not wanting to expend any unnecessary breath on talking. There would be time to abuse him when we got to the cemetery and I got my wind back.

But by the time we reached the cemetery, we'd begun talking about the college courses he was taking that semester and then we stopped at Alonzo Tillotson's headstone, the place I'd first met Eddie, for a view of Janay Lake and beyond to Lake Michigan.

"Nice," Ash said, leaning on his handlebars.

"Sure is."

We stood there, side by side, drinking in the scene. The sun had just pulled itself up over the horizon and was bathing the waters with the bright golden-red of morning. It could have been a romantic scene, maybe even should have been, but it . . . just wasn't. I didn't feel a spark of anything resembling passion for the man standing next to me. Didn't feel any sense of overwhelming love. Didn't feel anything except a sense of friendly companionship and the well-being that came from exercise.

Then, without a warning, Ash leaped onto his bike and sped off. "First one to the trailhead gets to pick the next breakfast place!" he called over his shoulder.

"Cheater!" I shouted, fumbling for my pedals.

"Takes one to know one!"

And so, laughing, we raced into the day, but I was coming to think that our days as a couple were numbered.

A few hours later, I picked up my cell phone and called Leese.

"Hey," I said. "Are you okay? How's your sister?"

"It's a long story." She gusted out a sigh. "And I don't think there's a short version."

None of that sounded good. "When I told you I was a good listener, I meant it, so if you want to talk, just say the word. I can stop by tonight even."

"Do you mean it?" Her voice cracked.

"Of course. Even if you don't cook anything."

She managed a laugh. "You give the worst hints of anyone I've ever met. How do you feel about jambalaya?"

"I'll bring salad," I said promptly, and pulled into her driveway at six o' clock straight up. I grabbed the container of salad bar salad I'd assembled in the grocery store's deli section, knocked on her back door, and went in.

"There's nothing worse than a guest who's on time." Leese glowered at me as I came up the steps.

"Then it's a good thing I'm a friend with refrigerator privileges and not a guest, isn't it?" I smiled at her brightly.

"What are you talking about?"

I opened the door of her fridge, put in the salad stuff, grabbed a pitcher of what I assumed was water, and shut the door. "Like this, see?" I held up the pitcher. "Having friends with refrigerator privileges means it's okay that they take stuff out of the fridge without asking because you know they're considerate enough not to take the last diet soda."

"Gotcha." She nodded. "I'm sorry for being so crabby. It's just . . ." She shifted her gaze, looking away from me but not at anything in particular, unless the blank wall held some special meaning for her.

"We'll talk later," I said. "After we eat, if that's okay with you."

"Very okay. I'd love to talk about something normal."

Normal, of course, was a moving target, but after she'd shown me around her house and I'd expressed jealousy over the handmade quilt she'd put up as a wall hanging in her office ("My grandmother's work," she'd said proudly), we'd sat down to eat and were discussing our all-time favorite movies when we heard car doors shut. Three of them.

Leese half stood to look out the window, then dropped back into her chair. "I am so sorry," she said heavily. "I had no idea they'd stop without calling."

"Who is it?" I asked.

The back door banged open. "Leese!" a high-pitched woman's voice called as multiple sets of feet tromped up the stairs. "We need you to talk some sense into your sister."

"My stepmother," Leese said, sighing. "Carmen.

And Brad and Mia. Carmen's . . . okay, just a little . . . intense."

Interested, I got to my feet as the trio made it to the top of the stairs. Carmen, brassy-haired and exceedingly thin, was holding the young woman I'd seen at the sheriff's office by the arm. Behind them trailed Brad, who, in spite of being a big, bearded guy, looked a lot like his stepsister. He also looked as if he'd rather be anywhere rather than where he was.

"Hello," I said pleasantly and introduced myself.

Carmen's gaze raked over me and went to latch itself on to Leese. "I can't believe you invited a stranger over for dinner on a night when your family needed you."

"Oh, Momma, leave her alone." Brad Lacombe stuck out his hand. "I'm Brad. Nice to meet you."

"Minnie?" The waiflike Mia stared at me. "You were the one with Leese last week when . . . when . . ." Large tears started to drip down her face.

"That's right." I turned my chair toward her. "Do you want to sit?"

"We're interrupting your dinner," Mia murmured. "We should leave."

"Don't be stupid." Leese handed her a napkin. "Dry your face and all of you sit down. I made jambalaya and there's enough to feed half an army."

In short order, she'd spooned out healthy servings of the rice-based dish and set the mounded bowls in front of us. I used my refrigerator privileges to add a few Leese-owned ingredients to make the salad stretch to five, and our hostess forbade discussion of anything serious until the food was gone.

Mia did more playing with her food than eating, so it took some time, but the five of us were drinking decaf coffee and digging into small bowls of ice cream as the sun started to slide down below the tree line.

"Okay," Leese pronounced as she watched a final spoonful go down Mia's throat. "Now."

The three of them all started talking at once and Leese held up her hands to silence them. "Let me summarize," she said. "Minnie came over to hear about the last twenty-four hours and I hadn't even begun when you three showed up."

At this, Mia looked at her lap, Brad grinned, and Carmen, between sips of her coffee, said, "Family doesn't need to call ahead."

Leese shot me a glance—which I interpreted as, *See what I ended up with in the family lottery?*—and didn't reply to her stepmother's comment. "Here's what I know," she said. "Mia, you went to the sheriff's office yesterday and confessed to killing Dad. No, let me finish, Carmen. I want Minnie to hear the order in which this all happened."

Her stepmother sighed dramatically, but otherwise kept quiet.

"Thank you," Leese said. "After Mia made her statement, she was arrested. Somewhere in there she was read her rights and I showed up to represent her, at least for the time being."

She stopped and this time the ticking of the refrigerator was the noisiest sound in the room.

"Right." Leese looked at Mia. "Today, you were released from jail because it didn't take the detective very long to determine that you were at an IT conference in Florida last week and that dozens of people could give you an alibi. Time-wise, it was impossible for you to fly home, kill Dad, and fly back to Florida."

"I know," Mia whispered.

"Then why did you confess?" her mother shouted, crashing her mug down on the table. I cringed, but no one else so much as blinked. "Why on earth did you do that?" Carmen demanded. "How could you be so—"

"Let her answer," Leese cut in firmly.

Brad stood, went around to the back of Mia's chair, and started kneading her shoulders. "Talk to us, Mee. It'll be okay, okay? Just tell us why."

Though Leese's napkin had stanched the earlier tears, it was not going to be able to handle the flood I could feel coming.

"It was my fault," Mia said so softly the words barely got past her teeth. "It was me, it was my fault."

"We heard you the first hundred times," her mother said. "It's bad enough that your father is dead without this little problem. You said you'd explain when we got to Leese's house. Well, we're here, so tell us."

Mia looked at Leese, who nodded. The younger woman bent her head. "Dad and I," she told the table, "had this big fight when he drove me to the airport. A huge fight."

This fact didn't seem to faze the other three at the table. I couldn't recall the last time my mild-mannered engineer father and I had argued about anything other than the importance of fiction in the universe. In spite of his ridiculous opinion that reading fiction was a waste of time if there was nonfiction at hand, I couldn't imagine having a knock-down drag-out with him. Clearly, this wasn't the case with the deceased Dale Lacombe and his offspring.

"What was it this time?" Brad was still working on her shoulders. "Your hair or your tattoos?"

His younger sister reached up and pulled at a loose strand of jet-black hair. "He kept saying over and over again that I was wasting my life, that if I ever wanted to meet a man who might actually want to marry me, I had to quit working a man's job."

I sucked in a quick breath, not quite believing what I'd heard. But once again, no one else at the table seemed surprised.

"Nothing new there." Brad very gently bumped the top of his sister's head with one of his fists.

"But this time I said he was wrong." Mia's shoulders rounded. "This time I told him that I was a grown woman, that I thanked him for his concern but my career decisions were mine and mine alone."

Brad and Leese exchanged surprised glances and Carmen stared at her daughter. None of them said a word.

Mia either didn't notice or didn't care. "He said he was my father and that he'd always have a say in what I did." She looked up and now the tears were flowing fast. "I told him he didn't have a say. I told him I'd been living on my own since college, that if I wanted his advice, I'd ask for it, but that I didn't see it happening. Ever again."

Though it sounded as if it had been past time for Mia to stick up for herself, the timing was unfortunate.

"Don't you see," she said wildly. "It's my fault he's dead. He must have been so mad at me, so upset, that he wasn't being careful on some building site and he . . . he fell. It's my fault."

That didn't make a lot of sense, since he clearly hadn't fallen straight into Leese's pickup, but I kept quiet. And how, exactly, had she known he'd fallen to his death? But even as the question popped into my brain, I answered it. Detective Inwood must have said something about it when he'd been interviewing her.

Leese hitched her chair around so she could sit next to Mia. "Sweetie, it's not your fault. There's no way it's your fault. Someone put him into the truck, so that same someone probably pushed him. We don't know what happened, but the one thing we do know is you didn't have anything to do with it." She wrapped her arm around Mia's slender shoulders and sent Carmen and Brad a look full of meaning.

"That's right," Brad said. "He died days after you left for Florida. How could there be any connection?"

Leese then looked pointedly at Carmen, who rolled her eyes and said, "Mia, stop being so dramatic. It wasn't your fault. I don't know why you have to—"

"Mia, have you talked to Corinne?" Leese cut in.

When Mia shook her head, her brother said, "Talking to Corinne is a great idea. If you want, I can call and make an appointment for you. Around lunchtime?"

"I don't want to," Mia said quietly.

"Of course you don't," Carmen almost snapped, "but it's what you need."

It suddenly dawned on me that they were talking about Corinne Napier, a psychologist with an outstanding reputation who practiced in Chilson.

Mia shrugged, but didn't say a word.

"Then it's settled," her mother said. "Brad, you call Corinne first thing tomorrow and let us know what time the appointment is. Mia, you know what's going to happen, don't you?"

"Yes, Momma," she said almost mechanically. "I have to be there ten minutes ahead of time and I have to ask Corinne to sign a note that I sat through the whole hour."

Seriously? I glanced around, but as before, no one else seemed to think this was unusual.

"Good," Carmen said and I watched the tension drain out of her face. She smiled and patted her daughter's hand. "Now, how about another bowl of ice cream?"

"Coming right up," Leese said, jumping to her feet.

"I'll help," Brad said, collecting the bowls from the table.

I got up and wielded the can of whipped cream and the talk turned to guessing what was going to be the peak fall color weekend, but though I played along with the conversation, I kept wondering about all the things this family hadn't said.

Mia had been a patient of Corinne's. Was it for her anorexia, or something else?

Their father apparently had a history of fighting with his adult children. Why?

But most of all, I wondered why they were finding it so easy to believe that Dale had been murdered.

Chapter 8

The next morning, my desk phone rang as I worked through the amazing number of e-mails that had accumulated since the last time I'd sat at my computer. Some were pure spam, some were solicitations, some were from other librarians, others were from patrons who thought an e-mail to me was the best way to get the library to purchase a new book.

And it probably was the best way, since the mention of any book I hadn't heard of sent me straight to the nearest search engine for more information. One of my New Year's resolutions had been to put all those requests into a separate folder and go over them when I had time, but here it was October and the habit had yet to get started.

"No time like the present," I told myself, and clicked on my e-mail program's "New Folder" function. After typing "Book Requests" as the folder's name, I started moving e-mails around. Three went into the new folder, six got deleted, and then there was . . .

I studied the subject line. "Software Pricing Request," it said, from a salesperson I'd met a few times.

Odd. I hadn't requested any software pricing. And I never would have requested anything from this particular company. Their stuff was fantastically expensive and was designed for large library systems with multiple branches.

Frowning, I clicked on the e-mail. "Dear Jennifer," it started. "Congratulations on your new position with the Chilson District Library. We're so glad you reached out to us regarding our new and comprehensive product line. Enclosed you will find materials that will explain what we can do for—"

My phone rang. Still reading, I picked up the receiver. "This is Minnie. How can I help you?"

"Have you read your e-mail this morning?" Jennifer demanded.

I sat back. "I have, and I was just going to call you."

"There was no reason for Dave to copy you on that e-mail," she said. "I certainly didn't tell him to." She waited, but since she hadn't asked me a question, I didn't say anything. "I suppose you've read it?" she asked.

"Yes."

"So you know why I'm trying to cut the library's budget."

"Not really," I said slowly.

She blew out an annoyed breath. "If I'm going to drag this library into the twenty-first century, we need this software. It can do a wide variety of things that we can't do now, and if we're going to grow, we need to make this kind of capital investment."

Absolutely it could do things we couldn't; the question was, did we need to do them? What was the return on the investment? What would we have to sacrifice to make the purchase, and would the sacrifice be worth it?

But I'd worked with her long enough to know that if I asked those questions, she'd accuse me of throwing up roadblocks instead of finding a way to make her idea work. So instead, I said, "The library board looked at this software during the renovation. At that point they decided it wasn't a good fit."

"Good," Jennifer said. "Then they're already familiar with the company. This is a more recent product line. It's much better than the old one. You should see all features it has!"

She sounded excited, so I sat up and started scrolling through the e-mail. Dave the sales guy, however, had made a strategic error—he'd put the price sheet first. I gasped at the five-figure number, but Jennifer was still talking.

"Once it's up and running, it'll save money. I'm familiar with the earlier version of this software system—the last library where I worked had invested in it and I'm sure the same thing will happen here."

As she went on, blithely talking about all the wonderful things the new system would do for us, I started thinking about all the horrible things that could happen.

Because I wasn't sure how spending thousands and thousands of dollars could save money.

Because we didn't have thousands to spend.

Because to find that kind of money—and the accompanying permanent service agreements, which were in the four-figure category—more than minor cuts would have to be made.

Which meant one of two things. Either programming cuts would have to be made, or staff would be laid off.

Permanently.

* * *

It took the rest of the morning for me to shake off the foreboding that Jennifer's call had created in me.

I considered writing a note to the library board, telling them how I felt about Jennifer's push for the new system. I considered it so seriously that I clicked the button to create a new e-mail, but just before I started typing, I came to my senses and deleted the entire thing.

If I were director, what would I think of an employee going to the board without my knowledge? Not much. Which meant that if I wanted to object to this potential purchase, I should make my objection to Jennifer. And to do that I needed facts and figures. Which meant a fair amount of work, but it had to be done if I wanted Jennifer to listen to me.

But first, it was time for lunch.

"Anyone want something from the Round Table?" I asked at the front desk.

"Onion rings," Donna said. "Double order."

The fat-laden order was completely out of character. "Really?"

She sighed. "No. I brought a salad. My knee has been a little sore and I haven't been able to do full workouts this week."

"Five-mile runs, then, instead of ten?" I asked.

"No, I'm still doing tens. Just not doing wind sprints in the middle."

I looked at her, but she seemed dead serious. "Right. Well, if you change your mind, I have my cell with me." I turned and almost ran smack into Mitchell Koyne.

"Hey, Minnie," he said. "Bianca said you stopped

by. Glad you two are getting along in spite of . . ." He kicked one foot against the other. "You know."

Many many months ago, Mitchell had asked me out on a date. My method of gently refusing him must have been confusing because he persisted in thinking that I harbored romantic feelings for him.

"She seems very nice," I said, carefully not looking at Donna. The entire library staff had eventually learned of Mitchell's offer and Donna was undoubtedly now grinning with great glee.

"Yeah." Mitchell beamed. "She sure is."

I edged toward the front door. "How's the toy store, now that you're the manager?"

"Yeah, the cool thing about that? I get to make the schedule. I need to work the weekends, because they're the busiest, you know, but I can come here on my days off." He grinned. "Especially now that I got my fines paid off."

He had indeed. We'd taken a ceremonious photo, which I'd promptly e-mailed to Stephen, who had yet to reply. "The only sure thing in this world is change," I said.

"What? No, I paid in bills. Mostly twenties."

I smiled. There was no one like Mitchell.

"Of course, now that I'm working so many hours, I won't have as much time to read." He sent the stacks a forlorn glance. "Kind of sucks."

"I know what you mean," I said. My childhood daydreams of becoming a librarian so I could read all day had been dashed early on. Though I wouldn't want to do anything else, I often wished I had more time to read the books I recommended.

Then I recognized the odd situation: Mitchell and

I were commiserating about our mutual lack of free time. Wonders truly never did cease.

"You hear about Mia Lacombe?" Mitchell asked.

"She was released," I said a little stiffly.

"Yeah, that's what I'm saying, you know?" He looked around then moved so close to me that I had to look almost straight up to see his face. "You working on it?" he asked in a loud whisper. "Dale Lacombe's murder?"

Not so very long ago, Mitchell had had delusions of being a private investigator. That phase, thankfully, was over, but for some reason he continued to think that I took part in active criminal investigations at the sheriff's office.

"Leese is a friend of mine," I said.

"Right." He nodded vigorously, which dislodged his baseball cap. "That's what Bianca said. If you need help, just let me know, okay? I mean, I'm pretty busy, but I'll do what I can."

The idea of a helpful Mitchell was more than a little appalling. "Thanks, but I'm sure the sheriff's office has it covered."

"Want to know what I think?" Mitchell resettled his cap. "I bet it was some guy who used to work for Lacombe. He was one of those guys that thinks he's always right, you know? He'd fire anyone who disagreed with him, over anything it seemed like. He was always working shorthanded. Half the time he had guys working for him that didn't know what they were doing."

Mitchell started telling a story about a buddy that Dale fired, and though I tried to pay attention, all I kept hearing was, "I bet it was some guy who used to work for Lacombe."

* * *

Since the previous night's conversation had been completely hijacked by Leese's stepfamily, I'd texted her that, if she wanted, I would stop by that night so we could have a one-on-one conversation. Her reply had been a thumbs-up, so after work I walked back to the houseboat and fed Eddie before I headed out to Leese's.

He ate fast enough to give himself indigestion, licked his nonexistent lips a few times, washed his whiskers, bumped my shin, then jumped onto the boat's dashboard and curled up for a nice long look at the seagulls.

"You realize that you'll never catch one, right?" I asked.

"Mrr," he said confidently.

I wanted to tell him how wrong he was, but I also didn't want to burst his little kitty bubble, so I kissed the top of his head and drove to Fat Boys Pizza to pick up our dinner order. Half a veggie sub for me ("Yes, Mom, I'm eating my vegetables"), half an Italian sub for Leese, and a full order of cheesy potato wedges for us to split.

The food was still mostly warm by the time I pulled into Leese's, so we dove right into our meal. This time, we were almost done eating when we heard the slam of a car door.

Leese, who'd been in the act of trying to convince me to eat the last three potato wedges, instead grabbed two of them. "To give me strength," she said.

Up the stairs came the brassy hair of Carmen. "Oh, good, you're here, too, Minnie. You can help with this." She dropped a box on the kitchen table. "Oof, this is heavy! But the police want me to go through everything. They want to know about any of Dale's clients, about anyone who might have held a grudge against him." She pulled out a chair and sat. "There are three more boxes in the car. I'll start on this one while you go get the others."

I pushed the last potato wedge over to Leese. "You might need this one, too."

She snorted out a laugh. "I say we split it."

Half an hour later, piles of thick folders were strewn across Leese's kitchen. On the table, on the chairs, on the half wall that marked the stairway, on the counters, even on the microwave. An hour after that, every folder was sorted into alphabetical order and checked to confirm that the contents matched the labels.

Leese stared at the largest set of piles. "Dad had this many lawsuits against him? I knew he had a few, but . . ." She shook her head, muttering something that sounded a lot like, "Could have used more potato wedges."

"Don't be silly." Carmen, her fingers and wrists glittering with jewelry, waved at the reams of paper dismissively. "Why don't you be a good girl and make me a margarita?"

"Because I don't have tequila, limes, or Cointreau," Leese said shortly.

"White wine, then."

After a long pause, during which I seriously considered making up a fast excuse and running for my car before the family tension became any tighter, Leese got to her feet. "Minnie, would you like anything?"

Um. "I'll have whatever you're having," I said, which was how I ended up drinking a Soft Parade from Short's Brewing out of a bottle.

Carmen sipped her wine and murmured, "I suppose it'll be better when it warms up." Then she said,

"I thought you knew almost all of these lawsuits were settled out of court."

"How would I have known that, exactly?" Leese asked. "I've been downstate since I graduated from high school. And it's not like Dad ever talked to me about his business."

"And whose fault was that?" Carmen asked. "All you had to do was pick up the phone."

Leese glowered. "Phones work both ways."

This was going nowhere in a hurry. "So," I said, pushing at the tallest pile, "none of these ever went to court?"

Carmen huffed, but said, "That's right. Dale was always trying to do his best for his customers"—I could feel Leese starting to say something, so I gave her a small kick in the shins— "but you just can't satisfy some people, no matter how hard you try."

"Ain't that the truth," Leese muttered.

"Right," I said quickly. "It's too bad, but there are a lot of unhappy people in the world. So all these cases were settled amicably?"

Carmen looked at the stacks of folders. "Well, I don't know about amicably. They were settled, though, and that's the important thing."

I pointed at the remaining piles. "And these are the cases that went to court."

Carmen flipped through the papers. "Some people, you know? Projects always start out so much fun, and then before you know it, they're complaining about something silly. I mean, who would think that a little problem with a septic system would make someone sue you?"

"If that 'little problem' was raw sewage backing up into my bathtub—" Leese began, but I cut her off.

"How about we sort these a little further?" I suggested. "Recent cases and old cases maybe."

Carmen shot Leese a glance, but followed my suggestion. Going with the debatable assumption that three years was enough time for home construction wounds to heal, I put aside any paperwork older than that.

I looked at the remaining pile. It was still more formidable than I'd hoped. Now what?

"Cases he lost and cases he won," Leese said. "See where that gets us."

Where it got us was two piles, one tall and one not. "These were so unfair," Carmen said, tipping her refilled wineglass at the higher stack. "The judge wouldn't listen to Dale, no matter what he said. That case there? That one cost me a trip to Italy."

"And these?" I pointed at the far shorter stack.

Carmen smiled. "Let's just say they didn't end well for the homeowners." She took a sip of wine and said, "We went to Italy after all, just a little later than I'd hoped."

I caught Leese's eye roll, but thankfully Carmen didn't. Leese pulled the papers toward her and started to flip through them. "Two cases, looks like," she said. "One was Daphne Raab and the other was Gail and Ray Boggs."

"Summer people." Carmen waved the names away. "Well, not the Raab woman, but the Boggses were classic summer people."

"So if they're not from here, they deserve to be cheated?" Leese asked.

"Who's talking about cheating?" Carmen put down her glass. "The judge herself said they didn't have a solid case. Dale didn't do anything wrong."

Leese drew in a breath, but I jumped in fast. “These are definitely names to give to the police, I’d say.”

For the first time in what felt like years, Carmen and Leese agreed on something.

“Excellent,” I said. “Leese, will you have time tomorrow to look these two over? See if you can find anything that looks, I don’t know, weird?”

Leese squared up the papers. “Sure,” she said evenly. “I lost three more clients today, so I don’t have much else to do.”

“Oh, honey.” Carmen reached over the table, jewelry tinkling, and put her hands over Leese’s. “I’m so sorry. I wish there was something I could do.”

“Thanks.” Leese withdrew one of her large hands and patted her stepmother’s far smaller ones. “There’s not, but thanks anyway.” She half smiled. “On the plus side, a Bob Blake called me today. He said he has a complicated estate and lots of friends he’s willing to recommend me to if I do a decent job.”

“Well, there you go.” Carmen smiled. “This will all work out, I can just feel it.”

I was happy she felt so positive because, as I stared at the stacks and stacks of folders, I was getting the creepy crawly feeling that things were going to get a lot worse before they got better.

Chapter 9

The next day, I pulled out my cell phone the instant I cleared the library's front door at lunchtime. Outside the wind was up and was bringing in a scattering of low, dark clouds. My personal opinion, substantiated by absolutely nothing except wishful thinking, was that it wouldn't rain until after I got back to the library, so I started pushing buttons.

"What?" Kristen snarled.

"It's early to be so cranky, isn't it?" I asked. "How could so much have gone wrong when it's barely noon?"

"You want a list?"

No, not really. "Would a gossipy question from me irritate you or make you feel better?"

She laughed. My best friend was nothing if not mercurial. "Depends on who you're asking the question about."

"Dale Lacombe."

"Hmm. Hang on." She covered the phone—pointlessly, since I could still hear everything—and bellowed, "Misty!

Harve! If we can't get that salmon, we're going to have to come up with something else. Start thinking."

I winced, glad I wasn't Misty, her head chef, or Harvey, her sous chef. Of course, I was also glad I wasn't Kristen, either, since if a "Least Likely to Own a Restaurant" Award existed, I would win it every year. But Kristen, in spite of her regular shouting sprees, also had an incredibly loyal and dedicated staff. I was starting to suspect her staff found a bizarre enjoyment in her hissy fits.

"Okay, I'm back," Kristen said. "What about Dale Lacombe?"

"Tell me more about him."

"Hmm."

"What do you mean, hmm?"

"It means methinks you're getting involved, once again, in something you don't need to get involved in."

Nothing new there. "Are you going to tell me about Leese's dad or not?"

"Of course I am. But there's no reason I can't give you some grief first."

"Don't you have a kitchen emergency?"

"Well, sure, there's that." She covered the phone again. "We have four hours to come up with a new special, folks! And that includes getting the ingredients." She came back. "Time is of the essence, so I'll have to delay my grief giving."

"So considerate," I murmured.

"Yes. Anyway, like I said, Dale Lacombe was a jerk. From top to bottom, inside and out, backward and forward. Everyone I knew who worked for him hated the guy within a few weeks, and the ones who stayed with him longer than six months only did because they couldn't find another job."

Okay, but, "How did he manage to keep his business going if it was so hard for him to keep employees?"

"Because people are stupid," she said. Then, before I could get on her for making sweeping statements that were statistically impossible, she added, "It helped that for about ten years his son, Brad, worked for him."

"I didn't know that." None of the Lacombes had mentioned it. Was that weird? Or not?

"That's because you didn't live here five years ago when the you-know-what hit the fan. I wasn't on the scene, but it's kind of like that basketball game when Wilt Chamberlain scored all those points. More people say they saw the fight than lived in Chilson."

I had no idea what she was talking about, but somehow I knew what she meant. "So Brad and his dad didn't get along?"

"Hello? Have you been listening? Dale was a jerk. How Brad and Mia ended up so normal with Dale for a father is beyond comprehension."

And then there was having Carmen as a mother. But even as I had the thought, I felt ashamed. I'd met her in the days following her husband's sudden death. Forming an opinion about someone's character based on that time frame wasn't fair. Or . . . was it?

I considered asking Kristen that question, but before I could, she said, "Misty just shoved me a note that she has an idea for the special. Can I go now, pretty please?"

"Sure. Thanks for the info."

"Yeah, yeah. I'll send you a bill at the end of the month. See you Sunday." And she was gone.

Still walking, I tapped a few more buttons to call Rafe. "Are you busy?"

"Me? Are you kidding? If I wanted to be busy, I would have taken a real job."

Why the man insisted on pretending that he didn't work himself ragged during the school year, I did not know. "Got a quick question for you. What kind of person was Dale Lacombe?"

He made a rude noise. "You're kidding, right?"

"I never met him."

"The man's dead, if you'll remember. Why are you asking about him now?"

"Do you really want that answer?"

"Probably not. Hang on." He covered the receiver and I heard muffled instructions to his secretary about an upcoming meeting. "Okay, I'm back."

"If you have to go, I can call later."

"This won't take long," he said. "Lacombe was an incredible jerk. People are saying the big question about his murder is why it took so long for him to get killed."

I blinked. "That seems harsh." And somehow, listening to Rafe be so unkind made me uncomfortable. It wasn't like him.

"Hey, you asked. And I'm just repeating what I heard."

After we disconnected, I made a few more quick calls, asking for people's opinions about Dale Lacombe from Denise Slade, the president of the Friends of the Library group, to Chris Ballou, manager of the marina. The response that every single one of them gave was, "He was a jerk."

But did it follow that being a jerk was what got him killed? Was it something else entirely? Or was it a combination of the two?

"What to my wondering eyes did appear," I heard

a familiar—and amused—voice say, "but a niece about to walk past her beloved aunt without so much as a hello."

"I'm pretty sure that's not how it goes," I said, coming to an abrupt halt, because my aunt and Otto were both standing in front of me so I couldn't move forward without either walking around or over the top of them. "Your version doesn't scan."

"Give me a minute and I'll come up with something," she said.

Otto smiled. "We're going to get some lunch. Would you like to join us?"

"Sure," I said. "That will give Aunt Frances time to work on her mangling of *A Visit from St. Nicholas*." I made a move in the direction of the Round Table, but they didn't move with me. "Are you going to the deli?" I asked, turning to go across the street to Shomin's.

"Dearest niece," my aunt said. "You do realize there are other eating options in this town?"

Of course I did. I was a regular patron of the pizza place and the Chinese-Thai takeout, but I was pretty sure that Otto wouldn't be interested in either of those. "There's the bar down by the water," I said hesitantly, "but I'm not sure . . ."

"It's obvious that your horizons need expanding," Aunt Frances said. "Come with us."

Suddenly I knew what she was talking about and I was very conscious of the state of my checkbook. "If you're talking about Angelique's, I can't . . . I mean, I don't—"

"My treat," Otto said. "Besides, since you have to get back to work, you won't be drinking any wine, and that's the expensive part." He grinned, and I was reminded again what a handsome man he was, if you liked the elegant Paul Newman type.

After a short walk around the corner, we entered the new restaurant that had formerly been a boutique. Since the store had sold women's clothing and accessories way out of my price range, I'd never set foot in the place. This meant I couldn't compare then to now, but the current decor of mismatched antique chairs, white linen tablecloths, and fabric-covered walls hung with pastel-based landscape paintings combined to create an atmosphere of understated quiet style.

The hostess seated us at a table near the front, gave us hand-lettered menus, and departed, saying our waiter would bring us water in a moment.

"Competition for Kristen?" my aunt asked, taking in the black-painted ceiling and the wooden floor.

I shook my head. "Different niche." I knew this because Kristen had obsessed ad infinitum about the new restaurant until I'd threatened to sneak diet soda into her glass of red wine. Only then did she grudgingly admit that a frighteningly expensive restaurant in town wouldn't change her customer base.

"It might work to her advantage," I said. "Even if this place gets busy enough to be a destination, it's not likely that people will eat here twice in a weekend."

Otto, a retired accountant with an astute business sense, nodded. "Clustering makes sense, particularly for a tourist town."

My aunt picked up her menu, gave it a short glance, then set it down again. "Before I even think about food, I need to ask if you're okay. I know you'll say you're fine, but it's been a week since you had that horrible experience of finding Dale Lacombe and I want to know if you're having nightmares."

I gave her a sideways grin. "I'm fine."

Aunt Frances looked at Otto—*See? I told you*—then back at me. "I notice you didn't answer the question about the nightmares."

The chair in which I was sitting was suddenly uncomfortable. Apparently my aunt knew more about my sleeping habits than I'd realized. I shifted a little and repeated myself. "I'm fine." Because I was sure that if I talked about the dreams that I was still having, the dreams with those staring blue eyes, the talking would fasten the images even deeper into my brain and that was the last thing I wanted. The dreams would go away. Eventually. They always did.

"Hmm." Aunt Frances studied me. Then, just when I was afraid she was going to play the Aunt Card (*Talk to me about this or I'll call your mother*), she said, "I like Leese. It's only because of her mother that she turned out so well."

"You knew Dale?" Of course she did. Though my aunt wasn't in the construction business, she was a master woodworker and there was overlap between the two circles.

"To my great regret, yes." She picked up her menu, but kept an eye on me. "You're going to work on finding his killer, aren't you?"

I grinned. "Might as well keep my eyes and ears open."

"Hmmph. The problem with Dale will be narrowing down the suspects. He was a miserable excuse for a builder. He lied to clients. He used cheap materials and billed as if he'd installed high end. He was an embarrassment to the building trade," she said, enunciating each consonant precisely. "He was a wretched employer and I'm sure he cheated on his taxes."

Otto glanced up from his menu. "Did he kick puppies, too?"

"I wouldn't put it past him," she said feelingly. Then she sighed. "But he didn't deserve to die like that. No one does."

It wasn't like my aunt to be so negative about someone. Her default tendency was to live and let live. "You sound as if you had a bad experience with him," I said.

"He owes me thousands for a custom dining table and chairs I made for him."

I went very still, suddenly nervous that my aunt was going to be a murder suspect.

"Oh, don't look like that." She smiled. "It was almost twenty years ago. If I was going to pitch him off a tall building, I would have done it then and there."

Relief blew through me. "Not that you're holding a grudge," I said.

"What would make you say that?" She laughed. "Speaking of the past, there's something we want to talk to you about."

"Oh?" I was delighted at the use of the "we" pronoun. My aunt had been alone for so long that I hadn't thought she would ever find a life companion. Or even look for one. "I know I'm too old, but I'm probably still short enough to be the flower girl at your wedding."

Aunt Frances ignored my gestures of tossing rose petals from a basket. "It's about the boardinghouse," she said.

"More specifically," Otto said, "it's about the future of the boardinghouse."

"Oh." I clutched my menu, making its edges curl around. "It's your decision, not mine."

"Duh," my aunt said. "But I still want your opinion. You have a stake in this, too."

"Don't worry about me. I'll find somewhere else to live during the winter. I'm sure it won't be hard to find some summer people giddy to have someone to rent their place in the off-season." And now that I'd come up with the idea, I was pretty sure it was a solid one.

"Good to know you won't be homeless," Aunt Frances said, "but that's not what I meant. What I want to know is, do you want the boardinghouse to continue?"

My throat was suddenly so tight it was hard to talk. "Please tell me you're not asking me to run the place in the summers," I squeaked out.

It wasn't just the thought of arranging breakfasts and dinners for the six boarders and myself all summer long, which was bad enough. It was also the thought of continuing my aunt's unspoken matchmaking projects. I still wasn't sure if I approved of the endeavor, but there was no denying that my aunt's careful perusal of applications and her subsequent selections had resulted in many permanent partnerships.

"Not what I asked," Aunt Frances said. "No offense, but you'd be horrible at it."

I put on a fake hurt expression. "Didn't you always tell me I could do anything I wanted?"

"And you can. But it also makes sense to play to your strengths, which are library inclined, not boardinghouse related. Back to my question. Do you want the boardinghouse to continue after I marry Otto and move into his house?"

Though her voice was matter-of-fact, I could tell she was deeply serious. So I thought about it. I thought about the front porch swing and the fireplace. I thought about the dining room that looked over the tree-filled backyard and the bathroom with the claw-foot tub. I heard the slap of the wooden screen door and the mealtime laughter that filled the dining room.

With a blink, I came out of my memories. "Yes," I said. "I want the boardinghouse to continue. I don't want the tradition to end."

"Okay, then." Aunt Frances nodded.

And that seemed to be that.

I spent the afternoon at the reference desk. My first customer was an elderly gentleman who wanted some help researching an ancestor who may or may not have homesteaded on property in Tonedagana County. After I sent him to the county building, the next person to ask for assistance was a seven-year-old girl who wanted to know how long it would take her to become a doctor.

Her thin shoulders sagged a little when she'd learned the harsh truth, but her chin had a determined look by the time she walked away. I watched her go, patting myself on the back once again for choosing the best job in the world, when I felt a presence at my elbow.

"Minnie, do you have a minute?" the presence said.

I turned. It was Brad Lacombe. "Sure. What can I do for you?"

"Leese said you were helping her and Mom go through Dad's papers."

"Sort of." Absentmindedly, I rubbed the backs of my knuckles. My skin still felt dry from shuffling all those folders. "Mostly I just happened to be there when your mom showed up with the boxes."

He shook his head. "Yeah. I wanted to apologize

for that. There's no reason for you to get caught up in our mess."

"I didn't mind." In retrospect, the entire exercise had been interesting. I'd learned a lot more than I'd ever expected to about lawsuits and court documents, plus I'd had the entertainment of listening to the bickering between Leese and her stepmother. There had been tension, certainly, but there had also been a strong current of respect and a feeling of . . . well, of family.

Brad gave a snorting laugh that was eerily reminiscent of Leese. "Either you're nuts or you're lying."

I smiled. "Since I'm a horrible liar, I must be nuts."

He instantly colored a dark red. "Oh, geez, I'm sorry. I didn't mean . . ."

"Don't worry about it," I said, laughing. "I've been called worse things. And besides, you might be right."

"No, I'm pretty sure I'm an idiot. My girlfriend says if I spent half the time thinking ahead than I do apologizing for not thinking, that I'd have time to read *War and Peace*."

His girlfriend sounded like a smart woman. I was about to say so, when another thought caught at me. According to Kristen, Brad had worked for his dad for years. If anyone would know about employee issues, it was him.

Then again, Kristen had mentioned a huge argument between Brad and his father. She'd said it was five years ago, but the fight could have been the result of an issue that had been festering for a long time and maybe the fight hadn't resolved whatever the problem was and Brad was still carrying a lot of anger toward his father and maybe that anger had gotten out of hand and . . .

I looked at Brad's open countenance. Spinning out possible scenarios was easy. Proving they had any basis in fact was something else altogether.

"What do you think happened to your dad?" I asked.

"Who killed him, you mean?" His face went tight. "Who killed him and tried to get my sister blamed for it? Who's trying to ruin her new business?"

His sister, I noted. Not his stepsister. And he seemed as angry about the damage to Leese as about the death of his father. Though I didn't want to cast aspersions on the dead, I'd heard enough stories about Dale to think Brad wouldn't take offense. "I hear your dad wasn't the easiest employer to get along with. Do you think maybe someone he'd fired could have done it?"

Surprisingly, Brad grinned. "If the cops are looking at disgruntled employees, I'm probably the best candidate. The whole town knows about that huge fight we had."

"Even I've heard about it," I said, semiapologetically, "and it happened before I moved here."

"Sounds about right. That fight had been a long time coming. I never wanted to be in the construction business. When you're a kid you do what your dad tells you, and the whole time I was growing up, he kept saying I was going to work for him when I got old enough. So that's what I did."

"You didn't like construction?"

"It was okay," he said, shrugging. "But it was just a job. And working with my dad sucked. Having me taking over the business was his plan, not mine. I had to quit to get him to see it."

Light dawned. "That's what your argument was about."

"I'd been telling him for days that I was hooking up with some guys who were starting a craft brewery. I kept saying what a great opportunity it was, going on and on about their business plan and projected growth and how important it was to be a part of the company from the beginning."

"He didn't catch on," I said.

"I should have known better." Brad grimaced. "Dad was never the kind of guy to take a hint. He probably knew what I wanted to do, he just wanted to make me say it straight out." He half smiled. "Eventually I did. At the top of my lungs. On a Saturday. In the summer. While we were doing an emergency repair job for the Round Table."

I blinked. "That's a little . . ."

"Public?" he suggested. "Yeah, that's what Leese and Mia said. I think part of me wanted it that way, though, so I couldn't go back."

I'd always heard you should never burn bridges when you left a job, but for Brad it sounded as if a scorched earth policy had been a necessity. "You're still at the same brewery?"

His face lit up. "Absolutely. There's this new recipe I'm trying. Flavorings of maple syrup and chocolate. What could be better, right?"

It sounded horrible, but then I wasn't a big beer drinker. But I also didn't see how a five-year-old argument that had ended with Brad in a career he clearly loved could also have caused him to kill his father.

I smiled and wished him well with his new beer. "Were there other guys who worked for your dad that might have . . . well, you know."

He shook his head. "I've been thinking about it, but I don't see it. What I can see is one of the guys blowing a gasket, killing dad in the heat of anger kind of thing, but not like this. Anyway, I can't think of anyone who would go to the trouble of implicating Leese. I mean, how many people even knew she was back in the area?"

Hundreds, actually. She'd joined the chamber of commerce and was attending Rotary meetings, not to mention that article in the newspaper.

"None of your dad's former employees were the kind of guys to carry a grudge?" I asked.

"Hard to say for sure." He shrugged. "I just don't see it."

I wished I shared his conviction, but it was my feeling that hate-filled grudges could last a long time.

"Well," he said, glancing at his watch. "I have to get to the brewery. I just wanted to stop by and say I was sorry that my mom socked you with all that work last night."

"Don't worry about it."

I watched him walk out and got the feeling that both he and Mia had probably done a lot of apologizing for their parents.

Ash's mom, Lindsey, smiled across the table at us. "It feels as if it's been ages since I've seen you two. Anything new?"

We were at the Three Seasons, sitting in what had been a parlor, back when the hundred-year-old building had been a luxurious summer residence for a wealthy family. Kristen herself had advised us on what to have for dinner, which in my case was more telling than advising. As long as whatever arrived didn't have mushrooms, I was good.

"New?" Ash repeated. "I've been working the

night shift. Do you really want to know what kind of thing goes on at two in the morning?"

His mother was a gorgeously elegant woman who made an extremely good living as a financial consultant. I had to keep reminding myself that there was no reason to be intimidated, and mostly the reminders worked.

Lindsay tipped her head to one side, considering her son's question. "Probably not. Unless you have some amusing anecdotes you can share."

"Nothing funny lately," he said, glancing at me.

Lindsey noticed the look. "Are you going to tell me what's going on right now?" she asked. "Or shall it wait until the salad course? Because I will find out, in spite of the fact that I was out of the country researching new investments for the last week and a half."

"Just tell her," I suggested.

"Nah." Ash grinned. "Make her wait. It'll be good for her and entertaining for me."

"You are a horrible son," Lindsey said. "What did I ever do to deserve you?"

The horrible son's dimpled smile bore a striking resemblance to his mother's. "Nothing. It was sheer good luck."

She paused, considering, then nodded. "Acknowledged, but the question remains. What's going on?"

Before Ash could continue baiting his mother, I said, "There was another murder."

"Oh, no." Her face fell into sad lines. "How awful. Someone from around here? A tourist?"

I looked at Ash, because I had no idea whether or not Lindsey had known Dale. Was this going to be a shock that we should prepare her for? And how does one do that anyway?

"Dale Lacombe," Ash said.

A variety of emotions passed over Lindsey's face. Most of them I couldn't catch, but I was confident of two. Surprise had been the first one, and finally resignation. Somewhere in there I thought I'd pegged satisfaction, but surely I was wrong about that.

"Well." Her expressions settled back down. "Isn't that interesting?"

I frowned. Her voice had been curiously flat. "It is?" I asked.

She flashed a short smile. "Hal Inwood and Ash are going to run themselves ragged trying to figure this one out."

Ash sighed. "Mom, let it go."

I looked from mother to son and back. "Let what go?"

Our waiter approached and there was a pause as water glasses were filled and drink orders taken, which was basically us agreeing to the bottle of wine that Kristen had recommended. When he'd left, Lindsey said quietly, "Marrying that man was the dumbest thing Bev Diesso ever did. Her parents told her not to. Her grandparents told her not to. I told her not to. But she was in love"—Lindsey sighed— "and she wouldn't listen to any of us."

Lindsey knew Leese's mom? One of these days I would have to stop being surprised at the interlocking relationships I kept stumbling over. "What was so bad?" I asked.

She laughed shortly. "I can tell you never met him."

"Mom—"

Lindsey put up a hand against Ash's mild protest. "To put it mildly, Dale was a misogynistic ass, and I was glad to offer Bev and Leese refuge when she left him. Yes, dear, I know Dale was your father's friend but he was never mine. Never."

It occurred to me that not only had I never met Ash's dad, but I didn't know anything about him. I tucked the thought away. Now wasn't the time. "You and Leese's mom are friends?" I asked.

"In a way," Lindsey said. "I'm good friends with Mary, Bev's older sister. Bev is a few years younger than us."

Small towns. "I know Leese, but I've never met her mom. Did she stay in the area?"

Lindsey nodded. "She went back to school and became a registered nurse. She's assistant director up at Lakeview Medical Care Facility."

"Never remarried?" I asked, hopping my chair to make sure I was out of the way of a gray-haired man using a walker who was being escorted to a nearby table.

"Not for lack of trying by a certain gentleman," Lindsey said, smiling. "Bev is a fantastic skier and goes out to Colorado regularly. Twenty years ago she met a man who proposed after she avoided a child who fell in front of her. She did this by going airborne."

I was a skier myself, but I couldn't imagine having either the presence of mind or the technical ability to do something like that. "Sounds like a reasonable basis for marriage."

"Better than many." Lindsey laughed. "Bev wasn't interested, though, and still isn't. But they've worked out a long-distance relationship that works for them." She made a very unladylike noise. "She would have been better off if she'd had that kind of relationship with Dale Lacombe."

The world was truly a strange place. And if Bev was happy in her post-Dale life, there was no reason for her to strike out at him decades later. Not that I'd suspected Leese's mom of killing her ex-husband, but it was nice to keep her off my mental suspect list.

Behind us, I heard the man with the walker murmur to the hostess that he'd prefer a table closer to the window, which was where we were sitting. I hitched my chair forward another couple of inches, just to make sure I was out of the way.

"What about the current wife?" Ash asked. "Carmen."

His mother studied him. "Am I being questioned by an officer of the law or by my son?"

"To which one would you give the most information?"

Lindsey, however, did not return the smile. She didn't say anything for a long moment. Then, when I was about to break the increasing tension with a comment about the weather, she said, "My darling boy. You're working to be a detective, a career choice I admire, but please think carefully about the questions you'll be posing to your family and friends and the complicated situations that might result."

She was absolutely right, and I hadn't once thought about the awkward positions Ash might put people into. He could potentially be asking the people he knew best to betray confidences. To spill secrets. To blab.

I slid him a sideways glance and wondered at what point I'd stop telling him things. Of course, we didn't exactly have many soul-baring conversations, which was another sign that the love I'd hoped would blossom was never going to burst into flower.

Ash nodded at his mother. "I know. Hal and I have talked about this. It's something I'm working on."

"Good," Lindsey said. "Since that's settled, I'll tell you about Carmen."

"And Leese and Brad and Mia?" Ash asked.

She considered the question. "The only thing I'll share about the kids is about Brad. He had a horrible temper when he was a child and I'll lay the blame for that at his father's cold feet. From what I've heard, since he broke away from his father, he has turned into a fine young man."

"Carmen," Ash said.

Lindsey glanced at our new neighbor, but continued. "Not from around here," she told us.

My chin went up the slightest bit. "Neither am I."

"But you fit with the way things work Up North," Lindsey said. "Carmen hasn't stopped complaining about the way things are done around here since the day she showed up." She shook her head. "She and Dale make an excellent pair."

"Not much of a pair any longer," Ash said.

"No." His mother sighed. "I couldn't stand the man, but I didn't wish him dead."

Though that seemed to be a common sentiment, he was undeniably deceased. Lindsey's information about Bev was reassuring, but I certainly hadn't wanted to know that Brad Lacombe's history included a horrible temper.

And that Lindsey hadn't wanted to say anything about Mia.

Or Leese.

At that point, Ash's phone started buzzing frantically. He pulled it out of his pocket and glanced down. "Sorry," he said, rising, "it's Hal. I have to take this." Thumbing the phone's screen, he walked out of the room and toward the front door.

I was trying to figure out why Ash's sudden and frequent departures didn't bother me nearly as much as the similar departures of my former doctor boyfriend had when Lindsey said, "Minnie, I need to use the restroom. Do you mind if I leave you alone for a moment?"

After shooing her off, I considered the options for the next few minutes of my life. Was there enough time to pull out the book I always carried with me? There wasn't much point in looking at the menu, but hope did spring eternal that I might someday be able to order something different from what Kristen wanted me to eat.

"Excuse me," said a male voice.

I jumped the slightest bit. It was the man sitting at the table behind us. I turned and smiled politely. "Hi."

"Were you talking about the Lacombes?"

One of his eyes was looking at me, but the other was staring into a slightly different direction. The poor man probably had horrible headaches "Yes," I said cautiously. In the years I'd lived in Chilson, I'd learned to accept the fact that personal conversations with strangers were commonplace, but I wasn't always comfortable having them. "Do you know them?"

"In a manner of speaking."

He smiled, and the skin over his right cheekbone drew up oddly. I was so distracted as I tried to think what could have caused the effect—Skin cancer? Plastic surgery gone awry? A bad burn? A congenital problem?—that I almost missed his next question.

"Leese has to be, what, in her mid-thirties by now?" he was asking.

"That's right." I wondered if I was about to be the bearer of bad tidings, and said, "Did you know that Dale Lacombe was killed just over a week ago?"

The man nodded briefly. "I hear Leese is an attorney these days."

"That's right. She's specializing in elder law."

"Interesting," he said, but I got the feeling I hadn't told him anything he hadn't already known. "Well, have a good dinner." He smiled again.

Choosing his left eye to focus upon, I smiled back. "You, too."

As I turned around in my seat, Lindsey returned. "Is now the time we talk about Ash?" she asked, sitting.

"Sure," I said. "Although I don't have any problem talking about him when he's here, either."

She laughed. "You two make a great team. Your senses of humor are so similar it's frightening. Are you sure you're not my own child?"

"If I'd come out of your gene pool, I'd probably be six inches taller," I said. "Then all my pants would be too short."

"Who are you calling short?" Ash asked, sliding into his chair.

"No one," Lindsey and I said together, and then laughed at the same time.

Ash shook his head in mock sorrow and murmured something about not being able to leave us two alone.

The rest of the meal passed in a similar lighthearted fashion, but underneath, I kept wondering the same thing: Exactly how uncontrollable was Brad Lacombe's temper?

Chapter 10

The next day, Saturday, was a bookmobile day, but instead of being my normal bright self, I started off the morning yawning and wishing for a couple more hours of sleep.

"Up late last night?" Julia asked. "Did you and Ash go barhopping?"

Barhopping in Chilson wouldn't have taken very long since there was only one establishment in town dedicated to the serving of alcohol. Half a dozen restaurants had bar areas, but I wasn't sure if those would count. "We had dinner with his mom and ended up back at her house playing trivia games."

Julia looked down at Eddie. "What do you think, my furry friend? Could there possibly be a more romantic way to spend an evening?"

"I like Lindsey. She's funny. And smart."

"Are you dating her or her son?"

I couldn't think of any response that didn't involve sarcasm, and since I'd recently promised my mother that I would try to avoid being sarcastic for at least a week, just to see how it felt, I flicked on the turn signal and said, "Is that Mr. Zonne's car?"

Julia looked at the church parking lot. "It is indeed. What kind of story do you think he'll have for us today?"

It was bound to be a good one. After the death of his wife, Lawrence Zonne, a sprightly white-haired octogenarian, had returned home to Tonedagana County from a retirement community in Florida. Mr. Zonne had vision sharper than an eagle's and a memory that retrieved information faster than *Wikipedia* and with far more accuracy.

I parked, Julia opened the door to Eddie's carrier, and we went about getting the bookmobile ready for business, which amounted to flipping open the laptop computers, unstrapping the chair at the back desk, and unlocking the back door.

Mr. Zonne bounded up the stairs. "My dears, I was so sorry to hear about your macabre discovery. What a dreadful thing!" He spread his thin arms wide and gave Julia a massive hug, which then got transferred to me. "More dreadful for Dale Lacombe," he said into my hair, "but then Dale was a dreadful man."

"You knew him?" I asked as I was released.

"In a way." Mr. Zonne paused and squinted at the ceiling. "The rat bast . . . sorry, that miserable son of . . . no, sorry . . ." He pursed his lips. Finally, he said, "Dale Lacombe was the low bid for an addition to our house some thirty years ago. And there was a reason he was low bidder."

"What's that?" Julia asked.

Mr. Zonne declined to answer, but after being peripherally involved with Rafe's home renovation for three years, I could guess. Dale had purchased cheap materials. Or he'd been late starting the project and even later finishing. Or he modified the floor plans without talking to Mr. and Mrs. Zonne. Or his subcontractors were rude. Or he didn't come back to finish the punch list. Or he didn't clean up the site. Or it had been all of that and he still demanded full payment.

"Have they arrested anyone for the murder?" Mr. Zonne asked. "No, never mind. I can see from your exchange of glances that they haven't. And with that particular victim"—he shook his head—"I imagine it's going to take a long time to winnow down the suspect list to a manageable size."

That seemed to be the common sentiment from everyone except the widow. Who, now that I thought about it, hadn't seemed to be suffering from an overabundance of grief.

Then again, everyone grieved in their own way. Maybe Carmen didn't like to display her sorrow to strangers, which I essentially was. Not that she seemed to have a problem communicating any number of other emotions, notably impatience and irritation, but maybe those were masking the grief.

"Mrr!!"

All three of us turned. Eddie was on the dashboard, standing on his back feet and pawing at the front window.

"What, pray tell, is your cat doing now?" Julia asked.

If he was Lassie, he would be trying to tell us that someone was in danger and we'd spend the rest of the time before the commercial break trying to figure what, where, when, why, and how. But since he was Eddie, other possibilities were far more likely. "He probably thinks that spot on the windshield is a cat toy."

"Really?" she asked doubtfully. "I've never seen him get so excited about a toy. A treat, yes. A toy, no."

I looked out the window. "New explanation," I said, nodding. "See?"

Julia and Mr. Zonne caught the direction of my glance, which was aimed at the lot on the far side of the church, where a house was being built. Pickup trucks filled the driveway and men wearing tool belts were hammering away. More to the point, one of the workers was throwing a ball for a golden retriever, who was happily tumbling after it.

"Such a plebeian response," Julia said, sighing. "I thought better of you, Eddie."

"Mrr!"

"I think you could be a little more understanding," Mr. Zonne said, not very seriously. "Not responding to an instinctive response is difficult."

"You hear that?" I leaned over the console and scooped up my cat. "We need to be more understanding."

"Mrr!"

He squirmed around, trying to get down. "How about a treat?" I reached for the cabinet that held the canister.

"Mrr," he said more quietly.

"Okay, how about two treats?" I asked, but before I completed the sentence, he started purring, giving me little choice but to snuggle him close and kiss the top of his head.

Cats. The world's best manipulators.

The rest of the bookmobile day went past quickly, as most bookmobile days did. We checked out books to toddlers and to grandpas. We assisted homeschooled youngsters with finding books that would help them write reports and we helped middle-aged folks find everything from a book on the history of Bolivia ("That's at the main library, but I'll bring it next time") to fiction that would help them while away the hours in a surgical waiting room.

"Another fine day," Julia said, yawning and stretching as we pulled away from the day's last stop, at a convenience store. The owner kindly allowed us to use his restroom and I, in return, purchased more cat treats. "The husband and I are headed to Petoskey for dinner. How about you?"

"Not sure," I said, which was mostly true, but not entirely, because all afternoon I'd been thinking about Dale Lacombe and how he'd died and some of the possibilities for why he'd died. I'd come to the conclusion that I needed to call Carmen, and did so the moment after I shut the door to the bookmobile garage.

"Dale's last job?" Carmen asked. "It's on Valley Street, a mile or so outside of town. The guys are trying to finish up before Thanksgiving. Why?"

I thanked her for the information and slid the phone into my backpack. "Do you want to go out there?" I asked my feline companion. When there was no reply, I leaned forward to look into the front of the cat carrier, which was buckled into my sedan's passenger seat. Eddie was sound asleep and snoring the slightest bit. All the adoration from his fans must have tuckered him out.

"Well," I said out loud, but quietly so I didn't disturb his beauty rest. "Looks like this decision is up to me. And I say there's no time like the present to talk to Dale's employees." Detective Inwood and Ash would no doubt have talked to them already, but since I wasn't law enforcement it was possible I might get different responses.

I started the car, aimed it in the direction of Valley Street, and soon found that Carmen's sense of distance was not the same as mine. When she'd said "a mile or so," I'd expected to drive roughly a mile before I'd see signs of a home under construction. At five miles, I was sure I'd missed it and was making ready to turn around when I saw a piece of plywood two feet square stuck on a post at the end of a rutted driveway and covered with the fluttering documents that were the various permits needed for construction.

"Are you ready?" I asked Eddie, but either he didn't have an opinion or he was still sleeping, because there was no reply.

I guided the car on a strategic path to avoid the worst of the ruts, which was impossible because the ruts had been created by vehicles much larger than my little car: pickups, delivery trucks, forklifts, bulldozers, and front-end loaders, for all I knew. As I neared the two-story house, I counted four pickup trucks. I also noted that the exterior looked close to completion.

This was good, considering it was early October and the weather could turn to winter any minute. What was bad was the fact that no landscaping whatsoever was in place. And if, as Carmen said, they were trying to get the house completed before Thanksgiving, and if the exterior wasn't done, it seemed unlikely that the interior had progressed very far. None of that boded well for the owners.

For me, it all combined to firm up a conclusion I'd come to a couple of years ago, when Rafe had dealt with a brand-new and really expensive furnace that didn't work: I never wanted to build a house. Some people loved the experience, but I was quite sure I wasn't one of them.

With that firmly in mind, I parked next to a white pickup that had the Tonedagana County seal on the driver's door, checked to make sure Eddie was still sleeping, and got out.

"I don't care what Dale told you," a man in khaki pants, work boots, and a nylon jacket was saying loudly. "I'm telling you that you can't do anything else on this house until I approve the mechanical inspection, and I won't do that until the water heater is working."

Three other men, all dressed in brown Carhartt jackets in various stages of age and grime, faced the man. "You got to be kidding me," said one of them.

"This doesn't make any dang sense," said the second guy.

"Yeah," said the guy standing next to him. "What does the mechanical have to do with plumbing? Running the pipes is all we want to work on."

"Take it up with the state," the first man said, who I was now certain was one of the county's inspectors, out on a Saturday, no less. "I can provide contact information for the officials who write the building code." The builders muttered darkly, but didn't ask for names and phone numbers. "Right," the inspector said. "As soon as that water heater is functional, give me a call and I'll come out."

He nodded, received none in return, and headed my way.

"Hi," I said, smiling brightly. "Do you work for the county?"

After a pointed look at the door of his pickup, he

said, "Yes, I do. Ron Driskell, building official and mechanical inspector for Tonedagana County."

"Is there a problem with the house?" I asked. To explain, I hurried on with, "I'm considering building and I'm trying to learn what to avoid."

He made a rude noise. "I'd say avoid getting your place built by Dale Lacombe, but since he's dead, that won't be a problem."

I wanted to say, Gee, tell me what you really think, but instead asked, "Do you mean his houses weren't built well? Or was he just hard to deal with?"

"Both." Driskell spat on the ground. "Lacombe didn't build a single house that didn't have some sort of permitting issue. It was either the foundation or the electrical or the plumbing or"—he turned and gave the house a hard glance— "mechanical. The guy just couldn't see it was easier to do it right the first time and save us all a lot of grief."

"Is that why he was so difficult, because his houses weren't built well?"

Driskell snorted. "He was hard to work with because he was a class A jerk. I'm no huge fan of that politically correct crap, but it's wrong to laugh at a guy in a wheelchair when he says he can't reach the bathroom faucet on the custom cabinet you built him."

I blinked and couldn't think of a thing to say.

"Piece of advice." Driskell opened the door of his truck. "Buy a house. Don't build one. It'll take five years off your life and make you wish you'd never been born." He climbed into his truck, shut the door hard, and started the engine with a roar.

Hmm, I thought as I watched him go. Driskell didn't appear to have a solid grasp on his temper. Could he and Dale have had a confrontation? One that had turned Driskell's temper into murderous anger?

Dale's workers, after incurious glances at me, piled into their own vehicles and trundled out the driveway, leaving me standing there, wondering.

As I drove Eddie back to the houseboat, I gave Leese a call and asked about the clients of her father's that we'd dug out the other day.

"Hang on," she said, and I heard the clicking of a computer keyboard. "I sent an e-mail to Detective Inwood . . . okay, here." She read off the names, Daphne Raab and Gail and Ray Boggs.

"Are they local?" I asked, not remembering the details.

"Daphne Raab lives here year round, out on Dawkins Road. I think the Boggses are seasonal. I'm not sure where their winter place is. Why?"

I hesitated, then said, "I know that Detective Inwood and Ash must be talking to them, but as a private citizen, I might get some different responses. You never know what might turn up."

"Minnie, I appreciate that you're trying to help, but you don't have to do this."

"It's Saturday," I said, "and my boyfriend is starting a twelve-hour shift in two hours. It's either this or start wondering if I've made a dreadful mistake with my life choices."

Leese laughed. "Well, since you put it that way, I'm glad of your help. It makes me feel a little less like I'm just sitting around waiting to go bankrupt." She laughed again, though this time it sounded forced. "I'd come with you, but considering my last name, I'd probably be a hindrance."

She was right, but the idea saddened me. "I'll let you know everything I find out," I promised, having full intentions on keeping that promise. However, half an hour later, when I was standing on a front porch that was sagging at one corner, I knew I wouldn't be telling even half of what I was hearing.

"Dale Lacombe?" Daphne Raab's face, which had up until that moment been one of polite curiosity about the stranger at her door, screwed up into a furious grimace. "I was raised not to speak ill of the dead, but there wasn't anyone more deserving of murder than that . . . that . . ."

"Jerk?" I supplied.

"Too mild," she said, staring at me fiercely. "I suppose I'm sorry for his kids, but that's as far as I'll go."

"His oldest daughter, Leese, is a friend of mine."

Daphne nodded. "My younger sister went to school with her. Nice enough, in spite of her dad."

I'd introduced myself as I had to Rob Driskell, saying that I was considering having a house built, and that I'd been told she'd had some troubles with her construction. It was an odd introduction, but it wasn't too far outside the realm of possibility.

"She's trying to start a law practice up here," I said.

"Another lawyer," Daphne muttered. "Just what we need."

"This is a little different," I told her. "She's specializing in cases for the elderly. Elder law, they call it."

Daphne sniffed. "Putting a fancy label on an attorney just means they charge more."

Ever so slowly, I was cottoning on to the fact that Daphne Raab was not a person filled with positive energy and general goodwill toward her fellow human beings. Moving away from the attorney issue, I said,

"Is there anything you can tell me about Dale Lacombe that would help me make a decision about building?"

"Not much point now in telling you not to hire him," she said, almost smirking, "but that's what I would have said if you'd asked me a couple of weeks ago."

Maybe Leese's father hadn't been an exemplary person, but enjoying the fact of his death was out of line. I tucked my irritation into a dark corner because, after all, I was the one who'd come to her. "He was murdered," I reminded her. "Have you thought about who might have killed him?"

"No idea." She laughed. "The police are going to have a heckuva time sorting this one out. It'll be easier for them to go at it from the other way around, to figure out who didn't want that . . . who didn't want him dead." She barked a short laugh. "Bet it was the wife. I don't see how anyone could have put up with him for more than half an hour without wanting to smack the living daylights out of him."

Her expression changed to polite blandness. "Really, though, I shouldn't say anything. I don't want to be the kind of person who says horrible things about people behind their backs."

Maybe she shouldn't have said anything, but she had, and had appeared to be enjoying herself immensely up until the last two sentences. Passive aggressive, thy name is Daphne Raab. "You know Carmen Lacombe?" I asked.

Daphne shrugged. "I know who she is. It wasn't long ago they were separated. I heard she was going to ask him for a divorce. At least she doesn't have to do that now."

I asked a few more questions about the construction of her house then thanked her for her help and drove away, my mind whirling with the new information.

Carmen and Dale had been separated? Why hadn't anyone told me that particular piece of very critical information?

Which led to an even more uncomfortable question: What else hadn't I been told?

"That's just not true," Carmen said. "I don't know how that story got around and it's just so annoying that Daphne Raab of all people—Daphne Raab!—thinks she knows anything about my marriage. I can't believe she would say that to you! No wonder Dale had to sue her to get paid for that job. Do you know what she said about him in the deposition?"

I did not, actually, not in the least, but Carmen was in full spate and there was no stopping her. On the plus side, we were talking on the phone and I was back home in the houseboat with Eddie on my lap, so at least I had some comforting purrs to soften Carmen's ranting.

"That woman," Carmen practically spat, "said my husband had the morals of a snake and the ethics of pond scum. Pond scum! The next time I saw her, you can believe that I told her exactly what I thought of her."

I did believe it, all too easily. "Do you know how the rumor started that you and Dale were separated?"

She heaved a tremendous sigh. "It got blown all out of proportion. You'd think people would have better things to do than talk about other people, but they don't. If we could harness the power of gossip, we'd have energy enough to light the world."

That was probably true, but I didn't want her to get off topic. "What was blown out of proportion?"

"Oh, it was just one of those silly things that happen in a marriage," she said airily. "It was nothing, and he was back in the house in less than a week."

"He moved out?"

"Of course he didn't. All he packed was a suitcase. You can't move out on a single suitcase."

I wasn't so sure about that, but let it go. "What had you been fighting about?"

She hesitated. "You know, I don't remember. I really don't. Isn't that funny? You'd think I'd remember our last big fight. But we don't get to pick what we remember, do we?"

We did not, and more than once I'd wished to forget certain things that were ingrained into my psyche. Being picked last for a kickball team in elementary school, for one. For another, tripping on the top step of the stage as I walked through high school graduation and falling flat on my face in front of hundreds of people. Still, I'd survived both episodes and the experiences had made me a more compassionate person. Or so I hoped.

"Do you know where he stayed for that week?" I asked.

"With Mia," she said, then laughed. "Maybe that's why Dale came back so fast this time. He was tired of eating Mia's cooking. Boiling water is about as much as she can do."

I latched on to the first part of what she'd said. "This wasn't the first time Dale left for a few days?"

"Well, I didn't keep score." Carmen sniffed. "Sometimes it was Dale and sometimes it was me. Every couple needs time away from each other."

I wasn't so sure about that, either. My parents had slept in the same bed every night of their marriage except for the hospital stays when my brother and I had been born. But every marriage was different, and if time apart was what had helped keep the Lacombes' union intact, who was I to say it wasn't a successful marriage?

"What do you think, Minnie?" Carmen asked. "Do you think that Raab woman killed my husband? I wouldn't put it past her, she's just a ball of hate."

The phrase was an odd one to apply to a human being, but somehow it was apt. "She did come across as a negative person," I said. "But here's the thing. If she was angry enough at Dale to kill him, it seems as if she would have done it when the lawsuit was under way. Why would she do it now, when everything has been resolved?"

"The legal issues might be over," Carmen said, "but there are things that the suit didn't settle. The woman only had to pay us seventy cents for every dollar we were owed. Where's the justice in that?"

Daphne's side of the story was different, of course. She'd told me she'd had to pay another contractor to finish her house because Dale never came back to finish the interior trim work and the final coats of paint, inside and out. If I asked Carmen for details, which I wasn't about to do, I was sure she would say that Dale would have eventually gone back to finish Daphne's job, but she had been too impatient.

Eddie bumped my elbow with his head and I started petting his sleek coat.

Where was the justice? The judge in the lawsuit had probably had a better grasp on it than anyone involved, and it was time to move the conversation on. "I've heard that your husband had a number of employees that he didn't get along with very well. Do you think any of them could have killed Dale?"

"The police asked me the same thing," Carmen said, "and I don't know why people are saying that. Dale was a great boss. Sure, he had turnover, but this is the construction business. It's hard work and lots of people can't handle it. That's all Dale wanted, was his guys to put in a good day of work. That's not too much to ask, is it?"

"Of course not," I said in as soothing a tone as I could, because I could hear the tense emotion in her question. She needed to believe that her husband had been a good man. That was understandable. But as I turned the conversation to the arrangements for a memorial service, my thoughts veered in another direction.

Carmen was an emotional woman who clearly had control issues. Could I envision her, in a fit of anger, going after Daphne Raab with the intent to maim and wound?

Yep.

And I was starting to see a scenario in which she had killed her husband.

Chapter 11

The next morning I woke up slowly. There was absolutely no need for me to get out of bed before noon, and I was seriously considering taking advantage of the opportunity. I was set to meet Aunt Frances and Otto for lunch at 1 p.m., but other than that, I had no obligations and nothing I absolutely had to do, so—

"Mrr."

I looked over at my cat. It wasn't far to look, because he was snuggled up inside the crook of my elbow, with his back half on the bed and his front half draped over my arm. He was staring at me with wide-open eyes and an expression that meant he was trying to tell me something.

"What do you want?" I asked. "Tell me and I will fulfill your every wish."

He lifted his chin the slightest bit. "Mrr!"

"Sorry, I don't understand. I'll just have to guess." I took my hand out from under the covers and patted the top of his fuzzy head. "Is this what you want? A little attention?"

"Mrr," he said.

Pats might not have been what he wanted, but he was purring, so he obviously wasn't rejecting them. I kept patting and he kept purring, which kept me from rolling over and looking at the clock. "What time do you think it is?" The light coming in the window was gray, but that could mean it was just before dawn or that the sky was thick with clouds. It was unlikely I'd slept through to morning's double digits, but it had happened before after a late night of reading.

And I had read late. Somewhere on the floor was a copy of Margery Allingham's *Black Plumes,* a book I'd picked up at the used bookstore. For some reason I now couldn't remember, I'd decided to start reading it after dinner the night before and hadn't managed to put it down until I'd finished.

Eddie, however, remained silent on the time question. "Well, if you're not going to guess," I said, "I'm going to have to play all by myself. Let's see, I think it's—"

My thought was interrupted by the ringing of my cell phone. I reached out, dislodging a protesting Eddie in the process, looked at the screen, and took the call.

"Hey, Leese. What's up?" I swung my stockinged feet to the floor and glanced at the clock. Not quite ten, which to me, if not my mother, was a perfectly acceptable hour to get up on a Sunday morning.

"Sorry to bother you," she said. "I didn't wake you, did I?"

"Nope." I stood. "Been up and out of bed for some time now."

"Great. I just got off the phone with Carmen."

"Right. About that." Last night I'd been so taken up with my new suspicions about Leese's stepmother that I'd decided I wouldn't call my friend until I'd worked it all through in my head. "I'd planned on talking to you, but . . ." But what? I hadn't left myself anywhere to go with that sentence.

Leese laughed. "But Carmen was being Carmen and you didn't feel you could take any more Lacombes in a twenty-four-hour period? I know the feeling. Believe me."

Though I felt a little ashamed of myself for doing so, I didn't contradict her. "What did Carmen tell you?"

"I heard the whole Daphne Raab story all over again."

"Did you wear yourself out from rolling your eyes?"

"Absolutely." She chuckled, then sighed. "Carmen also told me you think a disgruntled employee killed my dad."

"It's a possibility," I said. "Or do you agree with Carmen that your dad was the best boss in the world and the reason he had so much turnover was because kids today don't know what hard work means."

She snorted. "Brad's told me too many stories for me to believe in that fairy tale."

"Okay, so that's something to look into." I paused. "What do you know about Rob Driskell? He's a building inspector for the county."

"Not much, other than my dad didn't have a good word to say about him, which puts Driskell in the same category as ninety-nine point nine percent of the world's population."

"I met him yesterday," I said, and told her about the conversation.

After a short silence, she asked, "You think Driskell killed my dad?"

I almost said what I'd been told so many times by Detective Inwood, that I was exploring all avenues of investigation, but I stopped myself in time. "It's another possibility," I said. "I asked Carmen about him, but we got sidetracked."

"That happens a lot with Carmen," Leese said in a matter-of-fact manner. "I'll talk to Brad, ask if he knows anything."

By now I'd walked up the short flight of stairs from the bedroom and was starting coffee preparations. "Speaking of Brad, the other day I asked him about disgruntled employees. He said he was probably the best candidate of all."

"The fight," Leese said, "and that's a capital F. It was years ago, but people still talk about it." She paused, then said, "Minnie, so many people talk about the Fight that the story has grown far bigger than what actually happened. I'm afraid the police are going to start thinking that Brad is a good suspect."

I was afraid of the same thing. "Yesterday I ran across Daphne Raab and we talked about your dad a little. I'm sorry to say that she didn't have much good to say about him."

"No, she wouldn't," Leese mused. "Still, from what little I know of her, I don't see her as the murdering type. Not that I'd know what type that might be."

In the last couple of years I'd had the misfortune to run across more than one killer. Was there a type among them? I'd never seen it, but I hadn't been looking, either. Now that I was thinking about it, the only thing they seemed to have in common was murder.

"Let me know what Brad has to say," I said, pouring water into the coffeemaker. "Other than your stepmother issues, how are things going? Did you meet with that new client?"

"Bob Blake," Leese said. "We've had phone conversations, but we haven't scheduled a meeting. I think he has health issues—one time we talked I kept hearing hospital noises in the background. Anyway, he said he'd call this week to set up something. It sounded like Saturdays will work best for him."

I watched the caffeinated liquid dripping down. "Great. How about your other clients?"

"Things will work out," she said. "Isn't that what you always say?"

It was mostly my aunt Frances, and I would have given her the attribution if Leese's voice hadn't sounded so tight. "Is there anything I can do?" I asked.

"Thanks, but I'll be fine," she said a little grimly.

"Here's an idea." I got a mug out of the cabinet. "How about a presentation about elder law at the library?"

"Are . . . you sure?" Leese asked.

"Sure I'm sure." The more I thought about the idea, the more I liked it. "We could do a series of service-type talks for senior citizens, starting with you. No one's doing anything similar in the whole county, as far as I know."

Ideas were spinning around in my head. I'd get someone to talk about finances. Someone else to talk about health care. Maybe lots of someones to talk about different aspects of health care. I'd have to get Jennifer's permission, of course, but why would she object?

"Minnie, you . . . you . . ." Leese's voice caught. "You're the best."

"Can I pass that on to my new boss?" I asked, laughing. "Because I'm not sure she knows."

After making tentative plans, I hung up and looked at Eddie, who was sitting next to his mostly full bowl of food and staring at me with fierce concentration.

"She's worried about her law practice," I said. "She's not going to come out and say so, but she's worried. We have to figure out who killed her father and we have to do it fast."

"Mrr."

"I'm sure you're right." Not that I had any idea what he was saying, but it was always easier to agree with him than to start arguing. Then, as I poured my first coffee of the day, I got the nagging feeling that I was missing something about Dale's murder, that I wasn't anywhere close to figuring out who killed him, and that I was going to fail completely to help my friend.

"Mrr!" Eddie said.

"Absolutely," I told my cat. I opened the cupboard door and shook a couple of cat treats onto the floor. "All yours."

Eddie gave the treats a harsh glare, gave me a harsh glare, and stalked off.

"Love you, too," I called after him.

"Mrr."

I shook my head. Some days there was no understanding cats.

Three hours later, Otto Bingham opened his front door. "Frances is in the kitchen," he said, ushering me inside. "She sent me out here with orders that we leave her alone to cook for the next fifteen minutes."

I grinned as we sat on upholstered chairs in what Otto called the front room and I called a parlor. It was a small and elegant space occupied by a few chairs, a bookshelf, a few original paintings, and a fireplace. If this couldn't be called a parlor, I didn't know what could be.

After offering coffee from a side table, which I gratefully accepted since the Bingham coffee was outstanding, Otto poured and asked, "So what is the inestimable Eddie doing today?"

I reached down to scratch the chin of his small gray kitty. She and Eddie had met once and it hadn't turned out well. "Mr. Ed has become one with his slothfulness."

"It's good to recognize your strengths," Otto said, nodding.

Smiling, I said, "If sloth was a marketable cat skill, neither one of us would have to work again a day in our lives."

The small gray kitty, who up until that point had been lovingly accepting my scratches, had suddenly had enough. "Moww," she said loudly, and stalked off.

"What was that about?" I asked.

Otto smiled. "Isn't it obvious? You were doing it wrong. Yes, you may disagree, since you'd been scratching her the same way for the last few minutes, but what she wanted was something different starting six seconds ago. You did not respond appropriately, so she was compelled to voice her objections."

"My aunt," I said, "is marrying a man who understands cats. Does she know how lucky she is?"

He smiled. "I'm the lucky one. Surely you know that."

The lucky part was that they'd found each other. Though it had taken a little Minnie intervention to get the then-shy Otto to approach my aunt, things had turned out well for both parties.

"Speaking of strengths," I said. "How do you feel about giving a senior citizen–oriented talk at the library?"

His eyebrows rose. "About anything in particular, or would I get to ramble for an hour on whatever topic I choose?"

I laughed. "I'm sure you could give an interesting talk on the history of the phone book, but I was thinking about putting together a lecture series aimed at seniors. I thought you could give them tips on managing their finances." Though Otto's career as an accountant had been spent in the downstate corporate world, he'd also done pro bono work at his church and area high schools.

After considering the question for all of two seconds, he said, "I'm in. When do you want me?"

"Well, I only got the idea this morning. I need to get Jennifer's okay, but I'll get back to you."

He nodded. "Just let me know. Glad to help."

I looked at him. "You really are, aren't you? I mean, you're not just saying that."

"Honesty is far easier," he said. "Keeps you from having to keep track of different lies told to different people, and then what happens if the people get together?" He shook his head sorrowfully. "Much easier just to be honest in the first place."

"So tell me honestly," I said. "How do you really feel about the boardinghouse?"

A long and increasingly uncomfortable silence followed my somewhat abrupt question. Finally, Otto sipped the last of his coffee, set the cup back on the table, and faced me directly.

"I know it's a decades-old tradition, I know it's important to Frances, and I know that many people find comfort in its continued existence. I understand all that, but on a personal basis, I don't want to have anything to do with running it."

"Oh," I said blankly.

"If Frances has her heart set on continuing to run it," he went on, "of course I'll support her and do what I can to continue its success. And who knows?" He half smiled. "Maybe I'll come to love it." The slope of his shoulders, however, indicated that he was dreading the prospect.

But even as I noted that steep angle, he straightened and lifted his chin. "Enough about that. I shouldn't have burdened you with this knowledge, Minnie, and I apologize. Can you please forget I said anything?"

Though I murmured agreement, I knew—we both knew—that forgetting would be impossible.

I walked home from Otto's house with a tummy full of marinated pork tenderloin, steamed vegetables, redskin potatoes, cornbread, and more coffee served with a lemon square dusted with powdered sugar and topped with a dollop of whipped cream.

"It's possible I ate a little too much," I told Eddie as I put my container of leftovers into the fridge.

"Mrr." He jumped up onto the back of the dining table's bench seating and settled down to stare at me, all four paws in a short white row.

"How do you do that without falling over?" I patted the top of his head, which made it go up and down like a fur-covered bobble head. "No offense, pal, but you're not the most graceful cat who ever walked the face of the earth."

He adjusted himself slightly and continued to stare at me.

"Well, you're not." I slid into the seat across from him and stared back. "You have other strengths. Lots of them. It's okay to admit that you'll never be a candidate for the first feline gymnastics team to enter the Olympics."

Eddie's sides went in and out in a visible sigh.

"Don't worry," I told him consolingly. "You can always apply to be a coach. I'm sure they'd appreciate your advice."

"Mrr!"

"You're right, you're an excellent life coach for me and I don't appreciate your guidance as I should. I'll work on that."

Eddie slid down from his sitting stance into a lying down position. This relieved me, because I hadn't been certain his four-in-a-row was stable enough for the back of a bench seat. "Tell you what," I said. "Next time you give me advice I vow to take it seriously."

"Mrr," he said quietly.

"Good. That's settled, then." I turned and unzipped my backpack, which I'd tossed onto the far end of the bench the day before. "Right now there's some work to do. If you help, we'll get it done in half the time and then we can do whatever you'd like."

Eddie's yawn was wide. And contagious.

"None of that." I pointed my pencil at him. "There's work to be done. I promised Aunt Frances I'd make a list for moving up to the boardinghouse and I'm going to do it right now so I don't forget."

It was more a timeline she wanted than a list, but I wasn't sure Eddie would understand what a timeline was. Not that he knew what a list was, other than a piece of paper he could shred into bits the minute my back was turned. Still, pretending that he understood even a portion of what I was saying amused me.

I extracted a spiral notebook from the depths of the backpack. "Okay, are you ready?" I flipped to a clean sheet. "Goal number one," I informed Eddie, "is to get everything moved into the boardinghouse before the weather turns really cold. Everything includes you and me. Aunt Frances wants a date from us because she needs to plan the changeover."

Every fall that I'd lived in Chilson, I'd helped my aunt with numerous summer-to-winter tasks. Sheer curtains came down, insulated drapes went up. Light summer blankets were switched to thick comforters. Smooth cotton sheets were changed to cozy flannel. The furnace filter was replaced, the fireplace chimney was cleaned, white and pastel colored couch pillows were changed over to deep autumn colors.

And that was just the inside tasks. Outside there were oodles of leaves to rake, plants to cut down, furniture to store, screens to put away, and firewood to stack. Last, but certainly not least, we ceremoniously took the snow shovels out of the back corner of the garage and put them on the porch.

The whole enterprise took two full weekends if we worked hard. My bookmobile schedule of working on three of four Saturdays, however, made that a little difficult. "That's why she wants a timeline," I said to Eddie.

He, however, was more interested in playing with my pencil then listening to what I had to say.

"Speaking of timelines," I said, holding the eraser end of the pencil out for him to bat, "I'm wondering about the time of Dale's murder. If it was at the estimated two in the morning on Thursday, why wasn't he home, asleep in bed? It was a weeknight and he was working the next day."

Or was he? I realized I had no idea what Lacombe's normal hours had been. For all I knew, he'd been a night owl and was regularly up at that time. But if he wasn't, why had he been out so late?

"Something to ask Carmen," I said, but Eddie was still focused on my pencil and not paying any attention to me. "What do you think?" I asked him. "Does the fact that Dale was out in the middle of the night have anything to do with—hey!"

Eddie grabbed the pencil with his pointy teeth, gripped tight, and tugged it out of my hand.

"What exactly are you going to do with that?" I asked, stretching forward to get it back. "It's not like you can write with it. You don't have thumbs, remember?"

He sent a glare that should have instantly evaporated me, jumped to the floor, and ran off with my pencil.

I heard him thump down the stairs to the bedroom and leap up onto the bed. Shaking my head, I got a pen out of my backpack and kept on working.

On Monday, I kept trying to talk to Jennifer about setting up a library lecture series for senior citizens, but every time I went up to her office for a friendly face-to-face chat, she was either on the phone or cozied up with a library board member.

I spent the afternoon trying not to think about that and wasn't very successful. I didn't like that she was talking to the board members individually, didn't like it at all. It looked like she was manipulating the board, giving them her side of whatever issue she was talking about and preempting what should have been an open discussion during a full board meeting. Stephen, as annoying as he'd been in so very many ways, had never done that.

Halfway down the stairs, I stopped. Was it possible that I was actually missing my former boss?

I stood there, hand on railing and one foot in midair, considering the question, but it didn't take long to come to a conclusion. No. I did not miss Stephen. I missed one particular aspect of his management style, that was all.

Breathing a sigh of relief, I continued down the stairs.

The next day was a bookmobile day, and on the way to the first stop, I told Julia what Jennifer was doing.

"Interesting." Julia, who, as a successful actress, had endured more than her share of backstabbing, infighting, and alliances that shifted underfoot, made the humming noise that meant her quick mind was hard at work. "What did your coworkers say?" she asked.

"Didn't tell them."

Julia glanced over at me across the wide console. "Why?"

I shrugged. "They don't like her and I didn't want to give them any more reasons to not get along. Besides, it might be nothing."

"But you think it is something, don't you?"

"It kind of has to be. Otherwise, why would she be working so hard to talk to each of the board members separately?"

"I see what you mean." Julia leaned back and propped her feet on top of the cat carrier. Eddie, who was curled up in his pink blanket, took no notice. "Do you have a theory?" she asked. "No, let me rephrase that. Your name is Minnie Hamilton and of course you have a theory. On a scale of don't-be-ridiculous to stake-your-life, how likely is it?"

I considered the question. "Somewhere in the sure-enough-to-make-my-stomach-hurt realm."

"Do you want to tell your aunt Julia about it?"

Her overly warm concern made me laugh out loud. "I thought you were supposed to be a *good* actress."

"Only when I'm getting paid."

"Your husband must find that comforting."

"He does indeed," she said.

There was a short pause, then I said, "It's my guess that Jennifer is trying to persuade the board to buy that new library systems software."

Julia frowned. "Isn't the program we're using just a couple of years old?"

"Four and a half. It was installed just before the move to the new building."

"How time flies," she murmured. "But those systems are expensive, aren't they? Why would they change over to something new?"

An excellent question. "Jennifer thinks a different system would be more efficient."

"Let me guess," Julia said. "This other program is what she used at the library where she worked before she came here."

"Bingo!" The road, which had been narrow and tree-lined, widened to include a turn lane that led to a county park. For a few miles we'd been following a vehicle with a bright yellow kayak on top and now its right blinker and brake lights went on. Since the bookmobile was too wide to go around comfortably, I braked, too.

"I am a genius," she said modestly. "You, however, are stuck. As someone with more knowledge of library software than most library directors and, I daresay, every library board member, you know that what Jennifer wants to do is nuts. As her assistant, however, you're obligated to follow her lead, no matter how ridiculous it may be."

"That sums it up nicely." The vehicle in front of us, a midsized SUV, turned and I blinked as I recognized it.

"More proof that I am indeed a genius." She tapped her head. "What are you going to do?"

I had no idea what I was going to do about Jennifer's machinations, but I did know what I was going to do next. "Hang on," I said, "we're going to make a short stop."

Ignoring Julia's surprised look, I followed the SUV into the park's gravel parking area. I circled around, braked to a halt a few yards from the vehicle, told Julia I'd be back in a flash, and hurried out to meet Brad Lacombe.

"Hey, Minnie." He smiled. "I know I should read more, but you really don't have to chase me down."

"Whatever it takes," I said, laughing. "But as much as I'd like everyone to read more, including me, when I saw you in front of us, I thought I'd stop and ask a quick question about your dad."

Brad stroked his beard. "Sure. What's up?"

"It's the time he died. The estimate was two a.m., right?" Brad nodded and I went on. "So I got to wondering. Was he a night person and this was something normal? If not, what was he doing out at two in the morning?"

"That's a good question," he said slowly. "If he was

trying to finish a job, it wasn't unheard of for Dad to stay out half the night, or all night even. But I don't know if he was on deadline, or not. Have you asked my mom?"

"Not yet." I made a mental note to talk to both Carmen and Ash about it. Maybe Detective Inwood had already been over this, but maybe not. He was a busy man and it was hard to remember everything. Maybe it took a village to catch a killer. "Thanks, Brad. Sorry for delaying your kayaking."

He shrugged. "Right now I have all the time in the world."

Something about his expression caught at me. I'd been about to turn away, but I paused and studied him. "Is something wrong?"

"Just work," he muttered.

But Leese had told me that her stepbrother was a favored employee at the brewery. And that he loved his job so much he was in danger of losing all perspective about the relative importance of beer to the general population.

"What's the matter?" I asked.

Again, he shrugged, but this time I was watching his face closely and saw emotion etching lines into his face. Worry? Anxiety? Fear? I would have put it down to his father's murder except he hadn't looked like this the night at Leese's house. He also didn't seem inclined to talk, and since I barely knew him, I decided I'd let it go after one more attempt. "You sure you're okay?"

"No," he said wryly, and somehow he sounded a lot like his older sister. "Actually I'm not. I've been suspended without pay."

"What? Brad, I'm so sorry. What happened?"

"I have no idea." He stared off into the distance. "It's my blame to take and I understand why they had to do this, but I lay awake half the night trying to figure it out and I still have no idea what went on with that batch."

A crawly feeling was starting to creep over my skin. "Something went wrong with one of your beers?"

He nodded slowly. "The first batch of a new recipe I was trying. It tested fine when it was brewing, it tested fine when it was in storage, and I swear to God it tested fine when I put it into kegs for shipping. Then two nights ago, at that new tap room in Petoskey, we debuted it." He shoved his hands in his pockets. "It was contaminated. Fifty people got sick, nine went to the hospital, and one of them might . . ." He swallowed. "One might die."

The thought was horrible, and my heart went out to all who were sick, and to Brad. But a tiny idea trickled into my brain: Could this somehow be related to Dale Lacombe's murder? Could Brad have been the intended victim?

Chapter 12

Brad's sad news about the people sickened by a beer he'd made stayed with me through the day and into the evening, when I called Leese. She'd talked to her stepbrother earlier that day and had tried to get him to go out for dinner with her, but he'd turned her down, saying that he wouldn't be good company.

"I told him not to be an idiot," she said, "because he'd never been good company in his life and I certainly didn't expect him to start doing so anytime soon." She sighed. "He didn't laugh even a little. I sent Mia over. Maybe she can help."

By the end of the workday we'd both heard that of the nine people who'd gone to the emergency room, eight had been treated and released. The one remaining victim, the one Brad had been so worried about, had been diagnosed with appendicitis, not food poisoning, and was resting comfortably after an emergency operation.

But even if no one had been deathly ill, it was still a serious situation, and I didn't want to think what

Brad was enduring, knowing something he'd brewed had caused people harm.

That night I dreamed dreams of falling into vats of beer—a beverage of which I wasn't overly fond—and being reminded by a swimming police officer not to forget to register before I moved. "It was just weird," I told Holly and Josh, as I poured myself a third cup of coffee the next morning.

"Sounds more stupid than weird." Josh shook four sugar packets, dumped them into his mug, and looked at Holly, who was rummaging through the utensil drawer. "Please don't tell me you think her dream means something."

"Of course it means something," she said. "Hah!" She brandished what we all referred to as the Good Knife, and started using it to cut the pan of brownies she'd brought into squares.

"Yeah?" Josh pulled out a chair, making its feet screech against the hard floor, and sat. "What?"

"It means she was having stupid dreams about beer." Holly levered brownies onto the three paper towels she'd already set out. "Although that's redundant, since all dreams about beer are stupid because beer is stupid."

Josh took a brownie. "You're wrong, but as long as you keep bringing us food, I'm not going to argue with you."

"Silence of the Josh," I said, accepting my Holly-made confection. "Who knew it was even possible?"

"Anything's possible." Holly smiled broadly. "Even your husband coming home for a month."

"Hey, that's great!" Her husband, Brian, had a fantastic job working for a mining company fifteen hundred miles away. It was their hope that Brian would eventually find employment in Michigan, but for now they made due with occasional trips, video visits, and frequent packages sent to their two small children.

Though I'd long feared that Holly might get tired of the long-distance relationship and pack up and move West, she'd recently confessed to me that the idea of moving Out There, as she called it, was something she'd considered and rejected. "My family is here," she'd said. "His family is here. I don't want to take the kids away from those relationships."

Around a mouthful of brownie, Josh said, "If he's going to be here over hunting season, tell him to give me a call."

As the two of them talked about Brian's vacation, I started thinking ahead in the calendar. Soon I'd be moving up to the boardinghouse. Then there'd be Thanksgiving, Christmas, and skiing season. There would be an excellent new crop of books to read and—

"I forgot," I said out loud.

"Forgot what?" Josh asked. "No, let me guess. About twenty years ago, you forgot to keep growing."

"No," Holly said, "she forgot to get married. One of these days she's going to remember and we'll get invitations in the mail. I'm already planning what to wear."

"Wrong and wrong again." I got up. "I need to talk to Jennifer."

I heard the groans, but didn't see any facial expressions since I'd already started to walk out of the room. Temporarily working on the theory that what I didn't see I didn't have to deal with, I headed up to Jennifer's office and knocked on the doorjamb.

"Good morning," I said. "Do you have a minute?"

My boss, who had rotated her chair to face the window, turned around. "I have an appointment in a few minutes, but until then I'm available."

An appointment with another library board member, no doubt. "Great," I said, perching myself on the front edge of one of her abstract guest chairs. "I have an idea to run past you."

Jennifer's perfectly plucked eyebrows went up. "Oh? Please don't tell me you need another bookmobile."

"Need?" I asked, smiling to hide the sudden burst of annoyance exploding inside my head. "Sure, we could use another bookmobile. Just think of all the people we could reach that we're missing now." In truth, buying another bookmobile had never occurred to me. I was having a hard enough time operating one.

Jennifer shook her head. "Not possible," she said. "I can't believe you're even bringing it up. You should know that the library's budget can't possibly absorb the cost of another bookmobile."

I hadn't brought it up; she had. But instead of wasting my time and energy by pointing that out, I said, "My idea is to set up a lecture series that focuses on the needs of senior citizens. Finances, questions of law, health, nutrition. This morning I talked to the local senior center and they're not doing anything similar. They thought it was a great idea."

"More outreach," Jennifer murmured. "How does this align with the library's mission?"

This was a question I'd been prepared to hear and I quoted the mission statement's second sentence. "'The library serves as a learning center for all residents of the community,'" I said.

"A little vague." Jennifer turned back toward the window.

Undaunted, I said, "This applies to the first part of the statement, too. This would be a service that helps residents obtain information that meets their needs."

"One small segment of the population." Jennifer's tone was vague and I could tell she'd already lost interest. "I don't see this as a good use of the library's resources."

"It won't cost anything." I persisted, since I was determined to make a good case. "All it will take is a little bit of my time to arrange for speakers and the use of the conference room, which is empty most of the time anyway."

"Your time is valuable." Jennifer stood and went to the window. "You're already stretched thin and I don't want you taking on any new projects."

She'd said no, but had left a way open. "Would you be opposed to the plan if someone else was in charge of lining up speakers? I'd approve each speaker, but someone else would make all the arrangements." I leaned forward, waiting for her answer.

"Where are all the people?" Jennifer asked, nodding toward Chilson's downtown streets.

I blinked. "Excuse me?"

"The people." She reached through the venetian blind and tapped the windowpane. "There aren't any. When I arrived here, there were a lot more cars on the streets. The restaurants were full, the stores were full, there were concerts in the park, and some sort of event every weekend."

"This is a tourist town," I said, trying not to overstate the obvious.

"Yes, but that doesn't explain the emptiness."

Of course it did. What on earth was she talking about? "There won't be big crowds again until June."

Jennifer, never one for unnecessary movement, froze solid. "June?" she asked.

"Well, sure." When she didn't say anything, I expanded. "A few of the seasonal folks will hang on until Thanksgiving, then even they will head south for the winter. Some people come back for Christmas, Martin Luther King Jr. Day, and Presidents' weekend."

I smiled, feeling slightly evil and enjoying myself immensely. Bad Minnie. "March and April are the really quiet months. You could roll a bowling ball down the middle of Main Street at high noon and not hit anything except curb." It was an exaggeration, but not by much.

"But . . ." Jennifer wrapped her arms around her middle. "But there's skiing around here. Won't the skiers be coming soon? I was told Chilson was the Michigan version of Vail."

Not by anyone who'd ever been to both Chilson and Vail. "The ski resorts in this area are nice enough," I said, "but the best skiing in Michigan isn't close to the quality of skiing out West. We have hills. They have mountains."

"I'm not a skier," she murmured.

"Well, maybe you'll turn into one," I said cheerfully. "Finding something you like to do in the snow is the best way to deal with winter." And since she hadn't said I couldn't hand over my new senior talk idea to someone else, I made my exit before she realized she hadn't said no.

During lunch, I spent a few minutes looking up information about Gail and Ray Boggs, the other party involved in lawsuits that Dale Lacombe had recently won. The county website's property information database told me the Boggses had purchased a piece of property five years ago. I clicked on a "Find location on map" link. The aerial photography showed a house sited near a creek and neighbors close enough to be good friends, but far enough to feel private.

The phone book didn't have a Boggs listing, so after debating the wisdom of heading out to the house of a complete stranger, I walked home, wrote my intentions on a white board as I'd sworn to my mother I would always do when I went somewhere solo, patted a sleepy Eddie on the head, and got into the car.

Though there was still technically an hour and a half before the sun set, so much cloud cover had moved in that I felt compelled to turn on the car's headlights. I almost turned them off, but sighed and left them on. It would be dark soon enough and it was always better to be seen than not seen.

It was about ten miles to the address, and in spite of the growing murk, I enjoyed the drive over forested hills that opened up to a wide valley. All around were the bright colors of autumn or what would have been bright colors if there had been some sunlight. Even still, the reddish-orange of the maple leaves and the occasional yellow of birches and aspens penetrated the darkening sky with color that was both breathtaking and heartrending with its fleeting beauty.

"Get a grip," I told myself. It wasn't like me to wax poetic, especially with a melancholy tone. Maybe what I needed was a dose of Kristen. She'd been too wrapped up with preparations for seasonal closing of her restaurant to make dessert for me the other night, but we were set in stone for the coming Sunday.

I turned right on the road that led to the Boggses' house and, one mile later, bumped off the end of asphalt and onto gravel. After a half mile of bouncing over washboards and steering around potholes, I saw their house number on a mailbox in a cluster of five.

"Hmm." I studied the driveways, looked at the map I'd printed from the county's website, and aimed the car down the middle driveway. It was little more than two tire tracks through the woods, but the tracks were definite enough and I didn't have any trouble following them down the winding path. The driveway wasn't in any better condition than the gravel road had been, and as I bounced toward the house, I hoped my car's suspension would hold up on the return trip.

One last bump around one last corner, and a house came into view.

A dark house.

With a For Sale sign stuck into the front lawn.

I sat there, engine running, staring at the place. Clearly, there was no one for me to talk to. Not only was it dark and for sale, but it had that abandoned air that houses take on when their owners have departed. I hadn't even considered this possibility; now what was I going to do?

After a moment, I got out of the car, climbed the front steps, and peered in through the window in the door. "Huh," I said out loud. Dark, for sale, and vacant. The front hall didn't contain so much as a stick of furniture. The Boggses obviously didn't believe in staging a house.

I walked sideways down the porch. The only thing in the living room was the grate in the fireplace, and the dining room's only ornament was a hanging light fixture that was made from either driftwood or deer antlers. In the dark I couldn't tell, but if I had to guess—

"Can I help you?"

"Yah!" I spun and took a jump away from the voice, bashing my head against the house in the process. "Ow!" I held one of my hands to my chest in an attempt to keep my rapidly beating heart inside where it belonged, and with the other I rubbed the back of my head.

The man standing on the lawn chuckled. "Sorry about that. You didn't hurt yourself, did you?"

"Not enough to need an ambulance," I said, still rubbing. "But houses don't move much when you bonk into them."

"If any house would, it'd be this one."

I stopped my self-ministrations and looked at the guy. He seemed affable enough. Sure, I was looking at him through a half light that was growing darker every second, but his hands-in-pockets pose, along with an easy smile and a baseball hat that proclaimed him the WORLD'S GREATEST GRANDPA, combined for a nonthreatening persona. "What makes you say that? Are you Ray Boggs?"

"Neighbor. Or I was until they stuck that in the ground and headed off." He nodded toward the real estate sign. "I told them I'd keep an eye on the place, so when I saw your headlights, I came over to make sure that someone wasn't up to nefarious deeds."

By this time I'd walked off the porch and stood in front of him. "Minnie Hamilton," I said, offering my hand. "Assistant director and driver of the bookmobile for the Chilson Library."

"Fred Sirrine. Retired from Ford Motor Company." As we shook hands, he asked, "So what are you doing out here? Hope you're not chasing down overdue fines; the Boggses haven't been around in weeks."

"Not today." I debated how much to share. "A minute ago, you implied the house wasn't built well."

He glanced at the structure. "I shouldn't have said that. All I have to go on is what Ray and Gail told me. Secondhand information isn't a good way to form an opinion."

I started to wonder what Mr. Sirrine had done for Ford. "Sometimes secondhand information is the only kind available."

"The formation of an opinion should wait for solid data," he said firmly.

"Oh, dear," I said. "Then I'll have to take back the opinion I'm already forming that you're a nice man."

He laughed. "Point taken. But getting back to my question, what are you doing out here?"

"I'm not looking for overdue fees, but I would like to talk to the Boggses. Do you know where they moved?"

"They had a place in Royal Oak when they built this for a weekend getaway, but they sold that when they thought they'd stay up here year round. After last February, though, they'd had enough of snow and cold. They put it up for sale and rented a condo near Santa Fe."

"So they're in New Mexico?" If so, I didn't have much chance of finding them.

He shook his head. "That was only for the winter. They said they'd be staying at their other place in Michigan, but who knows?" He eyed me. "You going to tell me why you'd like to talk to my former neighbors?"

"Dale Lacombe, the contractor who built the Boggses' house, was killed two weeks ago." My new friend nodded, and I went on. "His daughter is a friend of mine and I'm just . . ." *Just what? Think, Minnie, think!* "Just following up on some of the clients he'd had troubles with."

Fred eyed me. "Following up," he said.

"Yes." It was my story and I was going to stick to it. "I'm trying to help," I said. "The family is . . . having a hard time."

"I imagine." He looked at me, at the house, then back at me. "You do realize that the Boggses and Lacombe ended up in court."

"Yes, and I was hoping to talk to them about that. To clear the air, if nothing else."

He pulled his hands out of his pockets and adjusted his Grandpa hat. "If Ray or Gail had been in town when Lacombe was killed, then you'd have some ideal candidates for the murder. They could hardly say his name without spitting. I assume that's what you're really doing here? Trying to find out who killed your friend's dad?"

Was I that obvious? I sighed. "Leese is a lawyer. She grew up around here and moved back home this summer to open her own business and . . . well, she's having a hard time right now."

Fred flicked another glance at the house. "Please tell me she's a better lawyer than her dad was a builder."

I smiled. "She and her dad didn't get along."

"Good to know. Well, good luck to you," he said. "It's commendable that you're trying to help your friend, but take care. Don't forget there's a killer out there."

And with that comforting thought, he gave me one last nod and headed back into the woods.

The next morning I woke up, put one foot outside the covers, then pulled it back with a yelp. "Hokey Pete! It's cold out there!"

I carefully reached out for my cell phone, keeping my hand under the sheet, blankets, and comforter until the last possible moment. Even then, my skin went all prickly with the temperature change. I ducked all the way back under the covers, turned on the phone, and opened the weather app, which showed a temperature of twenty-nine degrees.

That couldn't be right. The weather people had predicted a low in the mid-forties.

I poked at the phone and checked the current temperatures in Petoskey, Charlevoix, Mackinaw City, and Bellaire. All were hovering just below freezing.

"How could they be so wrong?" I asked out loud.

"Mrr," said Eddie's muffled voice.

"At least you have a fur coat," I said, then made a few more taps that resulted in my aunt's voice saying, "Let me guess. You want to move to the boardinghouse today."

"Yes, please," I said meekly. "Very much, please."

She laughed. "Come on up, dear heart. You know you're welcome any time."

Immediately after the bookmobile day ended, the Eddie delivery took place. He studied his surroundings, emitted a very loud "Mrr!" and promptly jumped onto the back of the couch, where he'd spent a large portion of the previous winter. I drove to the marina and started heaving things into boxes.

It wasn't the most organized of moves, but the unexpected cold snap was motivating and Aunt Frances, Otto, and I hauled the last item out of my car and up the stairs just past ten o'clock that night.

Aunt Frances surveyed the array of boxes, totes, and grocery bags strewn across my bed, the floor of my bedroom, and the hallway. "Do you know where anything is?" she asked.

"Not a single thing," I said cheerfully. "Except for

this." I hefted the small duffle bag that I used for overnight visits.

Otto looked around. "I'm surprised you could fit this much stuff into that little boat."

"Cabinets and drawers can hold more than you think. It's all in the packing."

"But why do you move everything back here in the winter? Couldn't you leave most of this down there?" He grinned. "Certainly the kitchen equipment we hauled up won't get used."

I laughed. "Are you kidding? I hardly use any of this stuff on the boat. To answer your question, though, the first winter I did leave a number of things in place. Then a squirrel got in."

"Ah." Otto nodded. "Thus the moving."

"Thus." I pointed at the boxes. "Aunt Frances, I promise I'll have everything organized and either put away in my room or up in the attic by Sunday afternoon."

"Take your time," she said. "That is, as long as you have everything out of the hallway before you go to work on Monday."

I held up my hand, Girl Scout promise style, and vowed to do so. I'd have to go down to the boat one more time to do what my brother called a Paranoid Check, making absolutely sure one final time I hadn't left anything behind, but I'd already called Chris Ballou, the marina's manager, and asked him to get it out of the water.

Otto rubbed his hands together. "All righty, then. I say it's time, don't you, Frances?"

"Way past," she said, and the two turned and started to make their way downstairs. "Minnie, are you coming?"

"Where?" I called after them. "To do what?"

Neither one of them answered. I did hear laughter, but since that didn't explain anything, I abandoned my unpacking without a qualm—after all, my aunt had invited me to follow them—and I wandered downstairs, curious and mystified.

By the time I reached the living room, where Eddie was still sleeping on the back of the couch, I'd come up with all sorts of theories about what it might be time for. An evening cocktail was a strong possibility, but somehow that didn't seem to fit. Other ideas ranged from going for an evening walk (a little late, but possible) to making a crank phone call (nine point nine on the unlikely scale of one to ten) to choosing colors for their wedding (about nine point eight on the same scale).

I followed the sounds of voices and tracked down Aunt Frances and Otto in the kitchen, where they were looking into the cupboard that held baking supplies.

"How about red?" my aunt asked.

Otto nodded. "Cheerful, yet not over the top. An excellent choice. Then again," he said thoughtfully, "with Minnie here, it's a sort of celebration. Perhaps we should go with gold."

"Or blue," my aunt said. "Choosing her favorite color might be appropriate."

Nope, I had no idea what was going on here. "What are you two doing?"

Aunt Frances glanced over her shoulder. "Picking sprinkles for the Thursday night ice cream, of course."

I blinked, then started laughing. "You sound like you're choosing a wine to go with a meal you're serving the president of the United States."

"Sprinkles are a serious business," Otto said with a straight face, which made me laugh even harder.

"When the last boarder left in September," Aunt Frances said, taking out the canister filled with gold sprinkles, "we had a dish of ice cream. It happened to be a Thursday night, so we've had ice cream every Thursday since. I don't remember why we started the sprinkles." She looked at Otto, who was getting three small dishes out of the cupboard. "Do you?"

"Already lost in the mists of time." He opened the utensil drawer and brandished the scoop. "Is it your turn to scoop, or mine?"

"Yours."

Amused, I watched the ice cream assembly. "You two have quite a tradition going here."

"One of many," my aunt said. "I'm sure you and Ash do things that are just as silly. Would you like whipped cream?" She took a closer look at my face. "What's the matter?"

"Nothing," I said quickly. "I'm fine. And yes, please, on the whipped cream."

We sat at the round oak kitchen table, ate ice cream, and chatted about nothing in particular, laughing and enjoying each other's company.

But all the while, part of my mind was far away. Ash and I had fun together, like Aunt Frances and Otto did, but they had something we didn't. They had sparkle. Together, they were more than the sum of their parts. So much love flowed between them, it was almost visible. Nothing flowed between Ash and me except friendship. We were good friends, but no more than that, and it was time to say so. It wasn't fair to either one of us to keep on going like this.

"Minnie," my aunt said, frowning. "Are you sure you're okay?"

"My feet are warm and my tummy is full of ice cream. What could possibly be wrong?" I gave her a bright smile. From the expression on her face, she wasn't convinced I was telling the complete truth, but she nodded and let it go.

Tomorrow, I told myself. I would have a conversation with Ash tomorrow.

The next day was just as cold as the previous day had been, and I stopped feeling weak-willed for moving to the boardinghouse early. Aunt Frances didn't care, the marina didn't care, and Eddie would yell at me no matter what I did, so why endure a few cold and miserable days for the sake of a self-imposed plan?

At lunchtime, I walked downtown, my head bent against the blustery wind. As I walked, I started composing portions of the long talk with Ash I needed to have as soon as possible.

"You're a great guy, but . . ."

No. That was a horrible start.

"Ash, we need to talk."

I winced even as I was saying the words. It might be possible to be more trite, but probably not.

"Do you think something is missing from our relationship?"

Still not great, but better. Satisfied that I had something to work with, I strode forward, head up and eyes forward. Which was why I noticed the efforts of a man wearing a floppy hat trying to maneuver something out of his vehicle. Whatever it was, it was giving him fits. He was yanking at it with great force and threatening it with unimaginative curses. He also looked vaguely familiar.

As I looked at him, trying to remember where I'd seen him before, he gave a loud grunt, a massive tug, and then he and his walker almost fell back into the street when it came free.

"Three Seasons," I said out loud, hurrying forward. That's where I'd seen him, the night Ash, his mother, and I had eaten together at the Three Seasons.

The man caught my gaze. "You have a problem?" he asked, practically hurling the words at me.

"Not right now," I said, smiling and stepping off the curb. He was still struggling with the walker, trying to unfold what looked like, but couldn't possibly be, seven legs. "Just wondered if you needed a hand, that's all."

"I don't need your help," he snarled. "What makes you think I can't take care of myself? Just because I have to use one of these things doesn't mean I'm an imbecile."

And just because he had to use one of those things didn't mean he had the right to be rude to strangers, either.

"My mistake," I said mildly. Giving him a nod he didn't return, I mentally shrugged and went back to my main mission, which was hunting down lunch.

Honk honk!

I jumped at the noise and turned to see my friends Cade and Barb in a small SUV, laughing hard enough to hurt themselves.

"You know," I said, stepping into the street because they hadn't pulled up to the curb, but were just sitting in the middle of the quiet road, idling, "don't you both have better things to do than to scare a mild-mannered librarian out of her wits?"

"We do," Barb said, smiling. "That doesn't mean it wasn't funny to see you jump like a rabbit."

I looked across her to Cade, who was still laughing. "Don't you have a masterpiece to paint? Or at least a greeting card?"

"Ouch," he said, putting his hands to his chest. "That got me right here."

"Pish," said his loving wife. "You don't seem to have any problem cashing the fat checks from the greeting card people. Don't go acting as if it's beneath you."

"My dear Barbara." He glared at her, but a smile tricked up one side of his mouth. "Nothing is beneath me artistically. At least that's what what's-his-name in New York said."

"Pish," she repeated. "Critics are clueless."

My ears twitched at the repetition of two *C* words in a three-word sentence. Was this the beginning of a new game? The McCades and I had a habit of randomly choosing a letter and then finding words starting with that letter to fit whatever ongoing conversation was at hand. Winning the game wasn't quite as much fun as beating Rafe at a five-dollar bet, but at least losing didn't cost me anything.

Honk honk!

This time it wasn't Cade; it was the car behind them. I glanced up and recognized the vehicle as Rafe's. I stepped back. "See you two later," I said to the McCades. "We'll get together before you head to Arizona, right?"

Waving and agreeing, they drove off and Rafe rolled down the passenger's window. "What's up, short stuff?"

I shook my head sadly. "At some point you're going to realize that you're not as funny as you think you are."

"Oh, I know I'm not funny," he said cheerfully. "But can I help it if other people think I am?"

"Yes." Then, before he could ask how, exactly, he was supposed to help it, I quickly said the first thing that popped into my head. "I moved up to the boardinghouse last night."

"Figured that when I didn't see any lights on in your boat this morning. I had a late meeting last night; otherwise I would have helped."

I rolled my eyes. "I know what your version of help is like. Supervision from a distance with a beer in one hand."

He grinned. "Someone's got to do it. I have to say, though . . ." His voice trailed off.

"Go ahead," I said, dramatically standing tall and jutting out my chin. "Whatever you have to say, I can take it."

Rafe smiled. "This may be too much for you."

"Hah. I come from a long line of strong women. I can take anything."

"Okay, then." He shifted his gaze away, and when he looked back, his face was clear of fun and laughter. He looked sincere and serious, which was so unusual that I steeled myself for anything from the worst joke in the world to the news that his mom had been diagnosed with some incurable disease.

"I'll miss you," he said quietly.

"You . . . what?" I stared at him, and the world around me shifted.

There was a slight pause, then he said, "Mostly Eddie, of course, but you, too. Who's going to hand me tools?"

The world righted itself; Rafe was back to joking.

"Try thinking ahead," I suggested. "I hear it can work wonders."

He grinned crookedly. "Like you'd know?"

I opened my mouth to respond, but a car was coming, so I stepped away from Rafe's car and waved him away.

Rafe drove off and I watched him go. He missed me. He hadn't been joking about that; he really missed me. "I miss you, too," I whispered after him. Because I realized that I did. We spent a lot of time together in the summers, living so close, and I would miss his banter and laughter and . . . him.

"Don't be stupid," I muttered. Rafe and I have been friends for twenty years. If there had ever been anything more, we would have figured it out years ago.

With that settled, I took one step in the direction of lunch, then came to a sudden halt. For some reason, meeting up with the McCades had reminded me of a small task that needed doing, and since there was no time like the present, I reversed direction and went into the toy store, the bells attached to the front door jingling merrily.

"Hey, Minnie." Mitchell, who was standing too close to the top of a stepladder for my comfort, waved at me. "What's up?"

I tipped my head back to look at him. "You, it looks like."

"Me? What . . ." Then he laughed. "Oh, I get it." He reached, readjusted the large hanging model airplane to a slightly different angle, then clambered down the ladder and looked up at his handiwork. "Bet no one dusted that thing in years."

I could see why, since it was snugged up next to a tall ceiling and no one would ever notice the amount of dust on it, but I was glad Mitchell was taking such a proprietary interest in the store he was managing. "You did a nice job," I said.

"You're the second person who said that to me in six months."

No one should get that little encouragement, and I made a mental note to compliment the library staff more often. "Who was the other one?"

"The contractor I worked for last summer." He grinned. "The county building inspector was doing his thing, and it was my framing he was looking at. My boss said he couldn't think of a time when that inspector walked away without writing him up for something."

My attention went sharp. "Was that Ron Driskell?"

"Yeah, that's him. My boss couldn't stand him, but I always figured he was just doing his job. Kind of a crappy one, if you ask me, but I suppose someone has to do it."

"How did Driskell feel about your boss?" From Mitchell's puzzled expression, it was clear he had no idea what I meant, so I kept going. "Did they get along? Were they friendly? Did they argue on job sites?"

"Oh, I see what you're saying. No, they were good, far as I ever saw. Talked about sports a lot. Driskell's a Lions guy and my boss is a Packers fan, but they were both fans of the Tigers, so it was all okay."

"Was Driskell like that with most contractors? Get along with them like that?"

Mitchell shrugged. "I only worked for that one builder. All I know for sure is that he's a black and white kind of guy."

So Dale Lacombe and Ron Driskell might have

had a special—and acrimonious—relationship. Interesting.

"Doing any shopping today?" Mitchell smiled down at me from his six-plus feet of height. "Something for Sally's birthday next month? If she's still into horses, I have the perfect thing."

Another astounding by-product of Mitchell's new job was the realization that his memory for arcane facts and figures was being put to productive use. My older brother, my only sibling, had two daughters and a son, and Mitchell already knew not only their names but also their birthdays, favorite colors, interests, and current career indications.

"She's all about horses," I said, "but I'll stop by some other time to talk about presents. I wanted to tell you that we have a small stack of books for you. I know Donna called a couple of times and I wanted to make sure you'd received the message."

Mitchell made a face. "I don't see myself coming in there for a while."

"But your fines are all paid up." I frowned. "You can check out anything you'd like. I even found a copy of Philip Dick's *Do Androids Dream of Electric Sheep?* for you."

"Yeah, well." He blew out a breath. "It's that new director. Jennifer what's-her-name. She's . . . she's not from here, if you know what I mean."

Ash's mother had said something similar about Carmen. "She could be from Timbuctoo and still be a good library director."

He shrugged. "Don't care where she's from. She just doesn't belong. All she wants to do is change things. Like everything we were doing before was wrong."

I did agree, actually, but felt compelled to defend my boss. "She's new and she's trying to impress the board, that's all. I wouldn't take her need to change things as a true criticism."

"Yeah?" Mitchell's hands flexed. "Then why did she tell me I shouldn't be reading stuff like Robert Heinlein's *Citizen of the Galaxy*? That I was a grown man and should be reading things to improve myself, not reading science fiction written for fourteen-year-olds."

"She did?" I asked weakly.

"And she said there was no reason for anyone over the age of ten to spend their time on a jigsaw puzzle, not when there were so many things in the world that needed doing."

The library's reading room had a table that was practically dedicated to the assembly of jigsaw puzzles. There was a tall stack of the puzzles up in the Friends of the Library book sale room, and they seemed to wander downstairs on their own.

I couldn't think of a time when there wasn't a puzzle going on that table, and there was almost always someone sitting there, putting in a piece or three. It was quiet entertainment for dozens of people and I'd seen everyone from third-shift workers at a local factory to a state legislator doing their bit.

"Well," I said uncomfortably, "that's just her opinion. She's entitled to thinking whatever she wants about jigsaw puzzles. Maybe she had a bad experience as a kid, or something."

Mitchell gave me a disbelieving stare. "With puzzles?"

"Um." I searched for a reason; any reasonable reason would do. "When she was a kid, she could have been doing a jigsaw with a great uncle who had a heart attack." Not a bad reason at all. Nicely done, Minnie! "He'd had a heart condition for years, but that fateful day he clutched his chest, gasping for air, and fell to the floor, right next to Jennifer." I was feeling quite sorry for the young version of my boss. "She called nine-one-one, but it was too late. He was gone. Maybe since then, she hasn't been able to look at a jigsaw puzzle without remembering how helpless and how sad and traumatized she felt that day."

He snorted. "And maybe I'm going to win the lottery. She's not a nice person and she doesn't belong here. I'm not going back to the library until she's gone."

"Stephen was here for almost ten years," I reminded him.

"Then," Mitchell said grimly, "it looks like I won't go to the library for ten years."

"We'll miss you," I said, as seriously as I could, because there was no way Mitchell could stay away from all our books and all our magazines. I gave him two weeks at the outside.

The next day was a bookmobile day, a fact that Eddie figured out the moment I pulled his carrier from the boardinghouse's front closet. Aunt Frances watched him stand at the ready while I opened the wire door and arranged his fluffy pink blanket.

"Most cats," she observed, "run and hide when the cat carrier comes out."

"Eddie is not most cats." I held the door open. "Sir, your carriage awaits."

"Mrr," he said, strolling into the carrier and flopping down into an Eddie-sized heap.

Aunt Frances laughed. "That was definitely a 'thank you.'"

"He is just a cat, you know."

"Eddie," my aunt said. "Did you hear what she said about you?"

"Mrr!"

Later that morning, when I passed on the exchange to Julia as we started the preparations at the first stop, she looked at Eddie, who was sitting on his new favorite perch, the corner of the front computer desk.

"Have you forgiven her yet?" she asked him.

He stared her in the eye and inched forward. "Mrr!"

Julia shook her head, sighing. "Sorry, Minnie. He might not get over this one for quite a while."

I rolled my eyes. "You and Aunt Frances are two of a kind."

"What kind is that?"

Julia and I turned at the familiar voice. "Leese, I didn't hear you come in," I said. "And of course I'm different from those two. I'm shorter, for one thing."

"Like that's a real difference." Leese plopped her pile of return books on the back desk. "At the core, you're the same."

She was so wrong. "I hate to cook, I can't do sudoku for beans, and the only time I watch the evening news is when someone I know might be on it."

Leese stood in front of the selection of new books and pulled out Louise Erdrich's most recent release. "Superficial. I only know your aunt a little, but I'd bet that all three of you would do anything for a friend or family member, that you have the kindest hearts I've ever come across, and that you find every possible opportunity to laugh."

It was an interesting point of view, but my brain danced back to the first part of her sentence. "Speaking of family, how's Brad doing?"

She slumped. "He's been better. The brewery is still trying to figure out what went wrong. They're running some sort of lab tests on that beer and those won't be done for a week or so."

Julia and I exchanged a glance at her tone. It was one of worry, anxiety, and concern. Which brought to mind something I'd been wondering about for a while. It probably wasn't the best time to ask, but if I waited for the perfect time, I could be waiting until doomsday.

"How is it that you and Brad and Mia are so close?" I asked. "You have the same father, but not the same mother, and you weren't raised together, but the three of you are as close as full siblings. Maybe closer."

Leese stared at the opening page of *LaRose* and didn't say anything.

Uh-oh. Clearly I'd stumbled smack into an uncomfortable subject. "Sorry," I said quickly. "I didn't mean to pry. Forget I asked, okay?"

"No." Leese shut the book gently and turned to face us. "It's all right." Her eyes tracked Eddie, who jumped down from the desk and walked a circuitous route around Julia and me to bump the top of his head against Leese's shins.

She hunched down and scratched the top of his head. "It was a long time ago," she said in a quiet murmur that Eddie must have liked, because he started up a loud purr. "I was at Dad and Carmen's for the weekend. I hadn't wanted to go, but Mom didn't give me much choice. This was when I was in middle school, a new teenager, sullen and unhappy with the world."

Smoothly, she shifted sideways out of her crouch to sit on the carpeted step. Eddie, still purring, jumped up onto her lap and all but burrowed inside her jacket.

She smiled, gave him long pets that wafted stray bits of Eddie hair into space, and kept talking.

"I was thirteen, Brad was nine, and Mia . . ." Her voice faltered. "Mia was only seven."

Julia and I didn't move; I was barely breathing from not wanting to interrupt what was so obviously hard for Leese to talk about.

"I don't even remember where we were going," Leese said. "You'd think I would; it was unusual for the four of us to be together without Carmen, but I really have no idea what we were supposed to be doing."

There was so much tension in the air, I could almost see it floating around with the Eddie hair.

"It's been years since I've talked about this." Leese flicked us a glance. "Everything is clear in my memory, but I haven't had much practice putting it into words."

"Take your time," Julia said, using all her stage powers to sound encouraging and comforting.

Leese snuggled Eddie into a hug, something he didn't particularly care for. He eyed me over the top of her arm, but made no move to escape.

"Brad was in the front seat," she said, "because it was his turn. Mia sat behind Dad, which put me behind Brad, and there couldn't have been a worse arrangement."

Her faint smile was brief. "We started fighting. I'm sure I started it. I was that kind of kid. It didn't take long before all three of us were arguing. He this, she that, it wasn't me, you know the kind of thing. Dad told us to be quiet, but we escalated. I started kicking the back of Brad's seat; he started thumping backward, trying to do I don't know what, and Mia was pinching me. All three of us were yelling, Dad was yelling, and then . . ."

She closed her eyes and the words fell out of her, one after another.

"And then Dad turned he was yelling at me at Brad at Mia at all of us and he wasn't watching the road and the car started to swerve and I saw what was going to happen I could see it and I screamed but he didn't know why I was screaming and he swerved and he crossed the centerline and we hit that car head-on it was just a little car and—"

The torrent of words came to a sharp halt. It should have been quiet in the bookmobile, but I could hear the horrendous echo of that long-ago crash, the rubber screeching, the metal crunching, the glass breaking.

After a long, terrible moment, Leese drew in a shuddering breath and opened her eyes. The noise of the accident faded away and was replaced by the sound of Eddie's purrs.

When Leese started talking again, her voice was long and thin. "Dad was driving a big SUV. We hit a little red convertible. A man was driving, and he wasn't wearing a seatbelt. He was thrown out of his car, and—" She stopped and buried her face in Eddie's fur. "I can still see him hitting the ground," she said shakily. "I dreamed it again last night, I . . ."

She sighed and rubbed at her face with the heels of her hands. "Anyway, that's why Brad and Mia and I have a different kind of relationship than most half siblings. We haven't had a single argument since the day of the accident."

The car crash hadn't been their fault, and on some level I was sure she knew that, but I also knew nothing I could say would convince her that she didn't deserve part of the blame. So instead of wasting my breath and her time, I moved to sit on the step beside her and put my arm around her waist.

After a while, she stopped crying, but my mind kept on whirring and went in a whole new direction. Could this accident be the reason for Dale's murder? Could there be a connection?

Then the rational part of my brain started working again. No, that didn't make any sort of sense. The poor guy had died, and it had been more than twenty years ago. What connection could there possibly be at this late date?

Most of me was convinced, but there was a small part of me that went on wondering.

Chapter 13

A bare minute after Leese had finished her story, a mother and her three homeschooled children jumped aboard the bookmobile, all three filled with boundless energy and enthusiastic questions about their current project of learning about the constellations. Julia shepherded the group to the appropriate section as Leese wiped her eyes with the tissue I offered.

"Sorry I came apart like that," Leese murmured, pushing herself to her feet. "I don't, usually. Thanks for listening."

"What happens on the bookmobile stays on the bookmobile," I said. "And I'm glad we were here." I also thought her mini-breakdown had probably been overdue. Even if she and her father hadn't had much of a relationship, Dale had still been her father and some grief would have to be worked through.

"And now," Leese said, tapping her pile of new books, "I need you to play librarian so I can go home and drown my sorrows in fiction."

"An excellent way to spend a weekend," I said.

She smiled. A weak version, but still a smile. "Is that what you're going to do?"

Not exactly. "Fiction is always a priority in my life," I told her, which was true, though it didn't exactly answer her question. Luckily, she didn't notice that particular detail and went away with her books.

Julia, who'd overheard my last exchange with Leese, gave me a look that was Oscar-worthy in its complexity. One glance, and she clearly communicated sympathy, skepticism, and curiosity, along with a small dollop of exasperation. "Let me guess," she said. "You're not planning on reading tonight."

I grinned. "Eventually, sure."

My coworker rolled her eyes, but Eddie, who had remained sitting on the step after Leese had deposited him there, came over to bump me on the shin.

"Mrr," he said.

I took his reaction as a clear indication that my plans for the post-bookmobile afternoon were good ones, so after work I dropped him off at the boardinghouse, kissed him on the top of the head, and headed out again.

This time I drove to a construction site on Janay Lake. My discussion with Mitchell about Ron Driskell, the building inspector, had got me thinking. The man himself had certainly seemed to harbor ill feelings toward Dale Lacombe, and I wondered how many people were aware of that fact.

Thus, my next step in learning more about the relationship between Dale and Ron Driskell was to trespass on a building site. Howard Upton, according to my local sources (Kristen, Rafe, Donna, and Aunt Frances) was one of the most reputable builders in the area. He was also one of the most expensive. One

Friday phone call to the county's building department provided me with the location of Upton's current construction projects, and the chatty staff person also told me that Upton was behind on the biggest house.

"Saturday?" the guy said. "Oh, I'd lay money he'll be working Saturday. Sunday, too. He promised the owner he'd have it done in time to host the family Thanksgiving dinner and they're still roughing in the plumbing."

Through hanging around Rafe's fixer-upper, I'd learned what that meant in a limited sort of way, and what it meant for certain was that Howard Upton had a lot of work to do in the next five and a half weeks.

The building department staffer gave me enough information to locate the house. ("Address? Well, I don't know if I can give you that. But it's past the gas station and across the road from that farm with the fieldstone barn. You know what one I mean?")

I did, and it didn't take me long to drive the few miles out of Chilson and locate the site. The raw dirt and bare foundation were big hints, as was the driveway that was filled by half a dozen pickup trucks with open tailgates and in-bed toolboxes with the covers raised high.

At the site where Dale Lacombe's crew had been working, the grounds had been littered with the detritus that came with construction: bits of cardboard and insulation, short snippets of wire, and stockpiles of dirt and stone. The workers' trucks had been parked higgledy-piggledy, and the trucks themselves had been coated with various combinations of rust, dirt, and dents.

This site was different. Here, there was no litter or debris of any kind. There was bare dirt, but it was raked smooth and looked ready to accept plants. The trucks were parked in an orderly fashion at the side of the house and every vehicle looked, if not new, at least clean and tidy.

By the time I walked halfway to the front porch, I'd already chosen Howard Upton as my future builder—assuming I won the lottery, of course, which wasn't likely to happen because I never played—and was toying with the location for my fantasy home when a woman who looked to be a few years older than myself walked out the front door and onto the porch.

My first assumption, that she was the owner, went by the wayside when I noted her work boots, tool belt, and nylon jacket, which was the same color as one of the trucks next to the house—the truck with an Upton Builders logo emblazoned on the driver's side door.

"Afternoon," she said cheerfully. "Looking for someone?"

Upton was definitely going to build my imaginary house. A contractor who hired personable help, female personable help at that, had to be something special. "Hi," I said, walking forward. "I was hoping to talk to Howard Upton, if he has a minute."

She laughed, making her brown ponytail bounce up and down. "Howie hasn't had a spare minute since 2011, but I'm sure he won't mind talking to you. Go on in." She tipped her head in an ushering motion. "Tell him Nan sent you in," she said, trotting down the porch steps. "And tell him I'll be right back with that corner piece," she called as she climbed into one of the trucks.

As her engine started, I turned to the front door and frowned. Though the opening was for a door with an arched top, the door in place was rectangular with a piece of plywood filling in the gap. Odd, I thought, but opened it and went in.

From outside, the noise had been a dull roar. Inside, my ears felt assaulted by a cacophony of noises, ranging from the whine of a circular saw to the *whunk whunk* of a firing nail gun to the metallic screech of ductwork being assembled. I counted five men and one woman hard at work, and from the sounds of the footsteps above my head, there were at least two more people upstairs.

I stood near the door, not wanting to get in anyone's way, and waited for someone to note my presence. Soon enough, one of the men, a guy wearing sawdust-covered jeans and a Ferris State University sweatshirt, glanced up. He nodded at me, put down the drill he'd been using, and motioned me outside.

Back on the front porch, he asked, "Can I help you?"

"Sorry to barge in when you're so obviously busy," I said, "but I was hoping to talk to Howard Upton if he has a couple of minutes."

"That's me." He took off a work glove, held out his hand, and we shook.

I was a little surprised by his age; I'd expected someone with such a stellar reputation to be in his fifties, but this guy couldn't be that much older than I was. I introduced myself, and before I could say anything else, he gave me a solid slap on the shoulder.

"You're Frances Pixley's niece," he said, grinning. "It's thanks to her that I got into construction. Before she started at the community college, she taught high school wood shop, remember? In two years I went from a kid who'd never touched a power tool in his life to a kid who won first place in the state woodworking competition with an inlaid dining table. She's a great teacher and it's a crying shame the high school dropped their industrial arts classes."

"She says the same thing." And she did, often. It was understandable why Chilson and so many other schools had done so—they were expensive to run and difficult to staff—but it was still a shame because the benefits were so obvious. I smiled at Howard Upton. "I'll tell her you said hello."

"Please do." He tipped his head at the house. "What do you think? Are we going to finish by Thanksgiving?"

It seemed unlikely, but what did I know? "You have lots of activity going on in there," I said. "It's like an ant hill that's been stepped on."

Upton laughed. "Sounds about right. Frantic, but with a method."

I'd been thinking more along the purely frantic lines, but I let him keep his version of the simile.

"So how can I help you?" he asked.

Instead of the thinking-about-building-a-house story, I said, "I was hoping to talk to you about Ron Driskell."

He studied me. "Why?"

"Sorry, it's just . . ." I sighed. "Dale's daughter, Leese, is a friend of mine. She just started a new business but she's losing clients left and right because of her dad's murder. I want to help, that's all."

A loud crash echoed inside the house, followed by shouts and laughter. Upton rolled his eyes. "Leave the room for one minute and what happens?" But he was smiling as he spoke and made no move to investigate. "Okay," he said. "I understand you want to help. What I don't see is why you're talking to me."

"Sorry." And I was, because I'd asked the wrong

question. Nicely done, Minnie. "What I should have asked was, what do you think about Ron Driskell?"

"Our beloved building official?" He smiled, but this time it had a distinct sardonic cast.

I began to scent a clue. "Mr. Driskell has a reputation?"

Upton shrugged. "He won't let builders cut any corners. He's black and white, no gray allowed."

"I don't see the problem. Isn't that what building inspectors are supposed to do?"

Another shrug. "Not for me, but for some guys, yeah."

"Because you don't cut corners?"

Upton grinned. "Let's go with that."

I suspected that I'd simply spoken the truth and that he hadn't wanted to do what might have been interpreted as bragging. My mental list of builders for my fantasy house went from a penciled listing with him at the top to a list of one with his name in permanent marker.

"Does Mr. Driskell have a temper?" I asked.

"Sure, if you poke at him with a stick."

"A stick?"

"Metaphorically speaking," Upton said. "Take last summer, for instance. There was this builder who needed a foundation inspection. Driskell's office said it would be three days before an inspector could get out there. The builder decided he couldn't wait and started laying the floor joists anyway."

"That's bad?"

"Very. When Driskell finally showed up, he went ballistic. Kicked at a pile of blocks and broke a toe." I expected Upton to laugh, but he shook his head. "That kind of thing doesn't do the construction trade any good. Sure, the builder shouldn't have started without the foundation permit, but Driskell shouldn't have lost his temper."

Hmm. "Was that an isolated incident, or are there other stories like that?"

Upton launched into a complicated tale about low-flow toilets being replaced by toilets from Canada. Though I lost the story's thread less than halfway through, I understood the ending of that and the three other incidents Upton told me about before heading back to work.

The ending, the conclusion being: Ron Driskell had a horrific temper that had, more than once, ended in an outburst of violence.

Thoughtfully, I drove back to Chilson. The sun was just starting to slide down below the trees when I parked in the boardinghouse driveway and went in through the front door.

"There you are," Aunt Frances said. "Your cat has been worried sick about you."

Eddie was, at that particular moment, stretched out long on my aunt's legs, which were up on the couch and covered with a new fleece blanket that I suspected she'd purchased because she thought Eddie would like it.

My furry friend, who didn't look worried about anything, picked his chin a quarter of an inch off the blanket and looked in my general direction. "Mrr," he said, and let his chin drop back down.

"He had a hard day on the bookmobile." I leaned over the couch and patted his head. "All that sleeping tires him out something fierce." I glanced at what Aunt Frances was reading. "Is that one of the scrapbooks?"

She nodded. "An early one."

On a rainy afternoon the first year my aunt had opened the boardinghouse, she'd unearthed a blank scrapbook in the attic, brought it downstairs, plopped it in front of two bored boarders, and challenged them to fill it up before the end of the summer.

They'd taken up the gauntlet with zest and from thence forth, every inclement boardinghouse day had become a group scrapbook activity day. Pages were crowded with handwritten notes, stick-figure sketches, beautifully drawn sketches, and maps to favorite places. Taped and glued in were cardboard coasters and napkins, ticket stubs, newspaper articles, pressed flowers, photos, and even small plastic baggies holding grains of sand from favorite beaches.

Since then, there had been a boardinghouse scrapbook for every summer—and for eventful summers, sometimes more than one.

I sat on the other couch. "Do I detect a wistful expression?"

My aunt smiled and turned a page. "It's that time of year. The guests have been gone long enough for me to recover physically, but not long enough that I've learned how to do without them."

"Physically?" I frowned. "I didn't know you needed a recovery time."

Aunt Frances laughed. "Dear niece. You do realize that I'm almost thirty years older than you are. Cooking and cleaning for six other people would take a lot out of anyone, let alone someone in my age bracket."

"Hire someone to help," I said.

She looked up. "As I recall, you suggested that last summer. And I still feel the same way as I did then, that any outside help would change the atmosphere, make it impersonal."

"But—"

She shook her head. "If it means we have to end the boardinghouse, then so be it. I am not going to budge on this one."

There was a short silence. "You shouldn't have to work so hard," I said softly.

"Don't you see?" she asked, just as softly. "I like to. I enjoy this and I always have. At least until now."

"Until Otto."

"Yes." She shut the scrapbook. "But Otto and I would never have met if it hadn't been for the boardinghouse. And what about all the other couples who have met here? It would be a shame . . ."

Sighing, she leaned over and tossed the scrapbook to the coffee table, slightly dislodging Eddie in the process. Though he gave a mild murmur of protest, he didn't do anything dramatic, like relocate.

"Distract me," she said. "I need to think about something else."

I put my feet up on the table. "Leese stopped by the bookmobile today. We got talking about her and her half siblings."

"Brad and Mia." Aunt Frances nodded. "In spite of their parents, they've grown into fine young adults. Who would have guessed?"

"Yeah, about that." I slid down into a comfortable slouch and tried not to be jealous that Eddie preferred my aunt's lap to mine. "Leese was telling us about a car accident from a long time ago. Leese was about thirteen, and Dale was driving. They crossed the centerline and hit a small convertible head-on."

Aunt Frances gave Eddie a long pet. "I remember. A lot of people turned against Dale after that. He tried to blame his children's argument for the accident." She snorted. "He should have pulled off the road, not tried to discipline them at fifty miles an hour."

"Leese says the accident was the last time she and her half siblings had a real argument."

"At least something good came out of it," Aunt Frances muttered. "The man driving the other car certainly suffered enough."

Eddie's head bounced up. "Mrr!" he said.

I patted my fuzzy pal, a little puzzled at her turn of phrase. "I suppose death is the worst kind of suffering."

"What?" Aunt Frances frowned at me. "He didn't die. Who told you that? He was hurt very badly, though. And didn't deal with it well, from what people said."

"Mrr."

My aunt looked at Eddie. "What did I do this time?"

"Mrr!"

"You breathed?" I suggested.

"Ah. That's it."

Eddie jumped to the back of the couch and glared at Aunt Frances. "Mrr!" He turned and gave me a hostile look. "Mrr!" Then he jumped to the floor and thumped his way up the wooden stairs.

Aunt Frances and I looked at each other.

"So," she said. "What are you up to tonight?"

I laughed, then remembered what was on the agenda for the evening.

And sighed.

After giving Eddie—who had crawled into the back of my closet and made a nest of my summer flip-flops—an air kiss, I hurried down the stairs and out the front door. Aunt Frances and Otto were already on their way out for dinner with friends, and if I didn't hurry, I was going to be late to meet Ash.

Late would be bad, but even worse was I still didn't have the right words to start the conversation we needed to have. I'd stopped by the Three Seasons the night before to talk to Kristen about it and she'd rolled her eyes at my attempts. "It's not a speech," she'd said disgustedly. "You can't rehearse this kind of thing. Just open your mouth and start talking."

"If I do that," I said, "I'll start talking about something that's easier to talk about. Say, the best way to achieve peace in the Middle East."

"Don't be stupid. All you have to do is focus."

In spite of the dire danger of receiving another eye roll, I asked, "Should I ease into it or do I start right in?"

"Focus," she'd repeated, and now that I was on my way to meet Ash, I was doing my best to keep her advice foremost in my mind.

The only problem was, my brain was filled with things to think about. There was Leese's dad, her brother and sister, her stepmom, and Leese's business. There was my new boss, the outrageously expensive software program she wanted to purchase, and Mitchell's refusal to enter the library until she was gone. There was the question of what Eddie might be doing to my flip-flops, my aunt's upcoming marriage, and the possible dissolution of the boardinghouse.

And there was the big question of who killed Dale Lacombe? Did I need to consider Carmen as a suspect, or would Ash and Detective Inwood be taking care of that possibility? Plus, there was the guy from the car accident, if I believed that an accident-based grievance could explode into murder decades later.

And what about Rob Driskell? And Daphne Raab? And the Boggses?

When I showed up at the location where I'd arranged to meet Ash, I climbed a few concrete steps, opened the door, and for the second time that day my ears were assaulted. This time, however, instead of construction noises, it was the thunderous crash of falling bowling pins that made the tiny bones in my ears work overtime.

Chilson's bowling alley had a grand total of eight lanes, but the amount of activity going on inside made it feel like sixty. Everywhere, people were milling about, talking and shouting and laughing. It was a gregarious scene of constant movement and Ash spotted me before I saw him.

He detached himself from a group of what I belatedly realized were fellow deputies—they looked much different out of uniform—and came over. "Just started to wonder where you were." Ash gave me a kiss on the cheek. "Hey, you're cold. You're not sick, are you?"

"No, I walked, is all. The temperature is dropping. I think it's going to freeze tonight." An inane comment, but I still hadn't figured out how I was going to get Ash away from his bowling team for a quiet talk and was hoping for inspiration to strike. Any moment would be good. Right that second would be even better. "Ash, we need to—"

But he was talking at the same time. "Minnie, we need to—"

We both stopped. In spite of the noise surrounding us, there was a short and uncomfortable silence. "You go first," he said, nodding.

I glanced toward his team, where a pitcher of beer had just arrived. "What about bowling?"

"The league before us is running late," he said over another crash of tumbling pins. "We won't start for another twenty minutes."

"Is there somewhere quiet?"

"In a bowling alley?" He grinned and for a moment I lost my focus completely. Ash Wolverson was the best-looking man I'd ever dated. He was smart. He was fun. He was active. He was interesting. Why on earth didn't I love him?

"Come on." Ash escorted me through the open doorway that led to an adjacent restaurant. He took us to a small table in the back corner, where he held out a chair for me and, once I was in it, slid the chair forward just the right amount.

"Would you like anything?" He sat across from me. "Food? Drink?"

Their largest glass of wine, I almost asked, but instead said, "No, thanks." And since I still didn't have the right words to start this conversation, I put my hands on the table and stared at them. Small hands with short fingers. Fingernails that needed trimming. Cuticles in need of maintenance. Some hangnails, too, and—

No. I had to say something. And I had to say it now. Still focused on my hands, I opened my mouth and the words started to spill out. "Ash, I'm so sorry, but—"

My voice combined with his, and I was pretty sure he said, "Minnie, I'm really sorry, but—"

I lifted my head to stare at Ash and found that he was staring at me. My mouth was hanging open the slightest bit, as was his, and I was starting to suspect that I didn't have to be too worried about breaking his heart.

"The last few months," I said, testing the waters, "have been a lot of fun."

"Absolutely." He nodded vigorously. "I can't think of a time when I've had such a good time with a girl-friend."

"But for some reason, there are no sparks when we kiss."

"No sizzle," he agreed. "I don't understand it."

I started to smile. "Me either. You're smart, you're good looking, you're funny, and we have so much in common. Why isn't this working out?"

"No idea. It doesn't make any sense. You're cute, and intelligent, and you're always ready to try new things. I don't understand why we're not a match made in heaven."

"Well." I sighed. "At least we tried."

He looked at me. "Want to try kissing again?"

"Not really." And I didn't. Not that I'd ever kissed my brother full on the lips, but if I ever had, I would have expected it to feel like it felt when I kissed Ash. "If there hasn't been any sizzle up until this point, why would it start now?"

"Good point."

We sat there a moment, each silently pondering the vagaries of romance.

"Okay," he said finally. "I guess that's it."

"I guess so."

As we both got to our feet, he snapped his fingers. "Say, are you up for a fat tire bike ride tomorrow? There's a new route I want to try."

"Sounds good," I said. "Meet at the Round Table first for breakfast? Say nine?"

"It's a plan."

After mutual nods, he went back to his bowling and

I headed out to the fresh air, ending the easiest breakup ever.

The next evening there was a party of three for dessert in Kristen's small office. Even with the normal two of us, there wasn't a lot of extra room. With Leese added to the mix, it had taken clever rearrangements by Harvey, Kristen's devoted sous chef, to provide enough space so that we could all eat the last crème brûlée of the season without bumping elbows.

I held my spoon above the ramekin, poising it to plunge through the crusty sugar and into the delectable custard underneath. "To another successful year."

The last consonant wasn't out of my mouth when I realized that my casual toast could have hurt Leese's feelings horribly. With suspicion about the identity of her dad's killer still hovering like an unwanted and socially inept guest, her year was not likely to be successful. And unless the killer was found and put in jail, her new law firm might not last another twelve months.

But Leese, smiling, was also holding up her spoon. "To Kristen and the Three Seasons."

"Ah, shucks," my best friend said. "You guys are going to make me blush."

I snorted in disbelief. The three of us tinked our spoons together and then the delightful sound of crackling sugar filled the air.

"When was the last time you were embarrassed about anything?" I asked as I worked to spoon up the perfect first bite, one that included caramelized sugar, custard, and at least part of a raspberry. Where Kristen had found local raspberries in mid-October, I did not know, but some questions were best left unasked. "You didn't turn a hair during the filming last summer."

In July, Trock Farrand and his son, the always impeccably clad Scruffy Gronkowski, had filmed an episode of *Trock's Troubles* at Kristen's restaurant. The show had aired a week after Labor Day and the ensuing rise in business had boosted profits not only for the Three Seasons, but also for much of downtown.

"Embarrassment is a waste of time." Kristen waved her spoon. "You would do well to remember that, little one."

"And you would do well to recall who showed you how to change the ring tones on your cell phone."

Leese laughed. "I said it before and I'll say it again. You two act more like sisters than friends."

"Sisters in spirit." Kristen leaned over and slung one of her long arms around my shoulders to give me a quick hug. "Friends forever."

I grinned. "That forever part is easier since she lives in Key West five months out of the year."

A laughing Kristen lightly thumped the side of my head. "Someday you're going to come with me and see why. Here it's sleet and snow and cold and boots. There, it's sunshine and sandals."

"There, it's big bugs," I said. "And snakes. Year round."

"Not if you stick to the city, where people belong." She eyed me and I sensed what was coming. I'd texted her about the end of the Minnie-Ash relationship last night and a discussion was inevitable. "So," she said. "It's over with the extraordinarily handsome Ash Wolverson? And yes, I told Rafe, just like you asked. Not sure why you didn't do it yourself, though."

Leese gave me a startled look. "Hang on. When did this happen?"

"Last night," I said. "And yes, we're no longer dating. We're still friends, though."

"Has that ever really worked?" Leese asked.

"Not in the entire history of the world." Kristen's spoon scraped the bottom of her ramekin. "I'm not sure why this one thinks this particular situation is going to be different."

"Because friends was all we ever really were," I said. "Just like . . ."

Kristen squinted. "Like what?"

Like Rafe and me, I'd almost said, but lately I wasn't sure what was going on between us. He'd said he missed me, which was more sentiment than I'd ever heard from him. And I missed him. Well, sort of. Okay, I did. But that didn't mean . . . well, what did it mean?

I put the question aside to think about later, because I was finally clueing in that something about Kristen was off. She hadn't quite met my gaze since I'd arrived and she'd started eating without uttering a single criticism of the food, which I wasn't sure she'd ever done in her life.

I pointed my spoon at her. "What's up?"

She turned a wide-eyed gaze on me. "The price of bacon, if the last invoice from my supplier is any indication."

Sitting up straight, I pulled out both stops; the Librarian Look and the Librarian Voice. "Kristen Jurek, there is something you're not telling me and I demand you tell me right this minute, because if you leave for Key West without spilling your guts, you'll regret it forever."

The silence lengthened and thickened. I continued

to stare at Kristen. She continued to eat her dessert. Leese looked from one of us to the other and didn't say a word.

Kristen scraped up a last spoonful of custard, swallowed it down, and tidied both the spoon and the ramekin. "I would have sent you a text, but I wanted to see your face when I told you. Then you break up with Ash, so now it's all a little awkward, and—"

That's when I knew. Shrieking with happiness, I flung myself at Kristen and wrapped my arms around her.

"Hey, now," Leese said with concern. "Minnie, leave the poor woman alone. Whatever's wrong, physical violence isn't the answer."

I burst out laughing. "This is a hug, not an attack. Do you know what's going on?"

"Clearly not," she said.

"The tall skinny blonde in the room got engaged last night." I gave Kristen one last crushing squeeze and let go. "Didn't you?"

My friend sighed ostentatiously, but her face was all smiles. "He flew in yesterday and did the one-knee thing with the biggest bouquet of roses I've seen in my life. I figured if he was willing to get dirt on his pants and spend money on flowers that were going to look like crap in three days, it wasn't a joke anymore."

Mild pandemonium ensued for a few minutes. At the end of it, Kristen said Scruffy had flown back to New York that morning with her request for an engagement ring—an emerald flanked by two smaller diamonds—and would be returning in another week with the ring and to help her close up the restaurant and pack for Key West.

Kristen called Harvey for a bottle of champagne. After the excitement faded and we sat back down,

Leese's earlier comment about sisters finally rattled around in my brain enough to remind me of something. "How's your brother doing? Is he back to work?"

Leese, who'd returned to scraping up the last of her dessert, sighed and put her laden spoon down. "Brad is still acting as scapegoat for the brewery."

Kristen and I exchanged a glance at her bitter tone, but before either one of us responded, Leese said, "I'm sorry, I shouldn't have said that. Brad says he understands perfectly why he can't come back to work." She half smiled. "He said if he was in charge, he'd do the exact same thing. That the reputation of a producer of a food product has to be above reproach."

I didn't quite put beer on the same level as bread or milk, but I was sure many people would disagree with me. It was Rafe's opinion that humankind had shifted from hunting and gathering to an agricultural lifestyle for the sake of brewing beer. After some research, I'd come to the reluctant conclusion that he might actually be right. And clearly the making of craft beer was becoming an important part of the economy in this part of Michigan. It was possible that the damage of one brewery's good name could reflect on all of them.

"But what about Brad's reputation?" Kristen asked. "If they can't figure out what happened, will he be able to work as a brew master?"

"He didn't do anything wrong," Leese said fiercely.

"Well, duh." Kristen rolled her eyes. "I'm just looking at the worst possible scenario."

"She has a tendency to do that," I told Leese. "It's nothing personal."

Leese nodded. "Okay, but he didn't do anything wrong," and this time we could hear the anxiety coating every word.

It was obvious that she was worried about her brother, but I thought there was a lot more to worry about. What about Leese's own reputation? What would she do if her name wasn't cleared of any and all connection to her father's murder? Was Brad being unfairly scapegoated because of the murder? How many Lacombes were going to suffer because of Dale's death?

Chapter 14

"Mrr."

I zipped shut my backpack and gave my cat a pat. "Sorry, but you're not going with me today."

Eddie laid his ears back and halted the purr action.

"You won't like it," I told him. "Trust me. I'm going to drive downstate, talk to some strangers, and drive back. Probably seven hours of driving for an hour of talking."

"Mrr."

"Yeah, doesn't seem worth it, does it? But it's Monday and I have the day off. It's a good day for a road trip. I've checked out a nonfiction audio book from the library so I get to listen and learn for hours and hours."

Eddie rolled to put his back to me and curled into a tight ball.

"Love you too, pal." I kissed the top of his head, picked up my backpack, and was on the road a few minutes later.

Shadow Divers, by Robert Kurson, kept me awake, interested, and occupied my brain so fully that I hardly thought about Rafe as I drove south on US 131 to Grand Rapids. At that point I hopped briefly onto I-96, then down East Beltline to where I turned off to find the address that my former boyfriend Ash had (sort of) helped me find.

When we'd paused to take a break on our bike ride the previous morning, I'd asked about the best way to locate someone who lived in an unknown city in Michigan. If I was going to help Leese and her siblings, I figured the first step was to talk to some of the people I'd put on my mental suspect list. In broad daylight, of course, and as much in public as I could manage. I was still shying away from Carmen as the killer, and I needed to work out the name of the guy from the car accident, so I'd decided to focus on Dale's lawsuit cases and learn what I could about the cranky building inspector.

Ash had laughed. "Someone who isn't in law enforcement, you mean?"

Since he was perfectly aware that was what I meant, I ignored his question. "If you were looking to talk to a couple named, say, Gail and Ray Boggs—that's Boggs with two *g*'s—and you were pretty sure they lived downstate somewhere, and they'd moved within the last few months and weren't showing up on any of the Internet searches you'd tried, what would be the best way to find them?"

"You've asked the neighbors?"

"That's how I know the Boggses are still in Michigan. But the neighbor didn't know where."

"Hmm." Ash pulled out his cell phone, tapped out a text, and tucked the phone into his jacket. "Ready?" he asked, putting one foot on a bike pedal.

One of my character flaws I was working to correct

was a lack of patience, so I nodded and we went back to riding. And lo and behold, when we were coasting back into Chilson, Ash's phone dinged with a return text, and my newfound—and most likely temporary—patience was rewarded.

"Okay," he said, reading the small screen. "If I was looking for Gail and Ray Boggs with two *g*'s, I'd check the phone listings for greater Grand Rapids."

Excellent. The only problem was, greater Grand Rapids included probably twenty-five different municipalities. Probably double that, if you were including the Holland–Grand Haven–Muskegon area. "Great," I said. "That would help a lot, if I wanted to find any Boggses with two *g*'s." We made the last turn and came to a stop in front of the boardinghouse. "But if someone wanted to find the Bogg people in a reasonable amount of time, should that someone look in Kent County?"

"Absolutely."

"Should that person look in the south half of the county?"

He squinted at the air, then said, "Yes."

"West of US 131?"

"No."

It took a few more pointed questions, but I narrowed the location down to East Grand Rapids, a city whose residents were, on the average, in a higher tax bracket than the rest of us. As a moderately paid librarian living in Chilson, however, I was used to everyone making more money than I did, so I drove through the well-tended streets of the town without feeling too much envy or awe.

Thanks to Ash's hints and a small credit card fee, I'd been able to use the online database of the Kent

County Register of Deeds to find an address for the Boggses. "There is no hope of privacy in this world," I'd told Eddie as I added the address to my phone, but either he didn't care or thought the statement was so true it wasn't worth discussing, because he'd continued snoring.

Where the Boggses now lived was an established neighborhood of large stately homes with tree-lined streets, and at eleven o'clock on a weekday morning, there wasn't a single human being to be seen. There were, however, a multitude of Halloween decorations. Pumpkins sat on hay bales, scarecrows and witches perched on tree limbs, and ghosts peeked from behind shrubbery. It was a charming display and it gave the feel of a community with a real sense of place.

I found the address and parked at the curb of the only place on the street without any Halloween ornamentation. The house of Bogg was Tudoresque, with steeply pitched roofs, big brick chimneys, and decorative half-timbering with stucco filling the space between the timbers. It looked substantial and prosperous and expensive.

It also looked unoccupied.

Well, maybe it just seemed that way. Maybe Gail and Ray were inside, planning their Halloween display. I got out of the car and walked up the brick path that led to the front door. I pushed the elaborate brass doorbell and listened to a deep bonging sound go through the house and fade away to silence. After waiting a bit, I pushed the doorbell again and got the same result.

Nothing.

There were no windows flanking the solid door, and in a neighborhood like this, traipsing around to the windows and peering in could easily trip a security alarm or send a watchful neighbor to the telephone to call 911.

"Rats," I muttered.

But speaking of neighbors . . .

Another advantage of being female and spatially efficient was that I didn't tend to project a threatening presence. I returned to the main sidewalk, looked at the adjacent houses, and spotted a house across the street and one door down that had interior lights on. Bingo! I headed on over and knocked, using the lion's head doorknocker provided for the purpose.

The door was opened by a dark-skinned man who looked to be in his mid-forties. He had a coffee mug in one hand and a pile of papers in the other. "Hello," he said in a polite, but cautious, tone.

I smiled disarmingly. "Morning. I was looking for Gail and Ray Boggs, but they don't seem to be home. Love your ghosts, by the way." I nodded toward the front lawn, where a group of five gauzy figures stood around one of the largest pumpkins I'd ever seen. Each ghost held a different sketch of a plan for carving their pumpkin and they were clearly arguing about whose design would win.

The guy grinned. "Reality becomes art. My wife, myself, and our three kids all wanted to do something different with the pumpkin we grew last summer in the backyard, so this is what we settled on."

I laughed. "Compromise can be funny."

"Well, the zombie versus ghost discussion was a little loud, but we worked it out," he said, smiling.

"It looks great," I said, then before he could start wondering about the stranger on his doorstep, I told him my name, adding, "I'm from Chilson, where Gail and Ray had a place up until a couple of months ago. I thought I'd stop by to see them."

"Chilson?" he asked. "You live there?"

"Fifty-two weeks a year. I'm assistant director for the library."

"No kidding. There's this restaurant I saw on one of those cooking shows a while back. Do you know it?"

I beamed. "Three Seasons. My friend Kristen owns it."

"That's the place," he said, nodding. "So you'd recommend eating there?"

"If you like high-quality local ingredients cooked by a perfectionist, presented by people who obsess about the size of the garnishing sprigs, and served by staff who know how often the parsley was weeded, then absolutely you should eat there."

Laughing, the guy introduced himself as Tim Soane. "We'll have to get up there next summer. But if you're looking for Gail and Ray, you're out of luck. They headed down to Florida last Friday."

"Oh." I glanced at the vacant-looking house. "They weren't here very long."

Tim shook his head. "Few weeks. Seems that's the way those two operate. A month at this place, a month in Florida, a month in one of their other places. If they get bored or don't like the weather forecast, they head out."

I blinked. "How many places do they have?"

"Depends on the day." He smiled briefly. "They build and buy and sell at the drop of a hat. From what Gail said, it ranges anywhere from three to six. Some of them are time-share condos, so you might count those differently."

I had a hard enough time moving twice a year. I

couldn't imagine the logistical difficulties of having multiple homes and having to fill them with multiple sets of belongings. I'd constantly be wanting something in another house. "Sounds like a complicated way to live," I said.

"Well, when you win one of the biggest lotteries in the history of lotteries, you can afford complications."

My eyes bugged out, then I remembered that, though I hadn't specifically said I was a friend of the Boggses', I'd certainly implied so and brought my eyeballs under control. "Well," I said, "thanks for your time. If I get to Florida this winter, I'll try to track them down there."

"Good luck with that." Tim laughed. "By that time they'll probably have moved on to Hawaii."

I nodded, thanked him again, and headed back to my car.

"What do you think?" I asked.

Eddie, sitting next to his food bowl, was staring at the kitchen counter and not paying any attention to me.

"Hey." I snapped my fingers. "Over here. There is nothing on that counter of any interest to you." This was a blatant lie, as he clearly was interested in the empty glass dishes that had held leftovers I'd scrounged out of the refrigerator for dinner, but he knew full well he wasn't allowed on the counter, so I stood by my statement.

I tapped my fingertips on the round oak kitchen table and he turned his head. "Right. Now that I have your complete and undivided attention, I have some things to discuss with you."

"Mrr."

"Don't worry, you're not in trouble for anything." As far as I knew. There was always a possibility that he'd done something horrible that hadn't yet entered my awareness, but since I was currently in blissful ignorance of any particular Eddie transgression, he had no reason to worry about punishment. Not that he would take punishment as a recommendation to modify behavior. His response would be more along the lines of a sullen teenager's shrug and a muttered "Whatever."

Eddie rotated his head, owl-like, to look at me.

"Right," I said. "Things to discuss. Sorry to say, they're not about you. Yes, the world revolves around cats in general and you specifically, as it should, but in this particular case I'd like you to just listen."

My fuzzy feline friend rotated himself a hundred and eighty degrees and settled his unblinking gaze upon me.

"Can you stop that?" I asked. "Please? When you look at me like that, I always feel like you're trying to tell me something and I'm too stupid to understand."

His stare hardened. "Mrr!" he yelled, his whole body twitching with the effort.

"Thanks," I said. "It's nice to know that you think I'm stupid. Anyway, I wanted to discuss my recent findings about people who had dealings with Dale Lacombe."

Until Eddie, I'd never known how talking out loud to a four-legged companion could help straighten out your thoughts. It helped that Eddie seemed to pay attention to what I was saying and inserted the occasional contribution, but I was under no illusions that he actually understood the one-sided conversations.

He was just a cat, after all. A lovable and personality-laden dork of a cat, but there was no way that any cat's brain power could match that of a human.

"Mrr," Eddie said agreeably.

"Right." I nodded. "So here's the thing. Dale Lacombe was a jerk of the first order and it was a surprise to basically no one except his wife that he wound up murdered by person or persons unknown."

The phrase, one I'd heard on television dramas and seen in print numerous times, rang oddly in my ears.

"You know," I said, frowning, "why am I working on the assumption that it was one person who killed Dale and is trying to frame Leese? Why couldn't it be two people? A whole host of people, like the *Orient Express*?" Drumming my fingers on the table, I considered, then rejected the idea.

"Nope. Too complicated, especially for a small town. Someone would have talked or confessed or acted weird enough that eyebrows would have gone up and next thing you know it would have been on Facebook or tweeted all over the place."

"Mrr," Eddie said.

"Glad you agree." I got up and opened the cupboard door that housed his treats. "But let's keep in mind that two people might have had a small conspiracy going. I know, I know, there's that proverb that two can keep a secret only if one of them is dead. Still, it's a possibility."

Eddie swiped a paw at the air and made a chirpy sort of noise in the back of his throat.

"Sorry." I opened the canister of treats and tossed one onto the floor. "We're going to skip the remote possibility that Dale's death was an accident. If it was, why bother moving the body to Leese's truck? If it had been an accident and someone had been afraid of being found guilty of negligence or something, it would have been far easier to drop the body in a lake."

By this time, the treat had long since disappeared down Eddie's throat, and the only sign that a treat had ever existed was a wet spot on the floor in the shape of a cat tongue.

I tossed down another moist tidbit.

"So we have the Boggses and Daphne Raab. As the people who Dale sued to get payment, they should be high on the suspect list. Daphne certainly didn't have a good word to say about him." I watched Eddie snuffle up the treat. Ms. Raab had been an unpleasant woman, but unpleasantness didn't equate to being a killer. Which was a good thing, because I'd met a number of unpleasant people in my life, and if they were all killers, it wouldn't be long before the human species would murder its way to extinction.

"And then there are the Boggses." The lottery winners. The couple who skipped from one house to another at the drop of a hat. I made a mental note to see if I could find out how long ago they'd won their pile of cash.

"Plus, there's Rob Driskell. You know, the building official. The guy with the temper."

I saw again Driskell's reddening face and clenched fists. If his anger could flare up so fast against a man who was dead, what could have happened if he and Dale had met face-to-face? A burst of violence seemed possible and even likely.

Eddie bumped the top of his head against my shin.

"And there's the guy from the car accident." I needed to call Leese and ask his name. I still couldn't think of a reason for a twenty-some-year gap between incident and revenge, but anything was possible, I supposed, and—

"Mrr!"

"One more treat," I said, "and that's it. Winter's coming. You don't get out as much when it's cold in spite of that fur coat and we don't need you getting any fatter or especially any sassier." I dropped a third treat to the floor and remembered what Daphne had said. "And I can't forget about Carmen. Remember? She and Dale separated not long before he was killed."

I knew there were statistics about the number of murders committed by spouses, but I wasn't sure I wanted to go in search of them. After all, what did statistics mean for any given for-instance? Well, a lot, really, because they provided odds for any given event happening, but it was hard to think in those terms.

"Everybody thinks they're going to beat the odds, right?" I looked down, but the only thing that remained of Eddie's presence was a tiny piece of cat treat on the floor. I looked up and saw the tip end of his tail vanishing through the doorway to the dining room.

"Once again," I told him, "you were no help at all."

"Mrr," he called back, which could only have been cat language for "Whatever."

"Thanks," I called. "If I ever have kids, it's good to know that I've had training for dealing with teenagers."

"Mrr."

The next day, since I'd scheduled myself to work a stint at the reference desk from midafternoon until the library closed at eight, I slept late and didn't leave the boardinghouse until almost ten o'clock.

It was one of those picture-perfect autumn mornings that you long for during the sweltering days of

August. The air had a fall tang and the leaves still hanging tight to their trees were so brilliantly colored, they almost hurt my eyes at the same time that I couldn't bear to look away.

The sidewalks were long emptied of the summer tourist traffic, and I knew most of the few people out and about by name. Yes, winter wasn't too far away, but Chilson once again belonged to its year-round residents. We had our town back. Life was good.

I could practically see the aura of contentment that surrounded me as I walked into the toy store. Before the bells had even stopped jingling, Mitchell popped out of the back room. "Good morning, sorry I was—oh, hey, Minnie." He grinned. "You back for Sally's birthday present?"

Someday I'd get used to the hatless, shaven, and socially presentable Mitchell, but today wasn't that day. It was a good thing that he'd found full-time employment, and an even better thing that he seemed to be enjoying it so much; it was the sudden change that I was having a hard time adjusting to. Who would ever have guessed that the perennially underemployed Mitchell would ever have found a career passion and true love in the same year?

"That's right." I leaned against the glass counter. "It's on Halloween and I've promised not to buy her anything black or orange."

"Gotcha." Mitchell smoothed back his hair, a gesture similar to the way he'd formerly rearranged his hat. "She's into horses, right? Does she collect Breyers?"

I frowned. "Isn't that ice cream?"

He ushered me over to a display of blue and yellow boxes. "And horses," he said, pointing.

"Huh." I studied the array of plastic horses, horse-type equipment, horse barns, and other horse-oriented paraphernalia that, since the closest I'd ever come to a horse was the carousel ride at the Ohio amusement park Cedar Point, I hadn't the least chance of identifying. "I have no idea if she's into these or not. Let me text my sister-in-law and I'll let you know."

"Isn't your brother an engineer?"

"Sort of." Matt thought he had the best job in the world, and since he was an Imagineer for Disney, it was possible he was correct. If you were an engineer.

"If that kind of thing runs in the family, how about this?" Mitchell stepped over to another area of the store, the one that displayed models of cars, boats, planes, and tanks, and held up the perfect present for Sally.

"A Visible Horse," I said softly, struck by the minimalist beauty of the skeletal model. "Mitchell, you're a genius."

"All part of the service." He grinned. "Want me to wrap it? I can ship it for you, too, if you want. I'm pretty sure we have the address on file."

I grinned back. If Mitchell 2.0 could provide this kind of service, I wasn't going to mourn the old version another minute. "I like the way you work."

"Yeah?" He flicked a glance my way. "Seems like you always thought I wasn't worth much."

There was enough truth in the statement to make it sting. But it wasn't the entire truth. "I've always thought you are a very intelligent person," I said honestly. "What I never understood is why you didn't care about using it."

Mitchell peeled the price tag off the box and stuck it to the counter. "I guess I can see why you'd think that." He leaned down and unrolled wrapping paper from a metal rod, giving it a yank to rip it off the roll. "But my dad, he used to work so hard he didn't have any time for anything else and then he died of a heart attack, sitting in his office chair before he turned forty-five. I didn't want to be like him, not that way."

So there it was. The reason why Mitchell had been a slacker most of his adult life. "And it's different now?" I asked.

"Bianca showed me," he said. "She works hard, but she leaves time for fun, too."

The fact that it had taken him this long to figure that out made me question my earlier assessment of his intelligence, but I let it go. "Well, you seem to fit in well here. The owners made a great decision when they hired you."

He didn't say anything, but the tips of his ears turned bright red. "Wish I could say the same about your library board," he muttered as he wrapped the brightly colored paper around the box. "That Jennifer doesn't fit at all. And don't ask about me going back to the library, because I'm not going to as long as she's there."

When he'd first told me he was boycotting the library, I hadn't believed it would last more than a couple of days, but he hadn't set foot inside for more than a week. "What about the bookmobile?" I asked.

His hands hesitated as he folded the last flap of paper, but only for a moment. He shook his head. "Nope. Can't do it."

Uneasily, I wondered if Jennifer's demeanor was driving other people away from the library. I toyed with the idea of talking to the board chair, then rejected the plan. If I had a problem with Jennifer, I would discuss it with her first. And right then and there, I vowed to do so that very day. If she pooh-poohed my concerns, I might be driven to speak to the board, but I wouldn't go over her head without telling her what I was doing.

"Sorry you feel that way," I said to Mitchell. "But I understand."

I wrote, *To Sally, From Auntie Minnie with oodles of love*, on the small birthday-themed tag Mitchell offered, pushed it back across the counter, and asked, "Have you heard anything else about the murder of Dale Lacombe?"

"You mean like who killed him?" He grinned, and the old Mitchell was suddenly back in the room. "Everyone says it's a toss-up."

"Oh? The police have two suspects?"

"Nah. It's a toss-up between half the guys in town who wanted to kill him because he was such a rotten builder and the other half, the ones who wanted to kill him because he was fooling around with their wives."

I blinked. "He was?"

"All I know is what I hear," Mitchell said. "And that's what I hear. Say, I also hear your aunt wants to quit the boardinghouse business, but won't because you want to hang on to it."

"What? Where did you hear that?"

He shrugged. "Dunno. Just heard it. Is it true? I mean, I don't blame you, that place is pretty cool."

This was the talk of the town? How on earth had the word gotten loose? Then I remembered that Aunt Frances and Otto and I had discussed it publicly at lunch that day in Angelique's. A number of people could have overheard us and repeated the conversation. Or . . . was there something going on that I didn't know about? "It's my aunt's," I said a little stiffly. "And it's hers to do with as she wants."

He took the credit card I held out. "Just asking," he said. "People wonder, you know?"

"Speaking of wondering," I asked, "do you remember a car accident the Lacombes were in? It was a long time ago."

"You bet." Mitchell zipped the card through the reader. "Everybody thought the guy was going to die and Lacombe would go to jail for manslaughter or something, but that didn't happen. The guy was from downstate, I remember that."

"Do you remember the guy's name?"

"Sure." Mitchell handed back the card. "No, hang on," he said, frowning. "I thought I did, but I guess I don't." He paused, looking at the ceiling, then shrugged. "Nope. It's gone. Why do you want to know?"

"No real reason." At least, not one I would tell him about. "Thanks for taking care of Sally's present," I said, and headed outside, only to see the floppy-hatted man who'd talked about the Lacombes at the Three Seasons on the sidewalk, using a cane this time instead of a walker. I gave him a small nod, he gave me an even smaller one in return, and when I'd walked half a block, I heard the distant jingle of the door bells from the toy store.

"Faber!" Mitchell called. "Simon Faber! The name of the guy in the car accident was Simon Faber."

I half turned to wave my thanks, and saw the startled gaze of the hat man, who was just opening his car door. He glared at Mitchell, glared at me, then slid into his car and drove away.

"That was weird," I murmured. Maybe hat man had been a friend of Faber's. I toyed with the idea that

hat man actually was Faber, but that seemed beyond unlikely. If Faber was back in town, word would surely have spread, especially with Dale Lacombe recently murdered.

I thought about this for a minute, then called Kristen. No answer, naturally. "Hey," I said into her voice mail. "Give me a call, will you? I have a question about the other night when I was in the restaurant."

As I walked up to the library it was Mitchell's gossip about Dale Lacombe that stuck with me. Was it gossip? Was it truth? Was it both? I'd already learned more unpleasant things about Leese's father than I was comfortable knowing, but this was a whole new level of discomfort. It was downright icky, and I didn't know what to do.

Should I call Detective Inwood? Call Ash? If what Mitchell said was true, they probably already knew, but what if they didn't? If it wasn't true, I didn't want to repeat gossipy rumors that could hurt Leese and her family. If it was true, and the sheriff's office didn't know, was I being remiss in not passing on the information? Was I not doing my duty as a citizen?

If I could have couched the question in a way that didn't involve murder, I would have called my mother and asked her advice. But she'd ask too many questions and would end up freaking out, in a motherly sort of way. I didn't want to put her through that, so the next best person to talk to was Aunt Frances. However, her mind was on Otto these days.

By the time I'd reached that point in my thoughts, I was in the library and at my office door. But instead of going inside, I turned and headed for the front desk.

"Hey, Donna," I said. "Do you have a minute?"

The gray-haired woman looked away from the computer screen and smiled. "For you? A full minute and a half."

"This isn't a library thing," I said.

"Even better." She stood and came to the counter. "Is this a private or public conversation?"

I considered the question. "Quietly public."

"So diplomatic. You could have a future in politics."

Fake shuddering, I said, "Please don't make me!"

Donna laughed. "What's up?"

"A gossipy question I don't want anyone to know I was asking."

My coworker's wise eyes studied me. "Have you considered the possibility that you shouldn't ask it at all?"

"Absolutely." I nodded vigorously. "It's just that not knowing the answer could do more damage than knowing. And it's not something I want to know, it's more that I think I have to."

"And at some point this conversation is going to start making sense?" Donna asked.

"It's about Dale Lacombe," I said. "And you know lots of things about people in this town that I don't."

She nodded. "Clarity is just around the corner. I can feel it."

I smiled. "Don't be so sure. From reliable sources, I know that Carmen and Dale had their disagreements and that they'd separated briefly more than once."

"This is true," Donna said. "Carmen and Dale are members of my church. We always knew when they were fighting because they'd sit in their regular spots next to each other, but they wouldn't share a hymnal. And we always knew when they were separated because they'd drive two cars."

"Right. Now what I recently heard, and this is from an unreliable source, is that Dale was having extramarital affairs."

Donna's gaze shifted away and past me. "Ah. If he was, that opens up a whole new list of murder suspects. Carmen, for one, if she wasn't already on the list, but also the husbands or significant others of the women Dale was seeing."

"Have you considered going into police work?" I asked.

"About as seriously as you considered becoming the new library director." Her focus returned to my face. "I can't give you an answer about Dale, because I don't know. Sure, there were rumors, but they were vague and I always thought they were generated from spite." She smiled wryly. "Dale wasn't the kind of man who had a lot of friends. Kind of like some other people we know."

I blinked, and then, as the *tap tap* of Jennifer's high heels came into my hearing, I understood what she meant. I also understood that if I didn't approach Jennifer soon, I'd come up with some task that needed to be accomplished that very day and never get around to discussing the Mitchell situation.

Our library director, today dressed in a silky gray jacket and skirt with four-inch heels and hair in a tight bun, crossed the lobby without a glance toward her employees. Donna shook her head. Softly, I said, "Mitchell Koyne says he's not coming back to the library until Jennifer is gone."

"He's not the only one," Donna muttered. "Half the staff feels like that."

"Sure, but I think Mitchell's serious."

"So am I."

I stood there, struck to silence by the quiet confidence in her tone. If the library had a mass exodus of employees, we would be in serious trouble. It was hard finding qualified people to work long hours for relatively low pay. Sure, working in a library, especially this library, was an incredibly rewarding job, but not everyone was willing.

"Donna," I said, "please—"

The loud call of my cell phone's ring tone cut into a plea to keep me abreast of any potential resignations. Somehow I'd forgotten to silence the phone when I'd walked into the building. I pulled my backpack around and fumbled through it, feeling my face burn hot with embarrassment. Me? I was the jerk who forgot to turn off her phone in a library? *Me?*

My fingers found the phone, but I couldn't stop myself from looking to see who was calling. "Weak, I am so weak," I murmured, pulling out the phone.

It was Leese.

Though I almost thumbed it to decline, something made me push the Accept button. "Hey," I said. "What's up with you on this gorgeous fall day?"

"Mia," she said with a gasp. "This time it's Mia."

My stomach clutched itself into a tiny hard ball. Waiflike Mia, who'd endured anorexia and who knew what else as a teen. Mia, who'd just lost her father. Who had felt so guilty over his death that she'd turned herself in for his murder even though she'd been hundreds of miles away at the time. "Is she okay?" *Please*, I thought, *let her brother be okay. Let Carmen be okay. Let all of them be okay.*

"Physically, I think so." Leese, big and strong Leese, had a voice full of tears. "Emotionally, I don't know."

"What happened?"

"Where she works. They're blaming her." Leese huffed out the words one by one. "She's responsible for the company's computer servers. It's all gone."

"Gone? What's gone?"

"She'd installed new servers last week. And they crashed. Crashed dead. All their data, all their proprietary software, all their designs and data. All of their everything. Along with all of their cloud storage. It's just . . . gone."

My mouth went dry. "Where is she now?"

"Here. At my house. In my spare bedroom, lying on the bed and staring at the ceiling." Leese swallowed loudly. "They didn't fire her, but she says it's only a matter of time. She's suspended. If this sticks, she'll get a reputation and won't be able find work like this ever again. Computers are the only thing she knows."

I made soft noises of comfort as best I could, but all the while my brain was shrieking at me, saying one thing over and over again.

This was just like Brad's suspension from the brewing company.

Just like. Was the Lacombe family having a horrible run of bad luck? Or was someone targeting them and picking them off, one by one?

Chapter 15

"There has to be a connection," I said. My right hand held the phone to my ear while my left was making broad gestures that could have endangered innocent library patrons if I hadn't removed myself to my office. "How could there not be?"

"Ms. Hamilton—"

I cut off Detective Inwood. "Yes, I know. You're going to say that in law enforcement there's nothing even close to a 'has to be.' You're going to tell me that you need proof and that you're exploring all avenues of investigation."

There was a short silence. "It occurs to me," the detective said, "that you've learned a tremendous amount about police techniques in the last year or two."

"Yet it isn't helping," I said, and my tone was close to snippy. *Back off*, I told myself. Getting Inwood angry would not be helpful. After pulling in a short calming breath, I said, "It seems way outside the realm of coincidence that both Brad and Mia could have made significant mistakes at their respective workplaces."

"Indeed it does," Detective Inwood said.

"Really? You agree with me?"

"And since both of them," he went on, "have suffered the recent loss of their father, a loss compounded by the tragic fact that he was murdered by person or persons unknown, it's not unexpected that they would be distracted."

"So you don't agree with me," I said flatly.

The detective's sigh blew into my ear, which was more than a little weird. "Ms. Hamilton, I'm not certain what you're asking me to agree with."

And suddenly, neither was I. My first inclination, which had been to call Ash, had faded as soon as I started typing in the phone number for the sheriff's office. Sure, we were still friends after the least emotional breakup ever, but it was early in the Friends Only phase and I didn't want to interfere with how that was progressing. So I'd asked for Detective Inwood when what I should have done was hang up the phone and thought harder about what I was going to say.

Luckily, Inwood hadn't paused for my response. "If the brewing company asks us to investigate a possible criminal act, we will. Likewise, if Ms. Lacombe's place of work asks the Charlevoix County Sheriff's Office to investigate a criminal act, I'm certain they will do so. It's not up to me to chase down theoretical crimes when I have enough to do working on the ones that are already in front of me!"

Another short silence filled the phone. "Yes," I said quietly. "I know." And I did. Ash had told me many times how hard Inwood worked and how badly they needed another experienced detective. "I'm sorry I bothered you."

The detective sighed again. "Ms. Hamilton, I'm the

one who should apologize. I shouldn't have raised my voice."

"And I shouldn't have bothered you about something like this."

"Please believe that we are working very hard to build a case for the arrest of Mr. Lacombe's killer," Detective Inwood said. "And please believe me when I say that I can't say any more."

I half smiled. "All avenues of investigation . . ."

He picked up the end of the phrase he'd told me many times. "Are being explored. Thank you for the call, Ms. Hamilton," he said. "I do appreciate your willingness to assist our office."

"Only maybe not quite so often?" I asked, but he'd already gone. "Just as well," I muttered, spinning my chair around to sit. As I flopped down, once again I had the thought that I was missing something, that I wasn't looking at something the right way, wasn't considering the right angle, wasn't remembering something critical, wasn't remembering . . .

Jennifer.

Not fifteen minutes earlier I'd vowed to talk to her that very day. Before I could convince myself that I was too busy, I stood and headed up the stairs to her office. There was no time like the present.

All the way up the stairs, I tried to come up with a way to broach the subject. The knee-jerk "Did you know Mitchell Koyne won't set foot in this place until you're gone" didn't work for a number of reasons. "I'm not sure I agree with you one hundred percent about the changes you've been making" was too vague and a little wishy-washy.

When I reached the second floor, a solid plan still hadn't materialized. "Won't be the first time," I muttered to myself, and knocked on the doorjamb of Jennifer's office.

She was sitting at her large desk, staring fixedly at the computer monitor. Either she was ignoring me or hadn't heard my knock. I was trying to figure out which it was, when I suddenly noticed that though her redecorated office didn't fit in Chilson, it did match something. It matched her.

Jennifer suddenly looked up. "Minnie," she said. "Just the person I wanted to see."

"I am?" The back of my neck stiffened even as I tried to relax. Because surely there was some reasonable reason that she wanted to see me. Maybe she wanted my opinion on the best place to eat. Or a favorite place to watch the sunset. Or—

"You're here to present today's update, correct?"

It took everything in me not to gape at her like a hooked fish. The daily update. I'd forgotten all about it. Completely and totally forgotten. But before I could panic and run, a stroke of genius burst into my brain, saving me from doom. "Since you haven't given me parameters," I said smoothly, "I thought we could talk about budgets this time. Have you had a chance to study the revised bookmobile budget I sent last week?"

"Next on my list," she said just as smoothly, leaving me to wonder if she was making up stuff as much as I was. She leaned forward, put her elbows on the desk, and rested her chin on her fingertips. "In the future, I'd prefer to get your daily reports late in the afternoon. That will give me time to make corrections if we're going in the wrong direction."

It seemed ridiculous to me. After all, how wrong a direction could a small library possibly go in one day?

But I nodded and kept my thoughts—and facial expressions—to myself.

"So," she said. "What else do you have to report?"

Right then and there, I decided to make my report full of the things I wanted her to know. If she wanted something different, she'd have to tell me. "Well," I said cheerfully, "this morning . . ." And I launched into stories of the little things that filled our days. The sad things: the stoic bravery of an elderly woman who had asked for books about dealing with a spouse's death. The inspirational things: a teenager who'd asked for advice on how to get accepted into law school. And the funny things: how Reva Shomin's youngest had wanted to take home a stack of books taller than he was.

Jennifer's fingertips started to tap together faster and faster, so I wrapped up my tales with a few facts about the numbers of books checked out and computer use. These were numbers I'd always studied every single day; I didn't need an update duty to force me to look at data.

Finally, I said, "So the current checkout trends are down, but that's still in line with averages over the past years. The only checkout numbers up are the bookmobile's."

"Interesting," Jennifer said.

At least that's what she said, but I wasn't sure she actually meant it. I suddenly had a sneaking suspicion that she was well aware of the numbers and was just testing my knowledge. Anger flared, but I did my best to tamp it down. Suspicion was not anything close to proof. Just ask Detective Inwood.

"There's one other thing," I said. "There have been a number of patrons who have told me they aren't interested in visiting the library any longer. I wondered if you might have some opinions about that."

"Me?" Jennifer's eyebrows went up. "It's your responsibility to communicate patron discontent to me. You should be explaining the whys to me, not asking for an explanation yourself."

My polite smile grew fixed. "Right. I have a few ideas about that. For instance—"

"Hold that thought." Jennifer pointed a finger at me. "I want to run this past you before the board makes its final decision. As I'm sure you know, there are a number of rare books owned by this library that haven't been viewed in years. My proposal is to increase revenues by selling off a number of them."

"You . . . what?"

"There's no reason to hang on to volumes that aren't being accessed by the public," she said in a "Duh" tone of voice. "Why should we allocate shelf space for books that haven't been opened in three years?"

I could think of all sorts of reasons. Jennifer, however, clearly wasn't interested in hearing anything I had to say.

"I've talked to each of the board members individually," she went on, "and I'm confident a majority favors moving in this direction. According to my calculations, selling off the unused volumes will raise nearly enough revenue to pay for our new software. Providential, wouldn't you say?"

What I wanted to say wasn't fit to be heard by human ears. My mouth opened and shut a few times and I finally asked, "When will the board decide?" Maybe I could talk to Otis, the board president. Call the vice president. Cling to the feet of the board treasurer and beg her not to sell our irreplaceable assets in exchange for a system we didn't need.

"Tuesday. I've called a special meeting." She smiled with clear satisfaction. "I'll need your help to move into action afterward."

I couldn't find it in me to say a single word that wouldn't create a potentially dangerous situation for one or both of us, so I simply nodded. My thoughts the first steps back down the stairs were full of internal shouting.

What? How in the name of all that is holy could she think this makes sense? We'd be like a museum selling artwork! What is she thinking? This is nuts!

After a few more steps, the shrieking thoughts started to calm down to a manageable level, but it wasn't until I reached the landing and made the U-turn that would take me to the main floor that I understood the impact of what Jennifer had told me.

She had the library board's support.

Which meant that speaking to them about Jennifer would gain me nothing. On the contrary, talking about their new hire in less than glowing terms would likely get me labeled as a malcontent, a troublemaker, and someone who wasn't willing to work with the board.

But how long would I be able to stay silent?

How long could I stand by and do nothing while the library changed underneath me?

All of which led me straight to a big and frightening question that I'd never before asked myself: How long was I going to be welcome at the Chilson District Library?

On the walk home that evening, I kicked at the leaves fallen on the sidewalk and tried to think happy thoughts. The sun wouldn't officially set until a quarter to seven, but the streetlights were on full force at a few minutes past six and not making much of a dent against the thick clouds. A cold wind blew down my neck and I could feel rain start to fall.

"Bleah," I muttered, zipping my jacket all the way up and wishing I'd worn my winter coat.

None of that was helping me shift to a positive mindset, however. I debated whistling a favorite song, but I wasn't sure I would have been able to hear it over the noise of the blowing leaves. I considered singing, something that always lifted my spirits even if I couldn't carry a tune in a bucket, but as I mentally scrolled through possible songs, the only songs that came to mind were Christmas carols and it was far too early for that.

But dire straits called for dire measures. Thankfully, just as I was about to start the first verse of "The Twelve Days of Christmas," my cell phone rang with Kristen's tone.

"About time," I said. "What have you been doing all day?"

"Do you really want to know?" she asked. "Because if you do, I'll tell you."

"What I really want is for you to get me the name of a guy who ate at your place a week and a half ago."

"You have got to be kidding," she said flatly. My normally energetic friend sounded tired and cranky.

"Sorry," I said, "I know you're busy with closing down the restaurant, but this is important. It was the night I was there with Ash and Lindsey. There was this guy behind me and—"

"Oh, him," Kristen said, and I could almost see the roll of her eyes. "I remember that guy. He was by himself, right? He wanted his steak well done."

"Such a travesty," I murmured, knowing from experience it was the appropriate thing to say.

"And he wanted fake whipped cream on his pie." She snorted. "Please. As if I'd have something like that in my restaurant."

"Do you remember his name?" I asked.

"Something boring," she said. "Bland."

"Not helpful."

"Give me a minute, will you? You know how horrible I am with names."

I hummed a few quiet measures of the *Jeopardy* theme song.

"Funny," she said, "but that's not helping—" She stopped. "Last name was Blake," she said. "I ran his credit card myself."

So, not Simon Faber. I blew out a small sigh of relief, then remembered the name of Leese's new client. "Bob Blake?"

"Pretty sure. Why do you want to know?"

I murmured a few vague words about looking into something for Leese and said I'd talk to her later. As I neared the boardinghouse, walking toward the welcoming light streaming from the windows, I thought about what Mitchell had said and knew there was something I needed to do earlier rather than later. As in right now.

I tromped up the steps, and as I opened the front door, a gust of wind yanked the knob out of my grasp and it went *bang!* against the wall.

Aunt Frances, who was standing in the living room, whirled around, startled. "Minnie! Are you okay?"

"Sorry," I said, reaching around for the door and pulling it shut. "That's the kind of day this has been."

Otto hurried in from the dining room. "What

was—" Then he spied me. "Minnie," he said, smiling. "I had no idea you could make such a tremendous noise."

"You should hear me dropping cutlery on the floor." I put my backpack on the stairs and my coat in the front closet. "Do you two have a minute? There's something I'd like to talk about."

Because there was one conclusion I'd come to amid my dark thoughts on the way home, and I wanted to get it out in the open before I chickened out. Or changed my mind. Or decided that it wasn't my place to say.

"This sounds serious." Aunt Frances gave me a speculative look. "Please don't tell me you're regretting your decision not to apply for the library director position, so regretful that you've applied for another director position in some other state, that they interviewed you over the phone and hired you on the spot, are paying you an exorbitant salary and moving expenses, and you and Eddie plan to leave as soon as the moving van shows up."

"Mrr," said a disembodied cat voice.

I put on a serious face. "You're actually very close."

"What?" My aunt, who'd been two inches away from a sitting position, froze in place. "Seriously?"

"No."

Aunt Frances sat down with a thump. "Did you hear that, Otto? My niece, the only niece I have in the entire world, is making light of my concerns."

Otto snorted and sat next to her. "Since your concerns were completely imaginary, I can't say I blame her."

"Glad you agree," I said, smiling, as I came around the end of the couch that faced them. I sat next to my furry friend and said, “Hey. Nice of you to greet me when I get home after a long day at work.”

Eddie, who was curled up on the cushiest cushion on the couch, opened one eye, then closed it again.

I patted the top of his head anyway, and he started purring.

“How long are you going to leave us in suspense?” Aunt Frances leaned against Otto and tucked her stockinged feet up underneath her. Otto shifted to put his arm around her shoulder. “I’m pretty comfortable here,” she said as their fingers laced together casually yet firmly, “so you can take your time, but we have dinner plans, so don’t take too long.”

I smiled at them fondly. It was clear they belonged to each other heart and soul. Romance had come late to them both, but it was never too late for love. They deserved to have a lot of time together and I was going to help.

“Everything comes to an end,” I told them. “The sands of time and all that. Nothing lasts forever, not even the sun. Sure, it’ll be around for a few billion more years, but someday that will be gone, too.”

My aunt gazed at me. “Otto, I think she’s trying to tell us something.”

“Yes,” he said. “I wonder what it could possibly be?”

I laid a hand on Eddie’s back and he immediately started purring. I mentally whispered a thank-you for his support and said out loud, “It’s time to let go of the boardinghouse.”

Aunt Frances and Otto went completely still.

“It’s time,” I repeated. “Your future is more important than the future of strangers, and yours will be better without the boardinghouse.”

"Are you sure?" my aunt asked quietly.

I nodded. "You don't need the money, and I now see that running it takes a little more out of you every year. You spend half the winter planning, all spring getting ready, and you work until you drop all summer long. You're tired even now. Sell the business to someone else or close it down entirely. Either way your life will be better, and that's what matters."

Otto reached forward to tuck a strand of hair behind my aunt's ear. "What do you think, Frances?"

My hardworking, smart, self-contained, and independent aunt sniffled and dabbed at her eyes with Otto's sleeve. "Minnie, are you sure? This is your home. If I sell this place, where will you go October through April? You can't stay on your houseboat all year."

The thought made me shiver involuntarily. "Don't worry about me. Like I said before, I'm sure I can find people willing to rent me their summer place." Who, I had no idea, but I wasn't going to worry about that. Not for a few months, anyway.

"It'll be strange to see this place in different hands," Otto said, looking at the maps that had been tacked up to the walls for decades, at the shelves filled with board games and worn books, at the mantel crowded with driftwood. "Frances, do you think living across the street will be too difficult for you?" He paused. "Frances?"

But my aunt wasn't paying attention. Instead, her face had taken on a thoughtful look.

"Aunt Frances?" I asked slowly. "What are you planning?"

"Me?" She blinked. "What makes you think I'm planning anything?" Her face was wide open and guileless, but I'd known her long enough to know one thing.

She was lying.

Half an hour later, I was still on the couch and Aunt Frances and Otto had left for dinner at the Barrel Back on Walloon Lake. They'd tried to convince me to go with them, but I'd pled the need for a long bath in a deep tub and they'd eventually left, hand in hand.

As the front door shut behind them, Eddie stood, stretched, and yawned. Then he rotated three hundred and sixty degrees and flopped down in the exact same position.

I watched the entire pointless exercise and said, "Do you know what happened just now? I may have talked us out of a place to call home."

Eddie didn't seem particularly worried, so I gave his tail a gentle tug.

"Did you hear me? If Aunt Frances lists the boardinghouse and someone buys it straightaway, where are we going to move? It's not like the new owner is going to let us stay."

"Mrr?" Eddie asked.

"No, not even if we ask nicely. Besides, it'll all be different." I glanced around at the wide pine paneling, darkened with age. At the fieldstone fireplace, birthplace of thousands of s'mores. At the faded and worn furniture older than I was. "We won't want to stay," I murmured. "Well, at least I won't."

My cat heaved a sigh and brushed the back of my wrist with his tail.

Smiling and oddly comforted, I patted him on the head. "You're not so bad, for an Eddie. Some days it really does seem as if you understand what I'm saying."

"Mrr," he said.

"Okay, yes, you understand me," I said, still patting. "Sorry I insulted your intelligence. But we need to have a talk about your activity level. If you keep on like you're going, all this flopping around and sleeping and hardly anything else, you'll weigh fifty pounds by springtime and that's going to shift the houseboat's center of gravity something fierce." It wouldn't, of course, but he didn't know that.

He also wasn't paying any attention to me, because the dulcet tones of his snores were starting to reach my ears.

I gave him a few pets and stood. There were choices to make and I had to get going on them. First, figuring out a dinner that wouldn't involve actual cooking. Then I had to choose between the upstairs bathtub and the downstairs bathtub. Downstairs was the deep claw-foot tub, but upstairs was a modern built-in version with massage jets. Which one would be better for thinking?

"Decisions, decisions," I murmured, and was halfway to the kitchen when I heard my cell phone ring.

I switched directions and pulled the phone out of my backpack just before the call slid into voice mail. The name of the incoming caller surprised me. "Hey, Carmen," I said. "How are you? How's Mia doing?"

"Mia?" She sounded surprised. "Fine, as far as I know. Why wouldn't she be?"

"No reason," I said, trying to sound casual. If Mia didn't want to talk to her mom about her suspension from work, that was her business. "Just checking."

"Are you still helping Leese?" Carmen asked. "Finding out who killed my sweet Dale?"

"Absolutely." Not that I'd made much progress, but you never knew; I could stumble across something any second that would solve the murder. And the sooner the better, because last time I'd talked to Leese, she'd eventually admitted that she was down to a small handful of clients with Bob Blake the only new one on the horizon. "Why do you ask?"

"Before, you asked about employees that didn't get along with Dale, about workers who might have hated him enough to kill him."

"That's right. The police asked you the same thing, didn't they?"

"I'd rather not talk to them ever again," Carmen said. "The last time they stopped by, they all but accused me of—" Her voice caught. "They asked me if I'd—"

"If you'd killed him?" I asked gently.

"I couldn't believe it!" Her outrage blew loud and strong into my ear. "Can you? I gave that detective a piece of my mind, believe me, and he went away with his tail between his legs. But now I remembered something, and the last thing I want to do is talk to that man."

"Carmen, if you have information, you need to tell the police yourself." I paused. "What did you remember? Maybe I can tell if it's important enough to tell the police."

"Back a few years, Dale hired this guy who was nothing but trouble. He didn't want to work, didn't want to pull his share. All he wanted to do on hot days was sit in the shade and put his feet up."

Her tone of outrage came through loud and clear. "Dale fired him?"

"Of course he did," Carmen said. "He had every right to. And what does the kid do but blow up at him, run on and on about what a horrible boss Dale was and how it wouldn't take much for an accident to happen on a dark night."

It sounded like a possibility, maybe even a strong one. "What's his name?"

"That Indian," she said. "You know, the one who works at the school."

Quickly, I mentally ran through the list of teachers and staff. The only Indian I could remember was Laila Mahajan, who'd taught third grade, but she'd only been in Chilson a year on an exchange program and I didn't see how she could have anything to do with Dale's death since she'd moved back to Mumbai in July. "Which school? The elementary school?"

"No, no," she said impatiently. "The middle school. I know you know him."

And how, exactly, did she know this? I wandered into the bathroom to choose a scent of bubble bath. "Sorry, I don't—"

"He used to be a teacher," she said, "but he worked for Dale right out of high school."

"If he's not there anymore, I doubt I'll—"

"Why can't I remember his name?" she asked. "He's still there, just not a teacher. He's . . . ah," she said with satisfaction. "Got it."

A sudden clench of my insides told me what she was going to say.

"It was Rafe," she practically spat. "Rafe Niswander. And you're right about calling the police. I'll do it myself first thing tomorrow morning."

Chapter 16

"It's not possible," I said. "It's just not."

My conversation with Carmen had left me so wobbly that I'd given up on the bathtub idea for fear of accidental drowning and instead huddled at one end of the couch with a blanket pulled over me.

"There's just no way," I said, repeating what I'd already told Eddie over and over again for the last half hour. "First off, it's just ridiculous to think that Rafe would kill anyone, even in the heat of anger." I paused, both in talking and in petting my cat. After half a second, he picked up his head and gave me The Look, so I started petting again.

"Sorry, I was just trying to imagine Rafe getting really mad at someone. He's the calmest person I know. I've never seen him more than mildly frustrated at anyone or anything."

The worst display of his temper I'd ever witnessed had been when the local lumberyard had delivered the wrong length of wooden siding to his house. It was special-ordered siding that had taken weeks to arrive. Rafe had looked at the vast piles of wood, uttered one heartfelt curse word, and called the lumberyard to calmly tell them what had happened.

"So there's no way he could have killed anyone," I reminded Eddie. "It's silly to even consider that."

My cat gave a huge sigh.

"Well, exactly. It's just ludicrous. He might have mouthed off to Dale, because he is kind of a smart aleck, but the idea of him making a real and serious threat is just . . . is just . . ."

"Mrr."

"Thanks." I patted Eddie's head. "That's just what I was trying to say. I'll have to talk to Detective Inwood, or maybe Ash, because I promised Carmen to let them know what she's remembered, but it's pointless. Yes, people can change, but that was a long time ago, way too long ago for a spoken threat to still carry any serious weight, and anyway, I've known Rafe since I was twelve. He's the same now as he was then."

"Mrr."

"Okay, maybe not exactly the same," I said, admitting the truth. "He's not so skinny anymore, but other than that, he's the same guy Kristen and I used to ride bikes with all summer long."

Eddie, temporarily a lap cat, rotated himself end for end.

"No, not skinny at all," I murmured, giving Eddie long pets that would soon create a small pile of cat hair on his back, on the blanket, and on me. "In some circles, he'd be considered trim and fit." Most circles, if I was going to be absolutely honest with myself. "And the odds are high that some women think he's good-looking." Actually, there were probably a lot of women who thought so.

"Really, he's not a bad guy." By all accounts he was

the best principal the middle school had seen in years. He was such a decent human being that he had friends who ran the gamut of ages, income levels, education, and ethnicity.

"He's actually quite nice."

I'd never once, in the twenty-plus years I'd known him, seen him be anything other than kindhearted and generous with his time. He was willing to drop everything to help a friend and do it with a grinning joke. Yes, he had an unfortunate tendency to act the part of an Up North hick, especially if there was some show-off downstater in the audience, and he didn't always take things as seriously as they needed to be taken, but as a whole, he was a genuinely nice guy.

I thought back in time to the previous summer. We'd sat side by side on his porch one warm evening and as our hands had brushed each other as he'd handed me something, I'd felt an uncomfortable prickling sensation. He'd touched my hair and the same thing had happened.

And even as I was remembering, my skin started to prickle again.

My eyes went wide and I sat up straight. "Oh, no," I breathed. "It can't be. It's not possible."

But as soon as the thought had entered my brain, I knew there was no way to unthink it, because it was true.

I was in love with Rafe Niswander.

And had been for years.

After a restless night of sleep, I crawled out of bed with eyes full of grit and felt the uneasy knowledge that my life had changed irrevocably.

"What do you think?" I asked Eddie, but my cat,

as per usual, didn't have any advice to offer when I needed it the most. On the other hand, he did purr like a champ as I slid him into his cat carrier, so I wasn't going to complain.

"Breakfast?" my aunt called as my feet trod the last few steps.

"No time," I called back. "Errands to run and people to see before I go into work." Plus, I didn't want her to see my troubled face. I would explain my newfound feelings to her at some point; just not yet. "See you tonight."

But in those few words, Aunt Frances had heard something in my voice. "Minnie?" she asked, walking into the living room. "Are you okay?"

"Fine." I closed the door to the front closet and put on my coat, not meeting her eyes. "There's just a lot to do today." Sort of. "Ready, Eddie?" I picked up the cat carrier and took hold of the front doorknob.

My aunt, however, put her foot against the bottom of the door, trapping me inside. "One minute, young lady. You're not leaving this house until I get a promise that you'll tell me what's going on."

I tugged at the unmoving doorknob. "Aunt Frances—"

"Promise. I'm bigger than you and I have nowhere to go. I'll hold this door shut all day if I have to."

"Fine," I said, sighing. "This week. We'll talk about whatever this is before another week goes by."

"Then you're free to leave." She stepped back from the door. "Of course, it would be nice if I could get a hint about the topic we'll be discussing. If I did, I could do any necessary research before you spill your guts."

"Research won't be needed," I muttered. "Trust me."

"Mrr," Eddie said, and then we were out the door.

Five minutes later, before I could lose my courage, I parked in a visitor spot at the middle school. "Be right back," I told Eddie, and headed inside. It was forty-five minutes before school started. If this was a normal day for Rafe, he'd already be at his desk, knee deep in whatever it was the principals did before school began.

I stared at the front door, took a deep breath, and went inside. "Don't let this be awkward," I told myself. After all, Rafe had no idea of the realization I'd come to twelve hours earlier. There was no way he could possibly know that I loved him, had loved him, would probably always love him.

"Don't," I whispered. If he'd ever had any interest in a romantic relationship with Minnie Hamilton, he'd had numerous opportunities to speak over the years. He'd never said a word. We were friends. And would remain only friends. It would take time, but I'd adjust to this new reality and would eventually move on.

I gave an involuntary moan of pain. Which sounded so pathetic that I was ashamed of myself. "Buck up," I told myself firmly, ignoring the bleak emptiness I felt, trying not to think about Kristen's upcoming wedding, in which both Rafe and I would undoubtedly be playing key roles, and opened the door to the school offices. "Hey," I called. "You in there?"

"Hay is for horses," Rafe called back. "I'd prefer steak and eggs."

"Oatmeal," I said, walking past the counter and his secretary's desk, still empty at this hour, "is a much healthier choice."

As I entered his office, a balled-up piece of paper popped me on the shoulder. "What was that for?" I stooped, picked up the paper, and fired it right back.

He batted it away and into the wastebasket. "Two points for the big winner. That's what you get for suggesting healthy food instead of something I might actually like."

"Is that what you tell your students?" I asked.

"I tell them to do as I say, not as I do."

"And how is that working out for you?"

He grinned. "That's for me to know and you to find out."

I looked away from his smile, that wide, easy expression I'd seen thousands of times but that was now threatening to undo me. "Maybe I will."

"You could, but you won't." He wadded up another piece of paper and lobbed it at a nearby chair. "Have a seat."

"Can't stay," I said, but took the time to perch on the chair's edge. "I just stopped by to tell you something."

"Let me guess." He whistled tunelessly for a moment, then said, "Eddie has finally found a way past his vocal limitations and is telling you exactly how you should run your life."

"He's been doing that for a year and a half," I said. "It's all in the interpretation. No, it's about Dale Lacombe. I talked to Carmen last night. A while back, I'd asked her if any of Dale's employees had ever been angry enough to kill him, or if any of them had ever threatened him."

Rafe snorted. "Most of them, I'd say."

"At the time, she couldn't think of anyone, but last night she called because she'd remembered one name." I paused, not wanting to say it out loud, knowing that I had to. "And it was yours."

He gave me a blank look. "What are you talking

about? I only worked for Lacombe once, the summer between high school and college."

"Yes, but Carmen said . . ." I tried to remember exactly what she'd told me. "She said you'd blown up at Dale, gone on and on about how horrible he was as a boss."

"True enough," Rafe said, leaning back in his chair and putting his hands behind his head. "I did say all that. He was the worst boss I'd ever had, and that hasn't changed."

"There's more," I said evenly. "She said you blew up at him after he fired you, and that you threatened him. That you told him it wouldn't take much for an accident to happen on a dark night."

For a long moment, there was silence in the room. Rafe's gaze met mine, and though I longed to go to him, to hold him tight and give him what comfort I could, I met his gaze and didn't flinch.

Then he started laughing. Loud and long. "Seriously?" he asked, through spasms of laughter. "She's going to take that to the cops?"

"First thing this morning, she said."

"Sweet." As his laughter faded to chuckles, he wiped his eyes with the backs of his hands. "Wish I could be there when she talks to Inwood, because that would be worth something."

"It was a threat," I said, getting a little annoyed. "And Dale Lacombe is dead."

"A threat, sure." He started laughing again. "What I told him was to take a long walk on a short pier. Not very original even at eighteen, but that was all I had. I mean, who fires a kid for picking up litter?"

"He . . . what?"

"I was cleaning up a job site," Rafe said. "He left

scraps of paper and wood all over the place, and he said I spent too much time cleaning when I should have been pounding nails."

"You were cleaning?" I found that hard to believe, knowing the typical status of his house. It was under construction, but still.

"Well, I haven't changed much, so imagine what Lacombe's job sites looked like if the mess was bugging me."

Good point. "Sorry about this. It was my questions that got Carmen thinking."

He shrugged. "Don't apologize. There's nothing there. It's not like I killed anyone."

Annoyance flashed through me. "Of course you didn't. But if she tells the police you made a threat, they'll have to investigate and who knows what could happen."

"Nothing," he said, yawning and stretching. "Absolutely nothing."

"What if the school board finds out? Aren't you worried about your reputation?"

"Cops coming in to talk to me?" He peered at the ceiling as if it held answers. "I'd say it would help my street cred."

I made a rude noise in the back of my throat, proud of myself for acting as if I didn't have deep unrequited love for the man sitting ten feet away from me. "You're so gangsta it frightens me. Why do I get the feeling you're not taking any of this seriously?"

"Because I'm not. Thanks for caring, though."

I looked closely to see if I could detect any hint that he was serious, but saw nothing out of the ordinary. "Do you mean that?" I asked, a little embarrassed about how tentative I sounded. The small silence that followed told me more than I wanted to know.

Rafe cleared his throat and leaned forward. "Minnie, there's—"

"I have to go," I said quickly, not wanting to hear him say that I had the wrong idea, that he was sorry I'd misunderstood what he'd said about missing me, that he hoped we could stay friends. "But before I go," I said, "write this down." I pulled out my phone and scrolled through the contacts list until I got to the downstate phone number I wanted and read it out loud.

Rafe picked up a pen. "What's that for?"

"Daniel Markakis," I snapped.

"Isn't that—"

"One of the best criminal attorneys in the state." I slid my cell back into my coat pocket, spun on my heel, and headed out, my heart near to breaking.

The rest of the day, I tried to keep myself busy so I didn't have time to think. I did, however, make a quick afternoon phone call to Detective Inwood and sounded him out about Carmen's accusation about Rafe. The detective said he had talked to Carmen, and though he didn't outright laugh, he seemed to take her report almost as seriously as Rafe had, for which I was extremely grateful.

"Not that I'm going to communicate that to Rafe," I told Eddie that night. "Did you count how many times Julia asked if I was coming down with something?"

Eddie, who was sitting upright on one of the kitchen chairs, looked at me with unblinking eyes and made no comment.

"Me, either," I said, "but it was a lot." Even a few patrons had asked if I was feeling all right. I'd spent a lot of time staring vacantly into space, and more than once, I'd jumped high when someone had tapped me on the shoulder.

I opened the refrigerator door and took out a container of leftover spaghetti. "But I'm not sick. Just distracted."

"Mrr."

"Glad you understand," I said, forking the spaghetti onto a plate and sliding it into the microwave. "There's a lot going on in my head, you know."

"Mrr!"

"You want me to list them all? Okay, Aunt Frances is going to marry Otto and move in with him. The boardinghouse will be sold."

Eddie jumped down and came over to bump my shins with the top of his head.

"Yeah, I know. It's sad, but like they say, all good things come to an end."

"Mrr!"

"Not done with my list," I said. "In addition to those big changes in my life, there's also this little thing going on at the library. You know, that Jennifer is about to sell irreplaceable assets for the sake of a computer system we don't need, not to mention the fact that she's making everyone's life miserable."

Or at least that's what Holly, Josh, Donna, Kelsey, and every staff member other than Gareth kept telling me. And if Gareth didn't do his custodial and maintenance work after the library was closed and everyone was gone, he would probably be complaining, too.

I was trying to convince my coworkers that we'd get used to her and she'd get used to us, but Jennifer had been director for almost three months now, and if anything, the situation was growing worse.

"We're going to lose Donna," I murmured. She'd already retired from one career and would do without the extra income if she got fed up with Jennifer. "I don't want to have to replace her," I said. "Finding someone with her range of skills will be next to impossible."

The microwave dinged and I pulled out my dinner. "Even if we did find someone, who else is going to work for the wages we can afford to pay?" Working in a library was, to my mind, the best job in the world, but no one did it to get rich.

I sat at the round oak table and twirled spaghetti around my fork. "And then there's Leese."

"Mrr," Eddie said.

His little kitty voice hadn't come from his chair. "Where are you?" I looked around, but didn't see him. "Anyway, Leese is worried about Mia and Brad, and I'm worried about Leese. Mia and Brad are in trouble at their respective workplaces, they're all working through their father's death, and the fact that no one's been arrested isn't helping."

I chewed and swallowed a forkful of spaghetti. "When I talked to Detective Inwood this morning, all I got was the standard response about investigating everything." Sighing, I ate another bite. "But from his tone of voice, it doesn't sound as if they have anything solid."

"Mrr."

"If you want, sure, I'll talk you through everything I've learned. First off, no one except Carmen seemed surprised that Dale was murdered. That makes narrowing down suspects hard from the get-go."

An odd noise emanated from the broom closet, whose door, I now noticed, was open a few inches.

"Detective Inwood and Ash were looking at all the employees that Dale had ever fired," I told the closet, "and they're talking to all his clients from the last few years." When I'd talked to Inwood, I'd obliquely mentioned the possibility that Dale and/or Carmen had been having extramarital affairs. There'd been a long telephone silence, Inwood had sighed, then I'd heard noises I'd interpreted as a new page in his notebook being flipped and a pen being clicked to writing position.

I was pretty sure that Inwood figured I was just trying to distract him from making a case against Brad or Leese as the murderer, and he was probably right. Then again, since there was no way Brad or Leese had killed Dale, the detective should be thanking me for saving him time and effort.

"If Brad was going to kill his dad," I said to Eddie, "it would have been while they were working together, not now. And Carmen and Dale had such an odd marriage, why would it explode into murder now? And it doesn't seem like it was anyone involved in one of the lawsuits.

"And then there's the building official, Rob Driskell. He was definitely not a fan of Dale's. Him killing Dale in a fit of anger makes a lot more sense than Brad or Carmen doing it." Not that murder necessarily made sense, but you had to start somewhere. "If the detective and Ash are going to keep looking at Brad, I'm going to have to work harder on—"

Zing!

A tiny toy car shot across the kitchen floor, caromed off a chair leg, and came to rest against my foot.

"I'm so glad," I said to my cat, "you've finally found

that Monopoly game piece. We've been looking for a year and a half."

Eddie pounded across the floor, slid into a dive, and slammed into the table's pedestal with a loud thump.

Wincing, I leaned over. "Are you okay? Because that sounded like it hurt."

Zing!

The toy car skittered to the other side of the kitchen. Eddie scrambled to his feet and ran after it.

Rolling my eyes, I went back to my food. If Eddie wasn't sound asleep, he was wide awake. There was no dozy middle ground. Were all cats like that? Or were—

I snapped my head around and stared at Eddie. Or more precisely, his new toy.

The car.

The jump my brain made had seemed reasonable when I'd explained it to Eddie, but the next morning, when I imagined an explanatory conversation with Detective Inwood, I wasn't so sure.

"A toy car," he'd say, his voice expressionless.

"No," I'd say, already impatient with him. "That's what made me think about it, is all."

"Your cat is helping you with a murder investigation?" he'd ask.

If I managed to get through that without crawling under the table from embarrassment, I'd move on to the important part. "A while back, Dale Lacombe was responsible for a head-on collision. Have you looked into that accident?"

Inwood would click on his pen. "I'm not familiar with this. How long ago?"

"Twenty-three years."

The pen would go back into his shirt pocket and I'd get a chillingly polite smile as I was ushered out of the interview room with an admonition to never again darken the door of the sheriff's office.

"Well, maybe he wouldn't tell me that," I said to Eddie as I got dressed, post-shower. "But he'd want to."

Eddie, curled up on my pillow, opened his eyes and picked up his head. "Mrr!" He closed his eyes and, a second and a half later, was snoring.

"No idea what that meant." I patted his head and headed downstairs. "Thanks anyway, though."

The kitchen was dark and empty, which meant that Aunt Frances had stayed at Otto's overnight. I smiled, wondering if she was rethinking her decision to wait until spring to get married. Then I frowned, because I wondered what the gleam in her eye had meant after I'd encouraged her to sell the boardinghouse.

Putting that aside for the moment, I planned how I'd get solid information about Dale Lacombe's car accident all those years ago. My most common sources for local history—Kristen and Rafe—weren't even teenagers at the time and they wouldn't remember much, if anything. Not to mention the fact that I didn't really want to talk to Rafe right now. I'd woken up that morning from a dream that featured him as the romantic lead and I was sure my face would turn an embarrassing color of red if I stopped by. I could do it over the phone, but he had an uncanny knack for sensing my discomfort.

"All right, Minnie," he'd say. "What's your problem today?"

"Me?" I'd ask, trying to sound surprised. "Nothing. I'm fine."

"Don't give me that," he'd say. "You're a horrible liar. Tell me your problems and I'll see if I can laugh at them hard enough to make them go away."

No, talking to Rafe wouldn't be a good idea, and Kristen was too preoccupied with the details of closing down the Three Seasons to be a good listener. I debated knocking on Otto's front door to talk to my aunt, but shied away from the possibility of seeing him in a bathrobe and fuzzy slippers. Or worse, no slippers.

But there were other sources, especially for this particular kind of information.

Twenty minutes after I'd scarfed down a bowl of cold cereal and headed outside, I presented myself at the office of the local newspaper, just in time to see the editor unlock the front door and hold it open for me.

"Hey, Camille," I said. "How are you this fine morning?"

Camille Pomeranz, a dark-skinned woman in her late forties, ran the newspaper office with a firm hand. She was a recent transplant, moved north after her large downstate paper slashed their staff by half.

Their loss and our gain, because the *Chilson Gazette* had gone from a lackluster publication little more than a gossip sheet to a news-gathering organization starting to win national awards. I knew Camille because I often sent her advertising for the library's events, everything from author talks to book sales, and we'd struck up a solid acquaintanceship that could easily become a real friendship if given proper food and water.

Camille grimaced. "Fine morning, nothing. Have you seen the weather forecast?"

"Never," I said. "Can't change it, so why bother."

"Wise woman." Camille smiled. "Except don't you find yourself dressed inappropriately for conditions every so often?"

I patted my backpack. "Travel umbrella, dry socks, and a fleece hat."

She laughed. "The Boy Scouts have nothing on Minnie Hamilton. What can I do for you?"

"Archive every article from every issue of your newspaper into a searchable database. Please."

Not missing a beat, Camille reached around and grabbed a small pad of paper and a pen from the nearby counter. "I'll get right on that," she said, scribbling. "What kind of time frame?"

"How about noon?"

"No problem," she said, nodding and still scribbling.

Curious, I sidled up to look at the pad of paper and laughed when I saw that she'd sketched out a stick figure with curly hair and carrying a backpack. Above that Camille had written a single question: *Has she lost her mind?!!!*

She finished off with an arrow pointing to the curly hair. "I added the exclamation points when you said noon," she said.

Camille often talked about the need for a database of the newspaper archives, but a lack of time, money, and personnel was going to keep it a dream for the foreseeable future. The only articles online were from 2009 forward, which was when the owner had made the leap into the twenty-first century. The library had the oldest newspapers, some of which were microfilmed, but the year that concerned me was housed here at the *Gazette*'s office.

"I'm looking for information about a car accident about twenty years ago," I said. Twenty-three, to be exact.

"We might have an article on that, and we might not." Camille made some finishing touches to her drawing, then tossed the pen and pad onto the counter and nodded for me to follow her. "Depends on what else was going on that week. Sometimes car accidents hit the front page, sometimes they don't."

She led me to the back of the office and up a creaky set of wooden stairs. A single light switch brought fluorescent illumination to the room, and I blinked at the number of shelves filled with boxes, books, newspapers, and dusty equipment that I didn't recognize.

"Twenty years ago?" Camille asked, walking toward the back corner of the room. She switched direction slightly when I said twenty-three years and motioned me over to a stack of newspapers.

"Look all you like," she said. "Use the table, take pictures, whatever. But if you rip a single page, the ghost of Katharine Graham will haunt you the rest of your life."

"Scout's honor," I said, performing the salute.

"Good enough." Camille gave me a steady look. "Are you going to tell me what this is all about?"

"If it's a real story, sure." Then I considered my words and made an amendment. "At least someday."

She scowled. "Not what I wanted to hear."

"Yeah, I know, but it's the best I can do right now."

There was a short silence. "Okay," Camille said, setting a foot on the top stair. "See you later."

And she left me alone with the dusty history of Chilson.

* * *

It didn't take long for me to find what I was after. I had the year and, knowing the other car had been a convertible, could assume that the accident had taken place during the Up North convertible season of May through September.

An hour after I'd gone up the steps to the newspaper's second floor, I was walking into the library, ready to hit the search engines.

"Hello? Are you in there?"

I started. "Oh. Hey, Donna. I didn't see you."

"Or hear me," she said from behind the counter, laughing. "That's the third time I said hello."

"Sorry." I stopped, a little embarrassed. "I was thinking."

"Anything you want to talk about?" She tipped her head in the direction of Jennifer's office.

"What? Oh, no. I was just . . ." My voice trailed off as it sank into my tiny brain that I was talking to a longtime resident of Chilson. "Do you remember when Dale Lacombe got into a bad car accident?"

"Now that was a long time ago." Donna leaned forward and put her elbows on the counter. "The kids and Dale were fine, as I recall, but the man driving that little car was hurt badly."

"Simon Faber," I said.

She nodded. "I didn't know the man, but my neighbor knew him through a golf league."

"Do you remember anything about him?"

"He was seasonal. Had a place on Janay Lake."

That much had been in the newspaper. "Anything else?"

"It was a long time ago," she said, her gaze shifting inward. "But if I recall correctly, his injuries from the car accident were the kind that change your life. Multiple operations, pins and screws in all sorts of places. Don't remember if he had internal injuries, but it seems likely."

"Is he still around?"

Donna shook her head. "He sold his place after the accident. All those surgeries took a lot out of him. Orthopedic, internal, eye, plastic, and who knows what else." She sighed. "That poor man was certainly in the wrong place at the wrong time."

I deflated a little, but decided to keep following through. "Could you do me a favor? Ask your neighbor if he's seen or heard from Simon Faber in the last few months. Any information would be good."

"Sure," she said, shrugging, "but why—"

I cut into her question, not wanting to explain. "Thanks, Donna." And with a quick smile, I headed to my office. There were all sorts of things I had to do that day, but now there was one more task.

Find out everything I could about Simon Faber.

Chapter 17

In my search for knowledge, I poked around with Google, used every type of social media in my librarian's arsenal, and made phone calls to everyone I could think of who might have any useful information.

What I found out from my lunchtime Internet efforts was a Simon Faber owned a house in Independence, Missouri, that had been listed for sale at $245,000. I found a Simon Faber who'd been listed as a speaker to the Rotary Club of Sacramento, California, on the topic of how increasing accessibility would increase retail sales. I also learned that Simon Faber had self-published a book on growing roses. Whether or not any of these Fabers was the right one, I did not know.

In the afternoon, all the voice mail messages I'd left at noon came rolling back. Kristen told me she remembered the car accident, but couldn't have given me Simon Faber's name if her life had depended on it. "I was maybe twelve years old," she said. "Did you really expect me to remember?"

"You can remember every amount of every ingredient in every dish you've ever cooked," I replied. "Why not one guy's name?"

"Duh," she said. "I care about the cooking. People, not so much."

There was a bizarre disconnect in her logic, but I let it go.

"Does this have anything to do with Dale Lacombe's murder?" she asked, suspicion strong in her voice.

"Not sure," I replied, and said a quick good-bye before she could start scolding me.

My aunt Frances was next to call back, apologizing for leaving me all alone the previous night in the boardinghouse.

"Eddie kept me company," I said. "Besides, it's expected that affianced couples spend the night together every so often. That's if they're not already cohabitating."

"Shacking up?" She laughed. "At my age?" Then she told me what she could recall about Simon Faber. "He lived out on the north shore road, a few doors down from a cousin of Everett's." She paused at the mention of her long-deceased husband, then went on. "I remember Everett's cousin saying Simon was strictly Memorial Day to Labor Day. Nothing before, nothing after. It was far more common back then. Now folks come up all year round." She sighed. "Almost makes you want to move to the Upper Peninsula."

I'd heard that comment many times from others, but no one ever seemed to pack up and go. I loved the UP, but I loved Chilson more. "Anything else?" I asked. "About Faber?"

"He was a big antique car buff," she said. "He built

a garage at his cottage, which in those days was very unusual, because he didn't want his cars to get any unnecessary exposure to sun and rain and wind."

Rafe's return call that evening, on the other hand, was less useful. I was on the couch reading, with Eddie on my lap, when my cell phone rang. I glanced at the screen and went all tingly when I saw Rafe's picture smiling at me. I took in a long breath and thumbed on the phone. "Hey."

"No idea what you're talking about," he said.

"You don't remember Dale Lacombe's car accident?"

"I'm lucky if I remember what I had for breakfast this morning."

"You always have the same thing for breakfast," I pointed out.

"See my problem?"

My laugh turned into an inexplicable sob that I forced into a cough. "You really don't know anything?"

"Nope. Why do you want to know?"

"Just looking into some things for Leese," I said vaguely. "Do you know anyone who might know what happened to Simon Faber?"

"Nope," Rafe said. "I was just a pup back then and he was a summer guy who lived out on Janay Lake. We didn't cross paths."

"You are no help," I said. "But thanks for calling."

"Anytime I can be less than useful, you know where I live."

I shut down the phone, knowing that my former habit of dropping by his fixer-upper was gone for the foreseeable future. To keep from dwelling on that depressing topic, I made myself think about who else might have information about Simon Faber.

"You know what?" I asked Eddie, who was happily putting my legs to sleep. "I should ask Dana Coburn."

A few months ago, the geniuslike young Dana had helped me with the history of one of the original Chilson families. Since then, she and I had texted each other on a regular basis (with her parents' permission, of course), and we were developing a solid friendship.

I sent a quick text to Dana. *Know anything about a Simon Faber? Car accident 23 years ago, east of Chilson.* Sure enough, a few seconds later, I saw the sequence of fading in and fading out dots that meant she was texting me back. Then the message came through: *No.*

Thanks anyway, I texted in return, and was about to tuck the phone away when she came back with: *Want me to find out?*

My reaction was immediate and instinctive. *No.* The last thing I wanted was for Dana to get mixed up in a murder investigation, even peripherally and from her winter home in Chicago. *Just wondered. Have a good night.*

After a short pause, she texted: *U 2. And Eddie.*

Smiling, I tapped Eddie on the head with the phone. "Hear that? The smartest kid in the world wants you to have a good night."

"Mrr," he said sleepily, and arranged himself deeper into the folds of the blanket.

My final lunchtime efforts had been to leave messages for two other people: my attorney, Shannon Hirsch, and Mr. Goodwin, a library patron in his mid-seventies. Donna had told me that she called her neighbor and he hadn't heard from Faber in years. "He sounded relieved," she'd said. "I asked him why, and he said Simon just wasn't the same after the accident. Too many scars, mental and physical."

Neither Shannon nor Mr. Goodwin called me, but as I told Eddie the next morning when hauling his carrier out to my car, "I just asked them to call if they knew anything. And I didn't say it was urgent. So I might never hear from them at all."

"Mrr!" Eddie said in a harsh way that sounded like criticism.

I shut the door on his second comment and we didn't speak to each other until we arrived at the bookmobile's garage, whereupon I apologized for slamming the door on what he had to say and he purred. I did a quick pretrip check of the vehicle, Julia arrived, and the bookmobile got on its way.

A few miles outside of town, Julia pointed out the front windshield. "What fresh you-know-what is this?" she asked in a deep, dark tone.

"Nothing," I said quickly. "Pay no attention to it and it'll go away."

Julia made a hmphing sort of noise. "Putting your head in the sand. Let me know how that works out."

"Mrr," Eddie said.

"Thanks so much," I told him. "The support and encouragement you provide is second to none. Without you . . ." I sighed and reached out for the windshield wipers, because it was now an undeniable fact that the low heavy clouds were releasing snow. Lots of snow.

"Time for a new theory?" Julia asked.

"It'll go away," I muttered. "Eventually."

In morose silence, we drove through the thickly falling white stuff and parked at a gas station and convenience store whose owner had been happy to have her place become a bookmobile stop. The first patrons aboard were two youngsters squealing with joy at the weather conditions. As their father climbed the steps, they ran to the front, where Eddie was perched on the passenger's seat headrest, gave him some pets, then ran back to me.

"Did you see, Miss Minnie?" asked the nine-year-old girl, who was grinning from large ear to large ear. "It's snowing. Isn't it pretty?"

I allowed that it was, in fact, pretty. And it was. I liked snow. And winter. And the three S's of winter: skiing, sledding, and skating. October was a little early to be driving through it, that was all.

"We're going to make a snowman," said her eight-year-old brother. "It's going to be this high!" He stood on his tiptoes, holding his hand above his head as far as he could reach.

His father smiled. "It's good to dream big," he told his offspring, then to me he said, "Of course, it doesn't hurt to have a backup plan."

Laughing, I asked, "You have one in place?"

"With these two? You better believe it. Most times I have three or four."

They moved forward to the shelves that housed the children's books, where Julia met them and guided them to the latest Timmy Failure book. As the kids pounced on the volume and started reading it aloud to each other, a number of things started tumbling around in my head.

The early snow, which was making me think about the prewinter boardinghouse chores. How the lottery-winning Boggses flitted from house to house, never coming to a long rest. Mitchell's comments about being underestimated. How Daphne Raab could be a poster child for passive-aggressive behavior. That Rob Driskell had been dealing with builders like Lacombe for years, if not decades. And about backup plans that involved children.

Children. Leese, Brad, and Mia were Dale Lacombe's children.

That was what I'd been missing. That was what I hadn't been taking into account when thinking about the murder.

I took stock of the action in the bookmobile. Julia was greeting a newcomer and the small family was settling down on the carpeted step to read more about Timmy's adventures, so I felt free to wander up front and pull my phone out of my backpack. I tried Brad Lacombe, but ended up in his voice mail, so I took a deep breath and called Rafe.

"You know it's Saturday morning, right?" he asked, yawning.

I squashed my mental image of him sitting up in bed, shirtless, his hair tousled with sleep. "Shouldn't you be up already, cutting big pieces of wood into little ones?"

"Why would I be doing something like that on a morning like this?"

There were too many possible responses to that, so I moved on. "Who do you know that knows a lot about beer?"

"Me."

"No, you just drink a lot of beer. I need to know about brewing. And not home brewing. I have a question about commercial operations. And it would be best if it was someone who works at the same place Brad Lacombe works."

"You don't ask much, do you?" He snorted. "But you did call the right person, because I know the exact person you need to talk to. Jake Yurgelaitis. Hang on, I'll get you his number."

As I sat on the edge of the console, Eddie jumped onto my lap and started purring. I half stood, Eddie clinging to my legs, and reached for the pad of paper and pen that lived in the computer desk. I sat back down and wrote as Rafe rattled off the number. "Thanks," I said. "Will it help or hurt to say I got his phone number from you?"

"Good question," Rafe said. "I won fifty bucks off him last week at poker, but he took me for sixty the week before, so I figure he still owes me ten—"

A loud *crash!* came through the phone. "Are you okay?" My breath caught tight in my throat.

"Me, yes," he said. "Not so sure about this light fixture, though."

"You're working? I thought I woke you up."

"Never said that. Silly you for making assumptions. You know you have a tendency to do that, right?"

And a tendency for spending the rest of my life alone. He started to say something else, but I cut him off. "Gotta go. Talk to you later." I pulled in a deep breath to clear my head and heart and punched in the number for Jake Yurgelaitis. When he answered, I said, "Hi, my name is Minnie Hamilton, and Rafe Niswander told me you're the guy to talk to about commercial beer operations."

"Niswander?" Jake asked. "What's he been saying about me?"

"That you took sixty bucks off him playing poker a couple of weeks ago."

He laughed. "But did he tell you he got fifty off me last week?"

"Actually, he told me that first."

"Sounds like Rafe," he said, and I could hear the smile in his voice. "What's the question?"

I gripped the phone tight. "In a commercial brewing operation, would it be possible for a nonemployee to intentionally contaminate a batch of beer?"

Jake didn't say anything at first. Then, he slowly said, "Are you talking about what I think you're talking about?"

Belatedly, it occurred to me that since Jake and Brad worked at the same place, they were likely friends. On the other hand, they could be enemies and maybe it was Jake who—I cut off my thoughts and asked, "Could you please just tell me?"

"Okay," he said after a pause. "First off, it depends on how tight your security is. Most places up here are pretty casual, so I'd say the odds are good someone could get inside a building without too much trouble. To actually contaminate a batch, you'd have to time things close, because the beer is tested every step of the way."

"But it could be done?"

"Well . . ." He hesitated. "Sure."

That was good, but I needed more. "Would it be hard? I mean, could someone who's never worked in a brewery do it?"

"I'd say so. It would take a little know-how, but someone could probably figure out how by spending a couple of hours on the Internet."

After thanking him, I ended the call and started another one.

"Hey," Josh said. "Don't tell me that bookmobile laptop is down again. I spent half the day yesterday doing the upgrade."

"It's fine." As far as I knew. "I have a question. Did you hear about all the servers at Bowen Manufacturing going down?"

"Yeah. Kind of weird. That shouldn't happen."

Exactly. I pressed on. "Could someone have done that intentionally? Someone who didn't work there?"

"Depends on their security measures."

It was déjà vu all over again. "But it could be done?"

There was a hesitation about the same length as the one with Jake. "Sure. If you knew what you were doing."

"What if you only kind of knew what you were doing?"

He snorted. "Then it might be even easier."

"Seriously?"

"No. You'd have to know something about computer servers, but if you had half a brain and knew what kind of servers they had, you could probably do some Internet surfing and figure out what to do. Might take a few hours, but it could be done."

I thanked him, ended the call, and sat there, thinking.

"Minnie?" Julia asked.

Blinking away the web of assumptions I was spinning, I got to my feet, deposited Eddie on the headrest, and went to do my job.

As soon as the returned bookmobile books were hauled through the snow and into the library and the bookmobile was tucked in for the night, Julia headed off and Eddie and I made our way to my car. Just as I was buckling the carrier in, my phone rang. It wasn't anyone in my contacts list, but it was a local number and seemed familiar.

"Minnie?" a man asked. "This is Jake Yurgelaitis. We talked earlier today."

Rafe's beer guy. "Sure. What's up?"

"Well, your question about maybe an outsider contaminating the beer got me wondering, so I started looking at the video from our security cameras for the week before those people got sick."

Video. Security video. Why hadn't I thought to ask if they had security cameras? Mainly because it didn't seem to me that beer was worth protecting, but I knew millions, if not billions, of people disagreed with me. "The police haven't looked at those?"

"Why would they?" he asked. "No one thought there was anything going on. Until now anyway."

The world went still. "You saw something?"

"These cameras only activate when there's movement, so it really didn't take long to review the files, but yeah, I saw a guy I've never seen before climb the stairs to the top of that tank. I couldn't see what he was doing—his back was to the camera the whole time he was up there—but when he came down the stairs, I got a good look at his face."

My chest was tight and I reminded myself to breathe. "What did he look like?" My words tumbled out. "Young? Old? Fat? Thin? Unique tattoo?" Preferably one with a name and an address.

"Old," Jake said promptly. "He was using a cane."

That narrowed it down a little, but the fastest-growing demographic in this part of Michigan was the upper age bracket. "But you saw his face," I said. "Do you think you'd know him again if you saw him?"

"You bet," Jake said confidently. "On one side he had this thing going on with his skin, like he'd had nerve damage or something. And his eyes didn't track together. It was kind of creepy, watching it."

Bob Blake? What on earth would he be doing there?

My brisk walking pace slowed as the connections finally snapped into place with a solid *click*. Donna's neighbor had said Simon Faber had gone through all sorts of surgeries, including orthopedic, eye, and plastic. Bob Blake had difficulties walking and had something odd with his face and his eye.

All of which meant, at least to me if not to law enforcement and the court system, that Bob Blake was Simon Faber.

And this meant that Simon Faber was Leese's new client. The client she was going to meet with on a Saturday, but which one? Today was Saturday. Was Leese going to be alone with the man who'd killed her father, the man who'd sabotaged the careers of her brother and sister? No. No no no . . .

I thanked Jake for his call, asked him to save the video for the police, cut him off practically in midsentence, and trying not to panic, called Leese.

"Hello, this is Leese Lacombe," said her voice mail.

"Call me as soon as you get this," I said. "It's an emergency." I tried her land line and got the same response. I looked at Eddie, who was sitting so close to the front of his carrier that his fur was sticking out through the wire gate.

"I have to go out to Leese's house," I told him. "What do you want to do? Go home to an empty boardinghouse"—because Aunt Frances and Otto were headed to Traverse City for a concert at the City Opera House—"or go for a drive in the snow?"

"Mrrowww!" he said.

"Glad you agree," I said, starting the car and turning the defroster on high. "No time like the present to remember how to drive in the snow. Steer in the direction of the skid, brake gently, anticipate what the other guy is doing. All that." I popped the trunk and rummaged around for the snow brush, finding it underneath a folding chair and next to the jumper cables.

By the time I cleared the hood, front windshield, roof, rear windshield, and dropped the brush into the backseat, the car was warm and toasty. "Timing is everything," I told Eddie, who, judging from the tone of his snores, agreed completely.

Driving my small sedan through five inches of wet, heavy, slushy snow was far different from driving the bookmobile, and I used the brakes tentatively as I approached the intersections.

"This isn't so bad," I said to an uncaring Eddie. "I'm glad you have such confidence in my driving skills that you can sleep through all of this. Some cats would be all tensed up and whining."

"Mrr," he said through what I assumed was a yawn.

I glanced over and saw that he'd repositioned himself and the tip of his nose was now sticking out between the wires. "Nice look. Could you possibly look any dorkier than you are looking right now?"

"Mrr."

"Wow, I could have sworn you said you could, in fact, look even dorkier, but I don't see how . . . oh, geez . . ." I stopped having a one-sided conversation with my cat and focused on my driving. A deer had tiptoed out of the woods and was standing in the middle of the road.

I tapped the brakes and felt the metallic rush of adrenaline surge through my body. The deer, a buck with at least six points on his antlers, stared straight at me.

"Move!" I shouted.

Either he heard me, or far more likely, he had already decided it was time to move, because he suddenly leapt into action. His hooves skittered on the road's snowy surface but eventually found traction, and he sped off the road and into the same trees from whence he'd come.

"Mrr!"

"Sorry," I muttered. "Didn't mean to yell. It's just that we almost hit a deer and . . . oh, never mind." Since he hadn't seen the deer, talking to him about it would make even less sense than our normal conversations.

For the rest of the ride out to Leese's house, though, my thoughts were a little jangled. Coming so close to hitting the deer had unnerved me; it was the closest I'd ever come. I'd lived Up North more than four years and everyone told me it was only a matter of time before I hit one, but I was planning on being the first resident of Tonedagana County to never ever hit a deer in her entire life.

"Of course, that's assuming I live here the rest of my life." The thought was a new one. I shook my head, but the idea stuck. There was no real reason for me to stay. Assistant library director jobs turned up all over the country at regular intervals. I might not be able to work driving a bookmobile into the mix—okay, almost certainly I wouldn't be able to—but you never knew.

"What's left for me here?" I murmured. The boardinghouse would soon be no more. Aunt Frances was getting married and wouldn't need my company. Kristen's single status was also on the edge of change. Jennifer was settling into place as library director, and she seemed intent on making so many changes that I could easily anticipate a future in which Minnie didn't play a part. And since Rafe was never going to be more than my friend, maybe it was time for me to think about moving.

I was young and almost debt-free. If I wanted to travel, if I wanted to live in another part of the country, now was the time. After all, I had no real reason to stay.

"Except I don't want to go," I said out loud.

Not in the least. Travel was all well and good, and as soon as I finished my last student loan payment, I wanted to plan a trip to Wales, with the primary intent of visiting Hay-on-Wye, a town famous for its plethora of bookstores. "Just imagine," I told Eddie. "A town of fifteen hundred people that has more than twenty bookstores. How cool is that? Then I want to visit all the horse race courses from the Dick Francis books. And remember when I read *84, Charing Cross Road*? I wonder if there really is something at that address. What do you think? Want to come along to find out?"

"Mrr," said my cat.

I smiled, then felt a wave of sadness. Who would travel with me? Though I had no real problem traveling alone, it would be more fun to go with someone. But who?

"Stop it," I told myself as I flicked on the turn signal to make a left into Leese's driveway. This was no time to feel sorry for myself. Leese and Brad and Mia were the ones who mattered at this point. I needed to stop the self-pity and focus on the situation at hand.

"Hey, look," I said, even though Eddie couldn't see much more than the car's console. "Someone's here."

"Mrr."

"How can I tell? There are lights on in the front room and there are some weird-looking footprints angling out of the tire tracks in the driveway and leading to the front door." Not only did the footprints look strange, but the very existence of footprints was odd because there was no car in the driveway. Maybe it was a neighbor, or—I had it!—an elderly client who had been dropped off by a caretaker or a loving family member. And that was why Leese hadn't answered the phone; she was busy doing lawyer stuff.

It was about time something good happened to Leese and I was smiling as the car slid to a stop.

"Okay, pal." I unbuckled my seat belt. "This shouldn't take long, so—"

"Mrr!"

"You'll be fine in here. It's not that cold out. Besides, you have a fur coat and—"

"Mrr!!"

My shoulders went up in a vain effort to cover my ears and protect them from the piercing sound of my cat's shrieks. "Eddie, geez, will you—"

"MMMMMRRRRRRRR!!!"

"Fine," I snapped. "I'll bring you with me, okay?"

He instantly subsided. "Mrr," he said quietly.

I shook my head as I unbuckled his carrier. "Some days it's really hard to believe you don't understand a word that I'm saying. Okay, maybe you understand 'kitty,' and your name, and I think you have a good idea what the word 'no' means, even if you pay no attention whenever I say it to you. And you know 'treat' and 'outside.'"

We were now out in the actual outside, and inside was clearly a better place to be. A stiff wind was blowing out of the northwest, bringing with it pellets of snow that beat against my face.

"N-not v-very nice out here," I said, my words coming out in a stuttering shiver. I'd dressed appropriately for a bookmobile day in late October, not for walking into the teeth of the season's first winter storm. We reached Leese's back door and I knocked, though if she was with a client in the front office, she might not hear. I hesitated about barging inside, but a thumping buffet of wind convinced me to move before Eddie and I became casualties of the storm.

I opened the door, hurried inside, and closed the door behind us.

"Leese?" I called. "It's just Minnie." And Eddie, but I didn't feel the need to announce that, especially if she was with a client.

There was no answering reply.

Huh.

Well, maybe she and her client were deep in a serious discussion and didn't want to be interrupted. I stood there, listening, and heard nothing except the hum of Leese's refrigerator.

"Now what?" I asked.

Eddie, however, had no words of advice.

"That's a first," I muttered as I walked up the few steps to the kitchen. I set the cat carrier down and gave my cat a long look. If I left him in the carrier, he was bound to start howling again, and I didn't want to interrupt Leese's consultation.

I set the carrier on the floor and unlatched the door. "Be good," I said, and set him free.

Eddie, being Eddie, continued to stay inside. As I watched, he pushed himself into the back corner and made himself small. Which is a hard thing for a thirteen-pound cat to do, but cats are amazing creatures.

I went to the cupboard for a bowl, added water, and

put it in front of Eddie, who didn't even sniff at it. I rolled my eyes at my contrary cat, returned to the cupboard, and got myself a glass of water.

Still, I didn't hear a sound from the front room.

Was it possible that Leese had gone somewhere and left the lights on? It didn't seem likely, but the complete silence was getting on my nerves. I tried to remember what the tire tracks in the snow had looked like, how filled they'd been with snow, but I'd been so busy with my thoughts that I hadn't paid much attention.

I stood at the sink, peering out through the window at the driveway, but couldn't tell. A tire track expert I was not. Besides, the afternoon was already growing dark.

"Well."

Leese was gone. She had to be.

Feeling a little like a creepy burglar, waltzing into someone's home when it was empty, I washed my cup, dried it, and put it away. I did the same with Eddie's untouched water bowl and was about to head out when I decided to poke my head into the front office, just to make sure everything was okay.

I crossed the kitchen and the formal dining room, which was functioning more as a library than anything else, and went into the front hallway, where there was a door to her office. It stood slightly open. By this time I was ninety-nine point nine percent sure that Eddie and I were the only ones in the house, so I pushed at the door with little concern.

Leese was sitting behind her desk, staring at me with wide eyes. She yelled something, but I couldn't hear what she said because her mouth was gagged shut. Her ankles were tied to the chair and her hands were tied behind her back.

I rushed forward, hands out, reaching for her gag, wanting to help, wanting to find out if she was okay, when strong male hands grabbed at me from behind.

"Don't move," growled a deep voice.

Chapter 18

I kicked and struggled and bit and clawed, but his strength soon overpowered me. He pulled my wrists behind my back and quickly looped duct tape around them.

"There," he said, panting a little from the exertion. He shoved me forward, making me stumble, and I discovered that it's remarkably hard to recover your balance when your hands are tied behind your back.

He pushed me again, this time into a chair, taped my wrists to the chair's back, then held my kicking legs down as he taped my ankles together. As he crouched to tape my ankles to the chair, he started talking. "What were you doing out there anyway? I thought I was going to die of old age in here, waiting."

I stared at our captor. This was the guy with the walker who had practically bitten my head off when I'd offered to help. He was the guy who had sat near Ash and his mom and me at the Three Seasons. Bob Blake. He must have heard everything we'd said. At some point we'd talked about the Lacombes, but had this guy been there for that part of the conversation? I couldn't remember.

Leese was making noises through her gag of duct tape.

"Now, now," said the man. "None of that. Your loving brother and sister will be here soon enough and then we can all have a nice long chat."

I stared at him. "You're Simon Faber."

"Nicely done, Miss Librarian!" He stood and clapped a few times. "Miss Lacombe here had no idea who I was. She was expecting Bob Blake and that's who she saw coming in her front door." He laughed. "You'd think an attorney would be more aware of the potential for personal danger, but there she stood and welcomed me into her home. If I'd known this would be so easy, I would have done it years ago."

His face suddenly darkened. "She should have recognized me. All of them should have. They ruined my life and now they don't even acknowledge me. What kind of people are these? How could they not know?"

I didn't like how his face was edging from bright red to white. His temper had been more even-handed a moment ago, so in hopes of returning to that more pleasant time, I asked a question. "Done what?"

Faber had been limping toward Leese with his hands balled up into fists, but he stopped and turned. "Sorry?"

"You said if you'd known it would be this easy, that you would have done this years ago. What are you planning on doing?"

"Killing them, of course," he said. "And I apologize in advance, Miss Hamilton, for being the cause of your early death, but collateral damage happens."

"This isn't a military operation," I managed to say.

"Ah, but it is war," Faber replied with a grin, his good humor apparently restored.

I studied him. A happy Faber seemed much less likely to lash out in anger, and at this point, keeping him happy was the only thing I could think of that had any possibility of bringing this situation to a positive conclusion.

"War?" I asked.

"Certainly." He limped to the front window and looked out toward the road. "They should be here by now. If they're Lacombes, I'm sure they're driving too fast, even on roads with so much snow on them. I hope they don't have an accident, not at this late date."

"Why is it war?" I persisted.

He spun. "Look at me," he ordered. "Just look at me."

So I did. He stood shifted to one side, favoring his left leg. His right hand was curled up into an odd shape. One shoulder was hitched slightly higher than the other. His unfocused eye, I realized with a start, wasn't his own; it was a prosthetic. His face, where it wasn't taut from plastic surgery, was creased with lines and wrinkles and I had no idea if they were the result of aging or pain. Or both.

"I'm not even sixty years old," he said, "and I look like I'm eighty. I was thirty-six years old when Dale Lacombe crossed the centerline and hit my car. Thirty-six. The prime of my life! My peak earning years still ahead of me. Decades of activity. And what do I get instead? Years of surgeries, years of pain, years of suffering, and half the time I can't even walk without the use of that thing."

He glared over my shoulder and I turned my head just enough to see his walker standing in the corner of the room.

"So, yes, Miss Hamilton," he said, "this is war. They invaded my life the moment of the accident, and they're all four to blame. Dale Lacombe said so himself. They took away everything I'd accomplished and turned it to dust, and I intend to do the same thing to each of them."

His face firmed with resolution. I quickly asked, "What had you accomplished?"

"Not nearly enough," he snarled. "I could have done great things. I was on my way to fame and fortune when this happened. My fiancée left me and my parents went to an early grave trying to take care of me. I'm alone and I know exactly who to blame."

I suspected I wasn't getting the entire truth, but I suspected even more strongly that this wasn't the time to accuse him of telling a one-sided story. "What kind of things were you working on?"

"What kind?" He blinked. "You want to know what kind of things?"

"Sure." Because I couldn't come up with anything else that would keep him talking that didn't have the name "Lacombe" attached to it, and that would be sure to get his temper going. "Tell me about them. I'd like to know." Sort of.

He pursed his lips. "At the time of the accident, I was top sales guy for the biggest computer company in the country. But that was only temporary. I had plans and they were about to come true."

"What kind of plans?"

"I was having conversations with venture capitalists," he said. "I had plans for half a dozen new businesses. All it would take was a little bit of seed money and I'd be on my way."

And I was growing more and more certain the guy was delusional. If he'd owned a place on Janay Lake with money left over for cars, he must have made a good living as a sales rep, but what he'd said sounded unrealistic.

"Wow," I said, doing my best not to sound sarcastic. "I'm not sure I've ever had one good idea about a start-up business, let alone six. Opening a bookstore is about as original as I'd probably get."

"Bookstore." He snorted. "No one reads anymore. I don't know how you keep your job."

The verdict was in: this guy was definitely delusional. I smiled politely. "Your ideas were better, I'm sure."

"Electronics," he said. "Twenty-three years ago, I knew where the world was going to go. All I needed was capital. Putting songs into digital form and selling them? That was my idea first."

"Really?" I made my face show surprise. From what I'd been told, a number of people had had that idea, but it had taken a while for technology to catch up with the dreams.

"Count on it. I had dozens of ideas that were stolen from me. Laptops were my idea. Those robotic vacuum cleaners were my idea. Cell phones were my idea." He waved his arms around. "Look around. Every personal technological device you see was my idea first."

"Tablets?" I asked. "Was that idea stolen from you, too?"

Faber frowned. "What? Don't be ridiculous. Those are a fad." He switched his attention back to the window. "I see headlights." He glared at me as he limped by the chair. "I should have taped your mouth shut. Keep quiet when they come in or I'll make your death long and lingering instead of fast and almost painless."

Almost? I couldn't breathe for a moment. This guy was a lunatic. A killer. And he was practically salivating at the chance to do it again.

I waited until he'd made his way to the front hallway. "Are Brad and Mia really on their way here?" I whispered to Leese.

She shook her head.

I closed my own eyes for a grateful half second, then snapped them open again. Either the headlights Faber was seeing were imaginary or there was a passing car. Then I had another thought. If Faber had forced Leese to make a phone call, maybe she'd done so to someone with whom she shared some sort of emergency code and that person was mustering a law enforcement team and rushing to our rescue.

"Is anyone else coming?" I asked. "Police?"

Once again, she shook her head.

Well, at least Mia and Brad wouldn't be walking into Faber's trap. "Can you move your hands at all?"

She nodded.

"Seriously?" Excitement flooded through me. "How much? No, you can't answer that with a yes or no. Do you think you can get them free soon?"

I could see the tape across her mouth crease as she smiled and nodded.

"Great." I felt a smidge of hope. Maybe we would get out of this in one piece. "Do you have a plan for when you get your hands loose?"

Her shoulders sagged a little and she shook her head.

After a short pause, I whispered, "Right. We'll work

on this together. I don't suppose you have a gun anywhere? No, that's okay, we can do without." Somehow. "There has to be something we can use as a weapon."

With an increasing sense of urgency, we both scanned the room for possibilities. The desk lamp? Maybe, but its aerodynamic capabilities were limited. Though Leese's laptop was heavier, it would be even harder to grasp, especially if her hands had, if mine were any indication, been losing circulation for some time.

"How about a letter opener?" I whispered.

Leese's eyebrows went up fast, then down again slowly. She nodded, but gestured with her chin to her desk.

"In a drawer?" I asked, and wasn't surprised when she nodded. "That'll work," I said confidently, or as confidently as I could manage at the time. "When you get free, give me a sign. I'll distract him and—"

Faber's returning footsteps cut me off to silence.

"Where are they?" he snarled at Leese. "You said they'd be here in thirty minutes and it's been over an hour."

"The roads are slippery," I said quickly, because I'd seen Leese's chin go up. We did not need her to go all defiant and let Faber know Brad and Mia were not en route. If he knew that, what was there to stop him from killing us right then and there?

A teensy part of my brain started to wonder how he planned to kill us. I'd had a recent and very bad experience with a long sharp knife and hoped that wasn't his plan. Of course, if I had to die an untimely death, did I have a preferred method? It wasn't anything I'd ever thought about in a serious way.

"They live here," Faber snapped. "They should know how to drive in the snow."

I nodded. "Sure, but this is the first snowfall. People forget the details."

He studied me for so long I had a hard time not squirming. "Is this a delaying tactic of some sort?"

Of course it was. "Just giving an explanation."

"Librarian." Faber grunted. "You probably give explanations every day. Here's a question for you. Explain why I'm here now, today, twenty-three years after the accident. Explain that, Miss Marion Librarian."

I hesitated. Had to, really, because I had no idea.

"Explain!" he screamed, and it came to me with a calm clarity that, for the first time in my life, I could well be talking to someone who was truly insane.

With no experience to guide me and no training, I had to rely on my instincts. My first instinct, which was to dive into research mode at the computer, wasn't useful in the least, so I went to the second tier of thinking out loud. I usually had Eddie for this—

Eddie! Where was my Eddie?

I pushed that fear away and tried to concentrate. This was suddenly even harder to do than it had been, because Faber limped over to stand behind Leese. He put his hands, strong from years of using a walker, around her throat and smiled.

"Explain," he said in a normal voice, "or I'll kill her right here and now."

My brain, which I'd always relied on to give me answers when I needed them, blanked out completely. All I could see was Leese's fear and those fingers pressing deeper and deeper into her neck.

"Something changed for you," I said quickly. "Something went wrong."

"Correct, but a little vague." He tut-tutted. "And here I thought librarians always had all the answers."

We did, but we usually had some resources at our disposal and weren't being faced with the imminent murder of a friend. I had to say something, so I started pulling guesses out of thin air. "Someone died. Your mother or father."

Faber kept pressing.

"You had a disappointment."

"My life has been a disappointment for the last twenty-odd years," he said. "Try harder."

Leese's face was turning a nasty shade of red. Guesses spilled out of me. "You lost your job. You can't find work. You're going bankrupt. You have cancer. Your house burned down. Your house was flooded and insurance won't cover it. Your driver's license was revoked."

Through all of my increasingly stupid theories, Faber smiled and gripped even tighter.

And then, with a sudden leap of certainty, I knew. "Your doctors have told you there's nothing more they can do for you. You're going to be in pain the rest of your life and there's no hope for improvement. The only thing that's going to make you feel better is getting your revenge on the Lacombes."

"Took you long enough." Faber's voice was back to a snarl, but he released Leese. Her breaths rushed in and out, and I watched helplessly as she attempted to swallow.

A cold anger settled down onto me. Yes, the man had problems, and I was sorry for the pain he'd been enduring for years, and which might have been the thing that had twisted his mind, but no amount of pain could provide justification for what he'd done to Dale and for what he planned to do yet tonight.

Faber smirked at Leese. "You don't look like such a high-and-mighty lawyer anymore, do you?"

More proof that the guy had lost the power of rational thought. Leese was about the least pretentious attorney in the world. Not that I knew all of the world's attorneys, but I'd met more than my fair share, and from that random sampling, I had a good idea of where she landed on the self-aggrandizement scale.

Distraction. What we needed was another reason for Faber to leave the room. Leese needed only a little more time to work her hands free, then she could grab the letter opener, and together we'd subdue Faber.

I fake-opened my eyes wide and darted a look toward the window.

"What do you see?" Faber asked.

"N-nothing."

"You saw headlights, didn't you? Didn't you?" he yelled.

"N-no," I stuttered, and this time it wasn't an act, because the reality of our situation was taking hold in the deepest parts of me. This man meant to kill us.

"You're lying," he said. "This is what happens to liars." He grabbed the roll of duct tape, ripped off a piece, and slapped it across my mouth. "Now sit tight, girls, and I'll be right back," he said cheerfully. "And this time I'll bring back a nice surprise." He limped off, whistling.

A surprise? There was no way that was going to be good. I started pulling at my bonds the second Faber left the room. Kicking my legs, pulling my arms, kicking and pulling, kicking, pulling . . .

The sound of the front door opening caught me up short. Leese and I exchanged glances. Was this guy's head so messed up that he'd just left? Maybe he had some bizarre neurological problem and his memory was short-circuiting. Maybe he'd switched from revenge mode to forgetful mode and he'd just left. Maybe . . .

Then the door shut, and his dragging footsteps came closer.

"There you two are," he said. "So glad you're both still here. The party wouldn't be the same without you."

He sounded like he was smiling, but I didn't look at his face, couldn't look, really, because the only thing I could see was the bright red plastic five-gallon gas can in his hand. And from the way he was leaning over, the very full five-gallon gas can.

"I'm afraid," Faber said, "that the party has to get started without Brad and little Mia. I have to get back to town to finish establishing my alibi. I'm sure you understand. Perhaps this is better in the long run. This way Brad and Mia have to live through the grief of losing their big sister."

He chuckled as he took the cap off. "And I'll get to watch. Did you know that I'm a brewing consultant? I must be, since I have a website and a business card that says I am. I'm also a nationally recognized IT expert." He sighed. "People are so trusting. Tell them you're up here on a long vacation and would like to see their operations and before you know it, you're being given a personal tour."

The smell of gas was wafting out of the can. My memory blinked in and out for a moment. Red plastic gas cans. Lawnmowers. Cut grass. Boats. The marina. Eddie. Rafe . . .

"Are we ready?" he asked. "Oh, dear. Neither one of you can talk, can you? Such a shame, but there's nothing to be done about that."

Of course there was. He could pull the tape off our mouths. He could also unwrap the tape from our wrists and ankles and go on his merry way. He could turn himself in to the police and get his lawyers to plead him as not guilty due to insanity. He could be committed to a psychiatric institution and get proper treatment.

Whistling again, Faber started sloshing gas around the room. Onto the area rug. Onto the hardwood floor. Across the wooden blinds. Across the papers on Leese's desk. Across Leese herself. He splattered gas across the front of the bookshelves and into the waste-basket. Then he held the gas can upside down and walked backward to the front hallway, creating a long thin trail of flammable liquid.

As I watched, still doing my best to break free, it occurred to me that five gallons was a lot of gas. Two would probably have done the trick. Five was overkill.

The front door opened once again and I heard the hollow sound of the empty gas can being tossed out into the snow. "All set." Faber limped into the room and wrinkled his nose at the smell. "Gas is malodorous stuff, isn't it? Well, at least you won't have to smell it for long." He laughed. "Miss Librarian, I know I said you'd have a quick death, but guess what?" he asked. "I changed my mind." Shrill laughter pealed out of him.

It sounded more like a ululation from a wild creature than anything created by a human being. One part of me was revolted by the sound; another part felt something almost like pity. That part, however, was quickly quashed by my primary emotion, that of white-hot anger.

"Now." Faber dusted his hands. "I'd like to say a few last words to Miss Lacombe. You, your siblings, and most especially your father, ruined my life. To even things up, I killed your dear father and—oh, I didn't tell you that story, did I?" He tsked at himself.

"As I said before, these things are so easy. I simply e-mailed him, asking him to meet me . . . well, not me as Simon Faber, of course, but me as Mike Davis, a prospective client, at one of his building sites. It was understandable that I would like to see his work, you see, but I was on a tight schedule and could only meet him at that particular moment, which happened to be a very unreasonable hour."

Faber chortled. "I'd chosen the tallest building, arrived early, and made my way to the top floor. When he arrived, I called to him and he came up. From there it was a simple push." He smiled at the memory. "The hardest part was moving him into my vehicle and then into yours, Ms. Lacombe. A dead weight, indeed."

Laughing, he moved to the room's corner and took hold of his walker. "Back to my earlier remarks. In order to even up a life turned to ashes, I killed your father and set out to ruin the reputations of his children. Putting his body in your truck, contaminating Brad's precious beer, and destroying young Mia's hard work. But killing Dale was so exquisitely satisfying that I've decided to continue in that vein. The best plan is one that can be adjusted on the fly, don't you agree?"

I did, actually, but it pained me to agree with anything Faber said.

"Now." He gave a perky grin. "Here's how things are going to work. Gas burns quickly and I need time to get away, so I'm going to light a candle by the front door. I've put some tinder around its base, and when the candle burns down, it'll light the tinder, which will light the gas, which will flame up nicely."

A candle? He was going to light a candle! Hope flared inside me. A candle would take time to burn down. Leese would get herself loose and put out the flame before it—

Faber reached into his pocket, searched around, and held up a birthday candle. "Just right for a party, I'd say. And though, thanks to the Lacombe family, I can't walk very fast, I'm sure I'll have time to walk to where I've hidden my car before the fire grows large enough for the neighbors to see and call the fire department. Plenty of time for me to drive away and not be seen, especially if I don't turn on the headlights."

He shuffled toward the door, then paused. "Have a good night, Miss Lacombe, Miss Librarian. Hope things don't get too hot for you." Cackling, he made his way to the hallway.

I cocked my head, listening. Maybe he was too far gone to be thinking clearly, maybe he'd leave and forget to light the candle, maybe he'd—

Leese and I both flinched at the sound of a striking match. "Ahh," Faber said. "Nicely done, if I say so myself. Toodle-oo!" The front door opened slowly and closed gently, so as not to let the cold air rush in and blow out the candle.

Silence settled over us, a silence so thick and deep I wondered if my ability to hear had been consumed by the sheer fright that was blooming inside me. Then I heard something.

On the other side of the room, Leese's shoulders were jerking up and down and back and forth. She was trying to get her hands loose, and what was I doing? Nothing but wondering about hearing loss. Leese was a far better person than I was, and it was just too stupid if she had to die because I couldn't be bothered to think of a way out of this mess.

"Mrr?"

I turned my head as far as I could, but didn't see my cat. If I'd trained Eddie properly, I could have instructed him to knock the candle over onto the floor, away from the gas. Of course, since I couldn't even figure out a way to keep Eddie off the kitchen counter, and since I was bound and gagged, that would have been difficult, but still.

"Mff."

This time it was Leese making the noise. Her shoulders had a wider range of movement; she must be getting close. I was making a little bit of headway with my feet, but my wrists were stuck together tight.

"Mff!"

Straining with my legs, working hard with my arms, I looked up at Leese. Only she wasn't looking at me; she was staring past me with eyes open so wide the whites were visible all the way around her irises.

There was only one thing that could make her look like that. I whipped my head around, turning far enough so I could see the door and saw . . . nothing. Then my brain jolted. A glow. There was a glow of light near the base of the door. A flaring glow that meant the birthday candle had reached the tinder and was burning it down.

With a horrified fascination, I watched as the glow grew and grew and then began to fade as tinder burned itself out. Then, just when I'd begun to hope that Faber's plan had gone wrong, I heard a *whoof!*

"Mffff!"

I knew Leese was shouting, knew there was a ripping noise, knew her hands were coming free, but there was too much gas poured in the room, too much on her, too much everywhere, and she wouldn't be able to get away in time, she would be burned, her clothes would burn, her hair would burn, she would . . .

Gathering everything I had, all my strength, all my weight, all my energy, and what was left of my courage, I flung myself to the side, leaning and straining with every muscle in my body, and tipped my chair, crashing to the floor hard, using my body to block the rushing run of fire.

Heat seared the small of my back and I knew the flames were eating away at my clothes. I rolled toward the fire, trying to squash it out, afraid that my efforts weren't enough, afraid that Leese was going to die, afraid that Eddie was going to die, afraid that—

A heavy weight was thrown over me and I suddenly couldn't see anything. "Mff mfff!" Leese shouted. "Mfff mfff!!"

I had no idea what she'd said, but I couldn't respond anyway since tape still covered my mouth and something was pinning me to the floor.

There was another ripping tape noise. "Hold still!"

Oh. Well, that I could do.

"The fire's almost out," she panted. "Hang on."

A few seconds later, the weight was gone and I could see again. Leese, still with her ankles taped to the chair, was on her hands and knees next to me, the quilt that had formerly hung on the office wall piled in a heap.

"He only got gas on the corner," she said, nodding at her grandmother's handiwork.

The quilt was a mess of scorch marks and blackened holes. "I'm so sorry," I said. "It's ruined."

Leese, who was untaping her ankles, snorted. "You should see your coat."

"It's just a coat," I said. "No sentimental value attached."

"Bottom line, that quilt saved our lives. Grandma would be pleased."

She kicked free of the tape and the chair and went to work on me. In short order, my hands were their own again, and so were my feet. Together, we scrambled to stand. "We have to get out of here," I said, grabbing her hand and pulling her toward the door. "It's too dangerous." Both from the danger of fire and the danger of Faber returning.

After one glance around her office, Leese came along with me.

"Eddie?" I called. "Here, kitty kitty kitty."

My cat, for once, actually came when I called, trotting into the formal dining room. I stooped to snatch him up, carried him into the kitchen, and pushed him into his carrier. "Let's take my car," I called to Leese over my shoulder. "I'm in front of your garage door."

"Be right out."

I picked up the carrier and started down the steps. "Leese Lacombe, get out of the house this minute."

"Behind you, I promise."

"If she's not," I said to Eddie, "as soon as I get you in the car, I'm coming back inside to drag her out."

"Mrr!"

We charged outside, where it was now full dark, and for the first time ever, I put Eddie into the backseat. "Hope you understand," I said, pulling the seatbelt around the carrier. "Because though you're on the biggish side for a cat, you're not anywhere near the size of a normal human, let alone Leese. She wouldn't fit back here for beans."

As I shut the back door, the dark shape of my friend came pounding down the stairs. She ran the few steps to my car and we got in, slamming our respective doors simultaneously.

I started the engine and pressed the gas pedal down hard. The tires spun in the slick snow. Muttering a curse, I let off the gas, used the transmission to rock the car back and forth, and slowly pulled forward through Leese's turnaround.

"Do you have your phone?" I asked. "Call nine-one-one."

"Can I use yours? Mine's in my purse."

She'd brought something with her from the house; I'd assumed it was her purse, but maybe she'd grabbed whatever she valued most, just in case the gas did ignite and her house burned to the ground. "Sure," I said, and directed her to my backpack, down by her feet.

"Mrr."

"Sorry about the smell, Eddie," I said. The car had almost reached the road and I was starting to turn right, heading for the safety of Chilson. "I know we reek of gasoline, but we didn't have much choice, and—"

"Mrr!"

"Will you quit?" I asked. "We have a guest in the car, you know. She's not used to your whining."

"MRR!!"

This time he was so loud my entire body cringed. My foot came off the gas and the car slowed. "Eddie, will you—" Then I noticed something. "Leese, there aren't any tire tracks on the road. Not any other than mine."

Her quick mind caught up to me in half a heartbeat. "Faber didn't come this way."

Our heads turned to the left. "What's down there?" I asked.

"Nothing," Leese said slowly. "Not a single thing. This isn't technically a dead end road, though. It turns into a seasonal road a quarter mile down, but it connects to another road on the other side of the ridge."

I'd lived in Tonedagana County long enough to know what that meant. "What kind of shape is it in?" Seasonal roads could be well-maintained gravel versions, or they could be little more than two tracks made by the occasional passing car.

"Horrible," she said. "I walked it last week and called the road commission because there was a fallen tree across it. They said they might get to it before spring, but wouldn't make any promises."

My foot hovered over the gas pedal. "He's probably still down there," I said.

"Yes." Leese stared at the snow.

"I mean, where else could he be?"

"Yes," she said.

"He could be hurt." I waited, but she didn't say anything more. "Call nine-one-one," I said. "Tell them about the gas in your house." I stared straight ahead. "Tell them we're on our way to check on the guy who did it, because he might be having a medical emergency."

"Yes," Leese said.

For a long moment, neither one of us moved. Simon Faber had killed my friend's father. He had tried to ruin her sister's, her brother's, and her own reputation. He'd done his best to kill her and had almost burned down her house. Now it was likely that he had either fallen in the snow or crashed his car or . . . or something else that wasn't good. No matter which way you looked at it, Simon Faber had intended to come out of the woods, and hadn't.

Then, at the same time I put my foot on the gas and turned left, Leese picked up my phone and pushed the three numbers.

Chapter 19

Sunday I spent doing four things: sleeping in, having long discussions with a variety of different law enforcement personnel, having dinner and dessert with Kristen, and looking online for a new coat to replace the one that I'd ruined the day before by having the foresight to use it to stop the fire instead of my face or my hair.

That had been sheer luck, actually, because I certainly hadn't planned my trajectory to the floor, but a white-faced Ash had said in a shaky voice that I'd probably done some fast calculations in my head without realizing it. I'd smiled, patted my former boyfriend on the arm, and let him keep his illusions.

Detective Inwood didn't say much the entire time I was in the sheriff's office, but when he was done taking notes, he stood and gave me a long look, which bore a strong resemblance to the way my dad used to look at me when I'd stayed up too late reading Dickens.

I braced myself, but all he did was sigh. Which was what my dad had usually ended up doing, too. "Did you notice?" I asked.

His eyebrows went up as he slid his notebook into his jacket pocket. "A little more specific, please."

Pointing at the table, I said, "I sat on this side." All the times I'd sat in the interview room I'd sat in the same spot. And since I'd spent a lot of time waiting for the detective to show up on previous occasions, I'd also spent a fair amount of time being bored, and had stared at the water stain in the ceiling tiles, eventually turning it into a dragon shape. I'd once mentioned this to Inwood and he'd commented that I should sit on the other side of the table and take another look.

I pointed at the ceiling. "You were right; it's not a dragon. It's a cat."

Inwood looked at me. "A cat."

"Well, sure." I kept pointing. "There's the tail, the ears, and the chin. What else could it be?"

Detective Inwood shook his head, sighed, and left the room.

Sheriff Richardson, who'd been sitting in on the last few minutes of my interview with the detective, said, "I have no idea what you two are talking about. It's obviously a loggerhead shrike."

I wasn't sure if she was joking or if she was dead serious, so I smiled briefly and asked what she thought the chances were of Simon Faber being incarcerated in a psychiatric facility instead of the prison's general population.

"He'll be evaluated by two doctors," she said. "If he's declared to be NGRI, the next step is to look for an open bed."

I worked out the acronym in my head; Not Guilty by Reason of Insanity. "Do you think he'll be declared insane?" I persisted.

The sheriff looked at me with a flat stare. "Minnie, I have no idea. Please don't ask me to predict the future. My crystal ball has been on back order for years." Then she sighed and said, "But if you'd like, I'll follow his case and let you know what happens."

"Yes, please," I said meekly. And true to her word, she did keep me apprised of Faber's trek through the justice system. It took some time, but he was eventually sent to a secure facility downstate that would be his home for the rest of his life.

Monday, I'd scheduled myself to work from noon until the library closed at eight. Mid-morning, I drove my car to a place Ash had recommended for detailing—which was Guy Code for a good, thorough cleaning—and walked the rest of the way to the library, pleased that they'd promised to find a way to get the stench of gasoline out of the car.

I swung my arms as I walked, happy that the sidewalks were already clear of snow. I was also pleased to see teensy breaks in the clouds that, even as I watched, grew wider and wider, showing the blue sky above.

I was near to smiling when I walked in the front door. Dale Lacombe's killer would kill no more, Leese, Brad, and Mia would be exonerated of all offenses, and winter was just around the corner. Life was good, except for the fact that I was going to die alone because the love of my life didn't know I existed (in a romantic sense), but I'd find a way to soldier on. With Eddie at my side, the bookmobile and I would range over new horizons, bringing books and knowledge to all. We'd sing songs of courage and bravery, and every syllable Eddie sang would sound the same: "Mrr."

"What are you so happy about?" Holly asked. She

was standing in the doorway to the break room, holding a mug of coffee in one hand and a plate of chocolate chip cookies in the other.

Since I couldn't very well tell her the truth, I said vaguely, "It's getting nice outside."

"Here." Holly handed me the mug and said, "You have a lot to tell us and you're going to need food before you get to the end."

I plucked one cookie off the plate. "How much of the story would you like?"

"All of it," Josh said, poking his head out of the break room. "And hurry. I'm supposed to talk to Jennifer's software guy in ten minutes."

The new software. I'd forgotten. My perky mood deflated a bit, but I pumped it back up by taking a bite of Holly's cookie.

Both of them had been well aware of Dale Lacombe's murder, so I moved quickly to how I'd considered a number of suspects and had eventually keyed in on Simon Faber. I skipped over the tied-up-and-almost-burned-to-a-crisp part, and finished off with us turning left out of Leese's driveway instead of right.

Josh rolled his eyes. Talking through a cookie, he said, "I can't believe you did that. I mean I can, because it's just like you to try and help a guy who was trying to kill you, but why didn't you just call nine-one-one and be done with it?"

I flashed back to something Detective Inwood had told me a few months ago. "You are not most people." I was still trying to figure out if that had been a compliment or not.

"Was he hurt?" Holly asked. "Or maybe he fell in the snow. With that walker, it couldn't have been easy to get through."

I shook my head. "He'd made it to the car, but he slid into a ditch, and couldn't get himself out."

After we'd made sure he wasn't injured, Leese stood guard next to his car door, her baseball bat raised and ready if he tried to make any sort of move to escape. The bat had been what she'd stayed back in the house to find because, as she said later, "I'm never going to be caught without a weapon ever again."

I'd directed the emergency vehicles, and Faber had been taken away not long afterward. Leese had gone to stay with Mia until her house could be made safe, and I'd gone back to the boardinghouse and finally enjoyed the bath I'd meant to take days earlier.

Josh stared at me, disbelieving. "She had that bat and didn't even take a crack at the car?"

"He wasn't going anywhere," I said mildly, and changed the subject. It had been an unpleasant few minutes, standing there and waiting for the emergency vehicles to arrive. Faber had gone from violent vocal outbursts to fits of sobbing to speech that sounded completely rational. Then the cycle would start all over again.

I shook the memory away and nodded at the man walking toward us. He was wearing a suit coat and tie and clearly did not belong. "Looks like your sales rep is here."

"Can't wait," Josh muttered.

"Isn't Jennifer supposed to be part of this?" I asked.

He shrugged. "Haven't seen her all morning," he said, and went to meet the sales guy.

"I haven't seen her, either," Holly said. "Maybe she's sick?"

Tsking at her, I said, "It's unkind to sound so hopeful."

Holly had the grace to look ashamed. "It's not that I really want her to be sick. It's just . . . you know."

I smiled. "See you later. It's time to check my e-mails."

And that was why I was the first one to know what had happened to Jennifer. The subject line of her e-mail was odd. "'Open Letter to the Chilson District Library Board,'" I read out loud. "That's weird."

"Dear Board Members," she'd written. "Thank you so much for the opportunity the last few months to be director of the Chilson District Library. However, it is clear that this climate and I are not compatible. Please consider this my resignation letter, effective immediately. I apologize for the short notice, but I cannot possibly stay here any longer. Your assistant director is more than qualified to step in as interim director or to be permanently elevated to director. She did, as I recall, make attempts to warn me about the snow, but I did not understand that eight inches could possibly fall in October! Human beings were not made to survive in this kind of situation. Yours sincerely, Jennifer Walker."

I read the e-mail through once. Then twice. Then a third time.

Reeling, I sat back. Which was when I noticed the subsequent e-mails from the library board members, calling for an emergency meeting at ten thirty, and would Minnie please attend. I glanced at the corner of the computer screen and saw that it was one minute past ten thirty.

I bolted out of my chair and ran upstairs.

"So what did they say?" Kelsey asked. "Are you the new director?"

Four of us were crammed into my office. I'd been

told by the board to talk to every staff member as soon as I could and was doing my best to comply.

"Not a chance," Donna said. "She didn't want the job last summer. She's not going to want it now."

The board had offered me the position, but Donna was right. I still didn't want to be director. Not yet anyway. "They're going to ask their second choice," I said. "Graydon Cain."

Josh scrunched up his face. "What kind of people name their kid Graydon? He's bound to be an uptight suit."

"Worse than Jennifer?" I asked.

His face scrunched even tighter. "We didn't think Jennifer could be worse than Stephen, but she was."

Though that had nothing to do with how Graydon Cain might run the library, I knew what he meant. But since there was nothing I could do about it, I decided not to worry. We'd deal with our new library director when he arrived. Why ruin the next few weeks with fussing over something we couldn't change?

"By the way," I said, "this morning I also found out the library board isn't really interested in that new software Jennifer was pushing."

"Wait. What?" Josh's face unscrunched.

I beamed. "She'd presented a proposal to the board to sell some of our rare books to fund the purchase, but the board told me they weren't in favor." The board president had said he'd told Jennifer the board would listen seriously to everything she brought them and she must have made assumptions from that polite policy.

"Yeah?" Josh grinned and started bouncing on his toes like a six-year-old. "That's cool. That's real cool."

"I'll say." Kelsey blew out a huge sigh. "If I'd had

to learn how to run one more system, my head might have exploded."

Donna's face was a mirror of my own. "The world is righting itself," she said. "It's about time."

Out in the hallway, I heard a familiar shuffle of large feet. I looked pointedly out my open doorway, and my coworkers turned in time to see Mitchell Koyne walking past, his head bent down to read the book he had in his hands.

A sense of peace settled over me, because Donna was correct—the world was indeed righting itself.

Even though I'd slept late two mornings in a row, Saturday's dramatic events caught up with me by the afternoon. Fatigue tugged at my eyes and I lost count of the times I yawned. Just before five o'clock, Holly, Donna, and Kelsey came into my office and stood in front of me in a solid row.

"Go away," Holly said.

I blinked. "Excuse me?"

Donna gave Holly an elbow in the side. "What we're saying is we think you should leave. Go home. We can cover the library until eight. You had a rough weekend, and now that you're going to be interim director again for a while, you're going to need your rest."

"That's right," Kelsey said, nodding. "We can't have you getting sick."

Their concern made my throat tight. "I appreciate your concern, I really do, but—" My protest was cut short by a huge yawn.

"Right," Holly said. "Ladies?"

Kelsey stepped forward and picked my backpack up off the floor. Donna took my old coat from the doorknob and Holly came around the desk, took my hands, and pulled me to my feet. "Leave," she ordered, and gave me a quick hug.

Donna held up my coat and shook it invitingly.

"Doesn't seem like I have much of a choice," I muttered as I slid my arms into the sleeves.

"Hello," Holly said. "That's the whole point. Get out and don't come back until tomorrow."

She was probably right. They all were. "Thanks, you guys," I said. "You're the best."

"Yeah, we know." Holly pushed me in the direction of the lobby. "Git!"

As I pushed open the library door, I was surprised to see the complete absence of snow. The day's sunshine, accompanied by temperatures that had crept up into the mid-fifties, had melted everything. I felt a small pang for Jennifer, who would never know the beauty of northern Michigan in winter, and whispered "Good luck" in her general direction.

Instead of taking the most direct route back to the boardinghouse like a good girl, I decided to walk downtown. It was too nice outside not to take advantage of the last hour of sunlight, and Holly's last directive had been simply to leave the library, not go home and go to bed.

The sun was casting lengthy shadows across the sidewalk, and I was enjoying the sight of my unbelievably long legs when someone called my name.

"Minnie!"

I turned and saw Leese climbing out of her SUV. Her broad face was wearing a smile that was even broader.

"You look happy," I said, understating the obvious.

"Hah!" She took a few long strides and reached out

in my direction. "Come here," she said, wrapping her arms around me. "This is what you get for now." She gave me a smacking kiss on the top of my head.

Squirming a little and wondering if this was how Eddie felt when I snuggled and kissed him, I said into her shoulder, "What did I do this time?"

She gave me one more rib-breaking pulse and released me. "Next time you need a favor, call me. The next ten times you need a favor, call me. Middle of the night, first thing in the morning, right after I get into my pajamas, doesn't matter, I'll come running."

I squinted at her. "At some point I'm going to know what you're talking about, right?"

She laughed. "Fred Sirrine. He called me this morning, and this afternoon he hired me as his estate's attorney. He also said he'll recommend me to all his old fogey friends, his words, not mine."

Fred Sirrine. The name sounded familiar, but . . . then I had it. Former neighbor to the Boggses.

"That's great," I said. "But I didn't do anything. All I did was mention your name."

"Sometimes that's all it takes, especially for the guy who used to have the title 'President of the Americas for Ford Motor Company.'" She gave me another crushing hug, declared everlasting appreciation for my help, and headed into the wine shop.

"Huh," I said to no one in particular. Then I suddenly remembered that, with Jennifer gone, I'd be free to start up the outreach lecture series I'd suggested, with Leese as the first speaker. I took one step after her, but again heard my name.

"Minnie!"

I turned and this time it was Aunt Frances who was

headed toward me. "Hey, there," I said. "Did you hear? I'm interim library director again."

"Old news." She grinned. "I heard that at the post office ten minutes ago." She waved a handwritten envelope. "This is the new news. Picked it up in the box just now."

My eyes tried to read the return address, but she was fluttering it too fast, and I was afraid if I kept trying to read it I'd get motion sickness. "Are you going to tell me what it is, or am I going to have to guess?"

She beamed. "It's from my late husband's cousin Celeste Glendennie. I don't think you've ever met her. She's a second cousin once removed, or is it a third cousin?" Aunt Frances pursed her lips, then shrugged. "Some sort of a cousin. She's been living in Nevada for the last thirty years and she wants to come back to Michigan."

"That's nice," I said.

Aunt Frances laughed. "I'm not to the good part yet. She has agreed, sight unseen except for the pictures and video clips I've e-mailed her, to buy the boardinghouse and to keep it running."

Um. "Does she know . . . I mean . . ."

My aunt laughed. "Yes, dear niece, she is fully aware of the amount of labor involved. She's a sucker for hard work, always has been. Plus she's more than ten years younger than I am."

"What about . . . you know?"

Aunt Frances tipped her head and considered me. "All that college education, a career among books, and yet you still have moments when you're about as articulate as a toddler. And far less articulate than Eddie." She shook her head. "Celeste is well aware of the arrangements of the boardinghouse, spoken and unspoken. She has agreed to continue my matchmaking efforts for at least a year if I help her with the guest selections. After that, it's up to her."

I nodded approvingly. "Well done."

"And," Aunt Frances said, poking me in the shoulder, "she said she won't mind a winter guest as long as said guest doesn't mind her."

On the surface, it sounded good, but I sensed there was more to the story. "And?" I asked, drawing out the word.

My aunt looked at the sky, looked at the sidewalk, and finally looked at me. "She has three little dogs," she said so fast, it sounded almost like one word.

"Three."

"I'm sure they're well behaved," Aunt Frances said. "I can't imagine Celeste having any other kind of dog. She's meticulous about housekeeping and is always concerned about doing the right thing."

She was sounding worse and worse. "Well," I said, putting on a smile. "I'm glad you've found someone in the family to take on the boardinghouse. Everything else is just details; it will all work out."

Aunt Frances blew out a sigh of relief. "I'm glad you think so." She gave me a quick hug. "I'm off to tell Otto the good news. See you later!"

I watched her go and slowly started walking again. Everything around me seemed to be changing. The library was shifting yet another time, and who knew what direction the new director would want to take? Kristen was going to marry Scruffy, and though she protested an undying commitment to her restaurant, with Scruffy based in New York, I could easily imagine her spending more and more time there. Aunt

Frances was going to marry Otto, and the boarding-house was going to be taken over by a cousin with three dogs. Change could be good, but so much all at once was a little overwhelming.

With so much going on in my head, I was afraid I'd absentmindedly walk into the middle of the street and become a traffic hazard, so I wandered down to the waterfront.

In summer, the wide sidewalk would have been crowded with people, strollers, and dogs. On this fall evening so close to winter, even though the sun was out and the air still, the only company I had were a few seagulls and a floating flock of Canada geese settling in for the night.

My aimless steps took me down to the marina, where there were only two boats left in the water. I stopped at the dock where my houseboat had been moored all summer and felt a pang of sadness for the months gone by.

It wasn't regret I was feeling, not precisely. It was more like nostalgia for a more innocent time. Which was ridiculous, of course, because I was just as naive about many things now as I was then, but at least last summer I hadn't—

"Minnie! Have you gone deaf, or what?"

For a moment, everything around me seemed to stop. Then I felt my heart beating, my lungs pushing air in and out, and my five senses sensing.

I turned around. Rafe Niswander was standing on his porch, hands in his pockets. "What do you want?" I asked. Because I really didn't feel like talking to him. What I wanted was to feel sorry for myself for a little while then go home to my cat. I'd pick either a book to read or a movie to watch—maybe make popcorn—and we'd snuggle together in front of the fireplace. What I did not want to do was talk to the man I loved with all my heart.

"Get over here," he said, motioning with his head.

I stayed where I was. "Why?"

"Because."

"Not sure that's reason enough," I said. But since it was clear he was going to hound me into doing what he wanted, I started walking. "Is this going to take long?" I asked. "There are things I need to do." None of them important, but he didn't need to know that.

Rafe, running true to form, ignored my question and opened the front door. "I want to show you something."

"The crown molding looks fine," I said automatically.

"You didn't even look."

Against my will, I felt a smile seep onto my face. "Well, no, but I'm sure it's fantastic."

"Of course it is," he said, "but that's not what I wanted to show you. Come on back."

He led me through the front room, through the formal dining room, and into his kitchen-like space. "I finally have a plan for this room," he said.

"Took you long enough."

He grinned. "You can't rush these things."

I loved him so much that I was afraid he would see it all over my face. Turning away, I said, "What's the plan? Although what I'd really like to know is why you're asking me. You know I avoid cooking if at all possible."

Once again, he ignored my questions. "Over here is where the refrigerator is going. A double-wide thing so there's lots of freezer space."

A bit of his enthusiasm trickled into me. "That would be nice," I said.

"Right. And over here, sticking with the work triangle theory of kitchen design, is where the sink will be. The electric oven goes here"—he pointed— "and the gas cooktop will go under that window."

"Six-burner, I assume?"

"Nah. Who wants to cook that much? I kept wanting to put the sink under the window, but I think this works better."

I looked around the space, trying to imagine the shapes. "You're right. This way when you're at the sink, you're facing the dining room." I stepped forward and mimicked washing a few imaginary dishes, which were my favorite kind. "What do you plan for cabinets?"

"Got a buddy who took down a bunch of maple he had milled. It's stored in his barn, gathering dust. He'll sell it to me cheap."

I looked around the large room. "Are you going to stain or paint them?"

"Not sure yet." He shrugged. "But it'll take me eight months to build the things. I figure by spring I'll have figured out what to do to them."

"Eight months?" I tried not to sound disbelieving.

"Yep."

"You seriously think you're going to build a full set of kitchen cabinets in eight months?"

"What, you think I can't do it?" He looked affronted.

"I'm sure you can. I'm just not sure you will."

"For your information," Rafe said loftily, "I have full confidence that this house will be completely done by the end of next summer."

I rolled my eyes. "You've been putzing around on this house for years. Why on earth would you suddenly start working hard enough to finish it within the next decade?"

"Well," he said reasonably, "where else are you going to live next fall, with a stranger running the boardinghouse?"

"Where . . . what?" I stared at him.

"I ran into your aunt at the post office and she told me about that cousin. I mean, sure, you might want to keep staying up there in the winter, but don't you think it's time?"

I kept staring at him. "For what?"

Rafe sighed. "For moving here."

My mouth hung open. Then I figured it out. "You need a roommate," I said flatly.

"How can someone so smart be so stupid?" he asked the ceiling. Then he took a step toward me. "I've been renovating this house for you all along," he said. "Why do you think I was always asking you questions about what I should do?"

"Because I was nearby?" I asked, and my voice squeaked a little.

"Well, that didn't hurt. But mostly I wanted to build the house of your dreams, a house you'd fall in love with . . . because then maybe you'd fall in love with me."

He'd moved closer as he talked, and now he was so close that I felt his warmth seep into me. "I like the house," I said so softly it was almost a whisper.

"Do you?" he asked.

"Actually, I love it." And I did. I'd loved it from top to bottom even before Rafe bought it. A wild thought occurred to me. "Back when this place was a mess of tiny apartments, I told you it was a shame and that what it needed to be happy was an owner who would fix it up properly."

"It was the summer before you went to college," he said quietly, coming even closer.

"You remember that?"

"Don't you?"

And I suddenly realized that I did. I remembered it exactly. I looked up at him, amazed, and he pushed back one of my curls. "I've loved you since the first time I saw you," he said, "back when you were twelve and not much shorter than you are now."

"Why didn't you ever say anything?" I whispered.

"I've wanted to for years, but you weren't ready. I thought after you got rid of that doctor, it might be time, but then you go and start seeing Ash." He smiled. "Have to say, that worried me a little."

"No worries," I said, smiling back with my whole heart. "Not today." Maybe not ever.

"So you'll try this?" he asked, so very gently that I almost cried. "See if we have a future together? Help me with cabinet colors and towels? All that?"

Instead of saying yes, I leaned into the kiss I'd been longing for. His arms circled me, and I felt as if I'd finally come home.

"So what do you think?" I asked.

It was hours later, and Eddie and I were getting ready for bed. Rafe and I had spent a fair amount of time talking, then not talking, then talking again, but since we both had to work the next day, he'd walked me back to the boardinghouse at midnight.

"Mrr," Eddie said.

"What are you doing? You're not going to fit, you know."

My cat had his head underneath my dresser and was squirming his way farther in. Weird didn't begin to describe him. "Anyway, I think you're going to like it at Rafe's house next fall."

But it wouldn't be just Rafe's house any longer. It would be our house, and the thought made my skin tingle with anticipation. "It's big, and it's close to the marina, so you'll be familiar with the territory." The houseboat details would be worked out later.

"Hang on a minute," I murmured. Rafe and Aunt Frances had met at the post office and she'd told him about the future of the boardinghouse. Had she known all along how he'd felt about me? Had she known how I'd felt about him? Had she played matchmaker for me?

I tossed the idea around for a bit, wondering how I felt about that likely possibility, then decided I didn't care. Rafe and I were together and that was what counted.

"Anyway," I said, "you'll be happy living with Rafe. Remember him? He's the one who puts your back foot in your ear, which you seem to enjoy."

"Mrr," Eddie said.

Or at least that's what I thought he'd said. It was hard to tell, though, because he was now all the way under the dresser.

"What are you doing under there?" I asked. "You have something and I'm guessing it's not a cat toy, or at least it wasn't a cat toy when it was manufactured." Eddie had a penchant for turning everything into his own possessions, and that included toothbrushes, short pieces of rope, and brooms.

Out of the corner of my eye, I saw something shoot out from under the dresser, skitter across the floor, and come to rest underneath the bed.

"Nice," I said, getting down on my hands and knees and reaching. "Having cats is a great way to keep limber. Did you ever think of . . . got it."

I sat on the bed. Eddie's plaything had been a pencil. "So this is where it went," I said, spinning the yellow pencil between my fingers. "I was unpacking the other day and—"

My words stopped short. This pencil was decorated with Eddie's teeth marks. This was an Eberhard Faber pencil. This Eberhard Faber pencil was what he'd yanked out of my hand that night on the houseboat when I'd been talking to him about Dale Lacombe's murder.

Eberhard Faber.

Simon Faber.

As I stared at the pencil, Eddie squirmed his way out from under the dresser and made one long leap onto my lap. He flopped down and started purring.

I looked at my cat. Looked at the pencil. Looked at my cat.

Could he really have been trying to tell me something? Was it possible that his cat brain had known something I hadn't and he'd been trying to communicate with me?

"Were you?" I asked.

Eddie turned his head and looked deep into my eyes.

"Mrr."